RELEASED

AMAZON BESTSELLING AUTHOR

JORDAN MARIE

DEVIL'S BLAZE
MOTORCYCLE CLUB

Copyright © 2016 by Jordan Marie
All rights reserved.

No part of this publication may be used or reproduced in any manner whatsoever, including but not limited to being stored in a retrieval system or transmitted in any form or by any means, electronic, mechanical, photocopying, recording or otherwise, without the written permission of the author.

This book is a work of fiction. Names, characters, groups, businesses, and incidents either are the product of the author's imagination or are used fictitiously. Any resemblance to actual places or persons, living or dead, is entirely coincidental.

Cover Design by Vicki Jones Portraiture
Cover Art by LJ Anderson of Mayhem Cover Creations
Model: Jared Caldwell

Interior Design & Editing by Daryl Banner

DEDICATION

To my dirty gang... I love you. To my street team who support me even when I'm not able to tell them how much I love them, and to anyone who has ever dreamed and kept the faith.

Thank you to Teena Torres for letting me play with your toes and making you evil. Thank you to Stephanie Sakal for your support. I hope you like your "part" in the book!

Xoxo
#BB4L and beyond.
J

RELEASED BY JORDAN MARIE
CONTENTS

THE BEGINNING..1
CHAPTER 1..3
CHAPTER 2..5
CHAPTER 3..9
CHAPTER 4..12
CHAPTER 5..19
CHAPTER 6..22
CHAPTER 7..25
CHAPTER 8..29
CHAPTER 9..36
CHAPTER 10..39
CHAPTER 11..41
CHAPTER 12..47
CHAPTER 13..50
CHAPTER 14..54
CHAPTER 15..58
CHAPTER 16..63
CHAPTER 17..66
CHAPTER 18..71
CHAPTER 19..73
CHAPTER 20..77
CHAPTER 21..81
CHAPTER 22..85
CHAPTER 23..89
CHAPTER 24..94
CHAPTER 25..98
CHAPTER 26..102
CHAPTER 27..106
CHAPTER 28..109
CHAPTER 29..113
CHAPTER 30..118
CHAPTER 31..122

CHAPTER 32	128
CHAPTER 33	132
CHAPTER 34	137
CHAPTER 35	140
CHAPTER 36	144
CHAPTER 37	148
CHAPTER 38	152
CHAPTER 39	155
CHAPTER 40	159
CHAPTER 41	162
CHAPTER 42	165
CHAPTER 43	170
CHAPTER 44	173
CHAPTER 45	177
CHAPTER 46	182
CHAPTER 47	187
CHAPTER 48	191
CHAPTER 49	198
CHAPTER 50	204
CHAPTER 51	206
CHAPTER 52	210
CHAPTER 53	215
CHAPTER 54	219
CHAPTER 55	223
CHAPTER 56	227
CHAPTER 57	229
CHAPTER 58	233
CHAPTER 59	236
CHAPTER 60	239
CHAPTER 61	244
CHAPTER 62	249
CHAPTER 63	253
CHAPTER 64	254
EPILOGUE PART 1	258
EPILOGUE PART 2	262
SNEAK PEEK OF "LEARNING TO BREATHE"	264
AUTHOR'S NOTE	266
GLOSSARY OF TERMS	267

FOREWORD

Dear Readers:

This book was a rough one for me. Everyone has such strong reactions and feelings. In the end, I hope I managed to live up to some of what you wanted, while remaining true to who I felt the couple was.

I would like to apologize for this last installment being late. My mother suffered a second heart attack and with all of the complications and other things, my writing time was cut to a third of what it normally is. This book is the last of my MC bad guys for a while. I want to take a slight break and try a different kind of book. Though my pen name Baylee Rose will have Marcum's story out soon. I will do Beasts in the fall.

Please check into www.jordanmarieauthor.com or sign up for my newsletter to keep up to date on my next release which is a contemporary romance I hope you'll love as much as I do.

xoxo
Jordan

RELEASED

AMAZON BESTSELLING AUTHOR
JORDAN MARIE

DEVIL'S BLAZE MOTORCYCLE CLUB

THE BEGINNING

It's dusty. There's so much dust that the air is literally brown and it dries out my throat with every breath. I hate days like today that remind me that the small area along the Mexican border is hell upon Earth.

I should hate my mother for bringing me here. I want to, but I can't. She did what she thought was best when my father left us. I miss Georgia, though. I miss the house we lived in. The smell of the magnolia trees after the rain. The taste of the air. It's all so different from here. I look at the small adobe-and-block *shelter* we are staying in. It's not a house. You can't call it that. There are big holes in the sides where walls should be. Our bed consists of a mattress that my *madre* sewed and filled with dried cornhusks. One day, I vow I shall have my own home and it shall have the softest beds imaginable. They shall be the best money can buy and my *madre* will have the very softest of them all. I will have magnolia trees all around the house and you can see them from every window. *Madre* will be so proud. I will make sure of it.

Most of all—I will never be alone as I am now. *Mi mama* is forced to leave me alone to go into town to work. I don't mind it so much because, as young as I am, I can still take care of myself. It's the silence that gets to me. At nine years old, there's never anyone here to talk to. All the other kids have gone into town to work or to school. I wanted to, but mama said she felt safer with me here.

So I sit here in the quiet and wait… Wait and dream.

Someday, I will return to Georgia. I will find the girl of my dreams. She will have hair like spun gold and eyes that capture me and remind me of the bluest sky there is. Bluer than even the one I saw in Montana when my father took us there. Most of all, my girl will laugh all the time because I will always make her happy. We will fish and hold hands. I'll have to put the worm on her hook because that kind of stuff grosses girls out. Then we will tell each other stories. Scary ones, because those are the best. She'll probably get scared because girls are like that too. I'll have to hold her and promise to make the bad dreams go away, just like *mi madre* does for me.

Well, she used to. I'm much too old for bad dreams now. I'm the man of the household. I'm strong. I have to be so I can defend my family. I will only get stronger, too. A man doesn't deserve a family if he can't keep it safe. I will.

I will be the man *mi padre* never could be. I will cherish all the things he threw away, and *mi esposa* will never cry at night like I hear my own mother do. I will always dry her tears and make her happy. Just like I do with *mi madre*.

This is my promise. This is my vow. I will not become the dog *mi padre* is… *Never.*

Chapter 1
Skull

"Boss? You ready?"

I shake the memory of my childhood away. I'm standing in my room looking out the window and watching the dust swirl around. Maybe it's the wind that brings old ghosts and memories to the forefront. More likely it is the memory of Beth's tears last night. I stood outside and listened to her cry. Her tears brought me dual sensations of hate and satisfaction. She deserves to cry. She deserves to feel pain. Yet perversely, I wanted to be the one to dry them. I wanted to pull her into my arms and…

And what? *Forgive?* There are things that cannot be forgiven in this world. Actions that cannot be undone. There are courses set in life that cannot be altered, no matter how you might wish them.

"*Si*. Did Dragon's men get here?"

"Yeah. They made it here about twenty minutes ago. He sent ten of his men. Dragon is with them. He seems to be planning on staying."

"I'll talk to him in a minute," I tell Sabre, unable to look at him. I'm mad at him. I shouldn't be. It's a sad fucker who can't be glad his brother is happy.

And I should be happy. Sabre has found his match in the innocent spitfire named Annie. Though admittedly, after Sabre and Latch have gotten to her, innocence probably has nothing to do with the games they play. Sabre never struck me as the kind of guy to share his woman full-time, yet that seems to be what the three have settled into. You would think that would leave the odd man out, but so far it hasn't. Latch seems just as fucking happy. One woman is taming two men I never thought would be tamed.

Women can make or break a man. Too bad I wasn't as lucky in the draw as they were. "I will be out in a minute. I want to see my daughter and take her to Beth."

"Are you going to let her have access to Gabby?" Sabre asks, sounding shocked.

"I never planned otherwise."

"That wasn't what it sounded like yesterday."

"I was mad. I wanted Beth's fear." I shrug, knowing it goes deeper than that, but not planning on explaining myself. My reasons are mine and mine alone.

"I'm glad. A child should have its mother," Sabre says, turning away.

I let him go without responding. He's right. My daughter will have Beth in her life, I'm the one who won't. I need to accept that and move on. The thought makes me want to scream and… *kill*.

I won't be letting go of her… at least not today.

Chapter 2
Beth

"Mo-om!"

Gabby's voice fills the room and instantly the emptiness in my heart is lifted. I look up to see Skull standing there, his face impassive. I can't read one thing that flickers in his cold dark eyes. Gabby pulls away from him and reaches for me.

I stand, wiping my damp palms on my jeans and reach for my baby. I'm surprised by the fact that Skull is here with Gabby, and maybe even more surprised when he passes her to me so easily. After his words last night, I expected him to keep Gabby away from me forever. Or at least try. I would have killed him or anyone who stood in my way before I would have let Gabby go. Well, that is, if I was able. If he gave me back to Colin and Matthew, I didn't figure I would live long enough to worry about any of that.

"Should I thank you for letting me see my daughter?" I ask, and it would probably be wise to keep the bitchy tone out of my voice, but I can't seem to.

Skull sighs, and I can see the circles under his eyes. I don't want to feel pity for him; I just can't seem to help it. I bite my lip before I blurt out something stupid. Skull doesn't need me to care about him. By his own admission, he has someone to do that already. The knowledge of that is still burning inside of me like a poison. I expected it, but it doesn't make it hurt any less.

"I will be going out of town for a couple of days. I've asked

Dragon to send some men over to help watch the compound, so you should be fine."

"Don't you have your own men?" I ask, confused and not knowing who Dragon is or if I should worry. I don't like letting outsiders close to my daughter.

"I do. I want to make sure *mi hija* is protected."

"If you would let me go, I'd make sure she was far away from Colin and anyone that might wish her harm."

"That is not happening, but then you know that. I am dealing with Colin."

His short, straight-to-the-point cold sentences annoy me. The look he wears on his stony face annoys me too. I want to scream at him, demand he acknowledge that there are things left between us that need to be dealt with, but I don't.

Skull turns to leave, and the stupid woman in me can't stop my mouth when I say, "Be careful."

Skull freezes and turns just enough so that I can see the side of his face. "Why would you care?"

"I don't know, but I do," I tell him, swearing that that will be the last bit of honesty he gets from me.

"Follow me out to the main area. I want to introduce you to Dragon."

I frown. The last thing I want to do is meet anyone. Still, it's a chance to get out of this room, and honestly, I thought I would be a prisoner here until Skull turned me over to Colin. So I give in, if for no reason other than needing to see something besides the four walls of this room.

I follow cautiously behind him. I have learned that around every corner, you can find a monster. Right now, I'm not completely convinced that Skull's not one of them. He's so different from what I remember. That's probably a good thing. I must focus on who he is now and give up the memories of the man I once loved. That's the only way I'm going to survive this.

When we reach the room, I hang back against the door frame. Gabby plays with her plastic set of keys and tries her best to stuff them into her mouth. I watch as Skull walks over to a large African-American man wearing faded jeans, a green t-shirt, and a leather vest similar to the one Skull wears all the time. He's tall—even taller than Skull, though not by much. He's lean and muscular and wears an easy smile. In fact, he looks happy.

He's got a little boy held close to his side. The boy is playing with the man's ear. It's cute, and somehow it makes this big man look even sexier. His other hand is draped over a blonde. She looks strangely familiar. Skull and the man are talking, but my eyes are on the woman. *Where do I know her from?* I take a couple of steps closer, still hanging back and not wanting to bring attention to myself if possible. She looks a lot like me. Actually, with Katie changing her hair color, I'd say people would mistake this woman as my sister even more so than Katie, except she's prettier. She has curves and hips that I could only dream of having. She's rubbing her very pregnant stomach and talking to Skull. He's smiling at her in a way that makes me ache. It's reminiscent of how he used to look at me.

"*Querida,* you are much too beautiful to be with this *hombre.* Run away with me and let me treat you like the *princesa* you are," Skull says, and I try to ignore the way his flirting hurts me. It cuts me that he calls her his dear one, as he once did me. The man with her doesn't look like it disturbs him that Skull is hitting on his woman. Scratch that, he *does* look pissed. Maybe he'll beat the hell out of Skull. I could cheer him on.

Do it. Do it! I urge him silently.

"Keep it up, Skull, and I'll kill your ass like I should have done years ago. You've been a thorn in my side for far too fucking long."

Skull just laughs it off. The blonde reaches up on her tip-toes and kisses the other man. "Behave, Dragon," she whispers in a soft voice that radiates with warmth.

He looks down at her and gives her a smile, the kind that makes you feel like an intruder.

"I'll show you just how good I am behaving when I get you home, Mama," he whispers, and the woman blooms in a deep blush.

Then he does something that surprises me and makes me ache. He leans down and places a small kiss on her forehead. It's so strange and seems out of character from this big man. It makes me instantly jealous of this woman, who clearly holds this man in the palm of her hand. I'm jealous of the love the two of them have and obviously cherish… the kind of relationship I wanted…

"Is this your daughter?" the man asks Skull, and then I'm instantly aware of all eyes on Gabby and me. I swallow nervously, wishing I had chosen to stay in my room instead.

Chapter 3
Skull

I'm ignoring Beth. It's not the most adult way to handle the conversation, but it's survival. I shouldn't have asked Beth to join me. It was a weak moment. I wanted to show off my child and her mother to Dragon. Seeing the way he and Nicole are with each other, though, brings home exactly what I've been robbed of—what Beth and her family took from me.

Today starts my revenge. When Dragon, nosy bastard that he is, asks about Gabby, I'm forced to acknowledge the woman who is the reason my insides are rotting away.

I turn around and take Gabby from her mom. The child cries and reaches for Beth.

Wanting her mother over me. Because she doesn't know me. Because I am a stranger.

Hate burns in my stomach yet again. I give in only because I can't stand to see my daughter cry. My daughter who doesn't know me. My daughter who doesn't want me to hold her. I've tried. It always ends up with her crying. Beth takes hold of Gabby and instantly, she stops. Anger wars with this feeling of failure.

Dragon slaps me on the back, moving beside me. "Dom is the same way. He'd much rather be on his Mama's hip than mine. Who can blame them? I'd choose them over our ugly faces any day of the week," he teases.

I know he's trying to make me feel better. He's a true friend and he alone knows how fucked in the head I am right now over all this shit.

Before I can respond, he's looking at Beth. "You must be Skull's wife." Hearing him call her that pisses me off even more. A wife is someone who stays by your side, who fights with you and holds their ground with you. A wife is someone like Nicole. Despite all of the shit her and Dragon went through, her love for him never wavered. She sure as fuck didn't run away and keep Dragon's boy from him.

"I've got to go. My men are waiting on me. You call me if there's trouble. Keep your family safe."

"Always, asshole. You know that," Dragon grumbles.

We might be friends, but he doesn't take it well when anyone tries to tell him how to take care of what is his. I'd be the same way if I had any claim over Beth.

I throw up my hand to say bye, then walk away without looking back. I feel like a fucking intruder in my own damn club. Just one more thing Beth seems to have taken from me.

"Skull?"

Beth. Her voice stops me. I can't bring myself to turn around.

"What?" My voice is cold, but it's nowhere near as cold as my heart.

"When will you be back?" she asks like she has a right to know. She doesn't. She doesn't deserve anything from me.

"After I kill your stepbrother," I tell her before walking out the door.

I move my hand over my chest in the vicinity of my heart. There's pain there. At this point, I can't tell if it's physical or in my head; I just know I am completely fucked up.

I walk out to the bikes where the men are waiting. I sit there for a bit after I climb on.

"Skull?" I look over at Briar. I can see the worry in his eyes. I don't know what the fuck to tell him. "You got your head in the game?" he asks.

I don't. I absolutely fucking don't. It doesn't make a damn bit of difference. I start my bike and give the signal to pull out. The air vibrates with the sound of the pipes revving. As we pull out onto the main road, I concentrate on that sound and the feel of the wind. Fuck everything else.

My club. That's all I need.

I just wish I believed that.

Chapter 4
Beth

The silence left behind as Skull slams the door is deafening. My face reddens. The babies are even silent, as if they too can sense the blackness and pain in the air. I bite my lip and look at the two strangers that Skull has basically left me with.

"He's upset," says Nicole.

Hello, understatement of the year. Nice to meet you.

"Don't you think he has a right?"

"Dragon, don't."

"What, Mama?" he exclaims. "I'm not saying anything but the fucking truth."

Gone is his easygoing attitude. Skull leaving was like a light switch going off.

"If you don't watch your mouth around Dom…"

"Damn it, Nicole."

"So you want to sleep alone tonight," she says, daring him to say anything else.

"You couldn't make it through the night without me either, Mama, so don't go tripping."

"Don't make me prove you wrong. I might miss you, but I'm stubborn…" She says it so sweetly that I hardly believe she's threatening Dragon with not sleeping with him. It's obviously a threat too, because the look on his face becomes deadly serious.

"You try keeping me out of our bed, Mama, and I'll turn your ass so red you won't sit for a week." I know my eyes go round as

I listen to them. It has less to do with what they're saying than the vibrating connection they seem to have. It's so powerful it lights up the room.

"You say that like it's a threat, Dragon," she whispers with a soft smile.

Dragon grabs Nicole by the back of her neck and pulls her into him. The baby in his arms acts like nothing is happening. I get the feeling he probably sees this a lot. His hold on her is almost violent as she grips his sides to steady herself and looks at him.

His face goes soft. "Woman, you're going to be the death of me."

"Dragon," she whispers, straining up towards his lips.

"I'm gonna go and make sure the men have the perimeter secure. You try to behave, Mama."

"I love you," she whispers, and my heart clenches.

"I love you, Mama. Forever," he whispers against her lips before taking them in the hottest kiss I've ever seen. It's the emotion you can hear in his words, though, that makes me feel like I've been gut punched.

I'm jealous of this Nicole. I can admit it freely. This is what I should have had with Skull. Would it have been that way if I had ignored my father's summons and threats? Would I have this kind of love now if I had confessed everything to Skull? Maybe... but then, if I had done that, my sister would be dead. That is truth. That is *real*. If I had ignored my father and alerted Skull, Katie would be dead.

I did the only thing I could have done.

I squash the little voice in my head that I should have tried harder when I had Gabby. I don't need to hear it again. I never seem to stop hearing it these days.

Dragon hands Nicole the baby and then leaves. I shift Gabby

to my other side, nervously. Will Nicole turn as surly as Dragon did? Will she take Skull's side immediately too? Am I doomed to be the enemy as long as I'm here?

Nicole watches every step Dragon makes until he goes outside and the door closes shut behind him. Then, she takes a deep breath that sounds more like a sigh. She turns around to look at me. She has a guarded smile on her face as she takes me in. "I'm Nicole, Dragon's wife."

When she turns her smile directly on me and I get a good look at her face, that's when it hits me. I know exactly where I've seen her before. She was the woman standing outside the movie theater the night I went into labor with Gabby.

"You dated Skull," I whisper, and I wish I could've stopped my stupid mouth, but I didn't hold it back—not even a little.

Nicole looks a little shocked. "Good Lord, no. Why would you say that?"

"I saw you at the movie theater the night I went into labor. You came outside of the theater with Skull. He was—"

"Flirting. Being Skull. I can assure you, we've never dated."

"But…"

"Never, Beth. Can I call you Beth?"

"Yeah, I guess. Though, I think I'm public enemy number one, so I'm not sure why you want to talk to me."

"Do you love Skull?" she asks, and wow, I guess that's a way to cut through the bullshit and get right to the point. How on earth do I answer that?

"I don't think I know who *this* Skull is," I tell her, which is the truth in a way. I still love the Skull I knew. I always will, but no one needs to know how stupid I am.

"Fair enough. But what you'll need to figure out, Beth—and in a hurry—is whether or not you want *this* Skull, because he's the one who's here now. He's the father of your child, and you need to—"

"I don't think there's any way to work this out, Nicole. In complete honesty, Skull hates me, and I'm not exactly sure how I feel about him."

"There's a thin line between love and hate, Beth."

"I'd really rather not talk about this with you. I think I'll take Gabby back to our…"

"Disappointing," Nicole says, studying my face.

The word irritates me and I jerk up to give her a look. "Disappointing?"

"How easy you give up. You think you would have learned that's not the way to handle things by now."

Her words are like a slap to my face. She doesn't know me. She doesn't know anything about me. And yet …

She's right. I'm really getting tired of that damn voice.

"Listen, I don't think you have the right—"

"Maybe I'm wrong? Dragon said Skull told him that you saw some pictures and took that as total proof that Skull would send not only you away, but also his daughter—"

"He did! I got a note…"

"A note from the man you love saying he wanted nothing to do with his daughter? Do you think so little of yourself?"

"I… what are you talking about?" I'm definitely annoyed and defensive now.

"Well, I mean you allowed yourself to get pregnant by a man who you obviously thought would be a horrible father," she says, as if it was completely simple.

My heart stalls in my chest. "I didn't," I stutter. "I mean, I didn't think I did. I got the note and it seemed…"

"With everything you had been through with your father and with Colin and Matthew—not to mention your grandfather—it didn't occur you to even question the letter? It didn't occur to your sister?"

My breath stops. It's not like I haven't asked the same questions Nicole's asking. I have. Katie did. It's just that I've never had a third party hit me with the questions. I've never had someone ask me pointblank before about my choices.

I find a chair and sit down, looking at this woman. I should hate her, but instead I am swamped with this horrible feeling that I fucked up. It's one thing to feel it, but another to acknowledge it completely.

"I was scared," I whisper, my feeble reason.

Nicole's face changes and she sits down across from me now. "Do you know what you were afraid of?"

I do, but saying it out loud will just sound lame. *Because it is.*

"I think if there was even the faintest possibility that Dragon had moved on without me, that he was in love with another woman, I would want to run away from ever seeing it."

I swallow, because that's it in a nutshell. "You would?"

"Definitely. It would kill me to confront that."

"But you would. Confront it, I mean."

I know I'm right. She's too confident, too self-assured. She's everything I've never been.

"Probably. But then again, I wasn't pregnant and alone at the age of nineteen. Betrayed by my father, who I thought was dead, then confronted by a sister that, again, I thought was dead."

"You know everything?"

"I know everything Skull told Dragon. It's just that I'm not a man, so I see things they miss, or they don't understand."

"You're on my side?"

She studies me carefully. "Skull is my friend. I want to see him happy."

"I see, so you don't—"

"I happen to think having his family together would achieve

that."

My heart speeds up. But then, why? There's no way that's going to happen and I don't know if I want it to, now. This Skull is not the man I remember. Plus, he has moved on…

"It doesn't matter. It's too late," I tell Nicole, occupying myself with playing with my daughter's beautiful hair. She's smiling and playing with her little set of plastic keys. She looks so much like her father that it physically hurts sometimes.

"I guess it is. Especially if you're not willing to fight for your family. Like I said, *disappointing*."

"You would fight to be with someone who hates you?" I question her, disbelieving.

"I think any woman would, if she cares about her daughter."

"It's not good for my child to be around people who hate each other," I tell her, getting pissed. She may have some valid points, but she doesn't get to tell me I don't know what is best for my daughter.

"True. But if there's a chance those parents could find their way back…"

"There's not. I respect what you're trying to do," I tell her, even though I'm lying, "but this is not your business, and since you haven't walked in my shoes, you can't really tell me what you would do."

"Point made," Nicole says, standing up with her baby. "But I'll tell you what I do know, Beth. I know that I would fight like hell to keep my man. It wouldn't matter how long we were apart, or what was between us. I'd fight."

"How nice for you," I tell her, getting up to leave. I definitely need to take Gabby and go back to my room.

"I just have one more thing to leave with you, Beth, then I'm done."

I sigh hearing her say that, but resign myself to listen. "Please just say it and get it over with, because I'm kind of done here."

"Will you be able to live with the fact that you didn't even try? Will it ever bother you to know that you basically just handed the man you love over to another woman?"

I swallow hard and turn away from her. I don't want her to see my face when I lie.

"I … don't love Skull."

"Then I guess it won't bother you at all when he finds someone else."

"No, it … it won't bother me," I whisper brokenly, walking towards my room and ignoring the tears that again threaten to fall. It won't bother me at all.

It will kill me.

Chapter 5
Skull

I hold my fist up in the air to tell my men to hold tight. I'm not about to ruin shit when I'm so close to getting Colin Donahue in my hands. He's the first step to my revenge. Pistol is a barely-breathing dead man. When I have Colin chained up beside him, maybe I'll be able to finish Pistol off. I'll center my rage on Colin, the fucker who truly deserves it.

When I got the intel that Colin was hiding out in this remote cabin in the backwoods of Georgia, I wanted to scream. The fucker thought he could hide from me? He wants to try and take what is mine? I'm going to make him regret the day he was born. All he fucking did was make things easier for me. I still would have stormed the gates of his pretty house on the hill. It doesn't matter. I don't give a fuck about anything at this point except revenge; it's the only thing that's keeping me going.

My men are tired. I'm driving them hard. We've been on the road for two days straight and, besides a quick nap in a fucking pig sty, we've barely taken a break. I can't help it. Being away from Beth is making me nervous.

No. *Gabby*. Being away from *Gabby*, not Beth…

I grab my binoculars and zoom in on the window that's closest to me. There's three heads in there. I can't tell that any of them are Colin. I need to just go in and make my move. There's something feeling off, though. I'm trying to ignore it because I'm so fucking raw about things right now. It's probably nothing.

RELEASED

Still… the lives of my men are at stake here.

"You're sure you checked the perimeter carefully?" I ask Beast.

He's back to doing things for me, but he's not adjusting great. He's letting his hair and beard grow out again. It's slowly covering the wicked scars that twist the skin on his neck and up the side of his face. He doesn't talk a lot anymore. His voice is hoarse and quiet. I haven't asked, but I'm sure that's beyond his control too. Just one more thing the explosion has taken from him… one more thing Beth's family has taken from him.

"It's clear." His voice is animalistic, like a growl.

I hold my hand back up using a series of numbers to signal the beginning of our plan. I've ordered radio silence. I can't take the chance that they have technology that might monitor that shit. Colin might not be fucking smart, but he has money, and money makes even the dumbest of men at least *look* more intelligent.

I've split the men up in teams of two. I'll charge in front with Briar at my side. Beast and Sabre will follow guarding our backs, then Shaft and Latch will follow and so forth. Hopefully by the time Roadkill, our newest recruit and last in the formation, follows in, there won't be a need for anyone to be watching his back. Hopefully by then I have Colin's neck in my hands and I'm choking the life out of the son of a bitch.

We start moving forward, staying in the brushy cover of the woods surrounding the cabin. When we reach the edge, I take a breath to move forward. I'm at the base of the steps along the small wooden porch when I see it. The small pinpoint red light flashing on my pants leg. It's connected to something that's mounted underneath the step. It's way too small of an area for a gun, but I've been in the military and I've dealt with this shit way too long. I also know what the Donahue's calling card is.

One word registers in my brain before I call out. *Bomb.*

"Fall back!" I scream. "Fall back! It's a—"

I'm still calling out while running backwards and pulling Briar with me when the bomb ignites. The force of the blast is a heated inferno at my back. It pushes us off our legs and up in the air as we're thrown a good ten feet. I slam hard against the rocky ground, feeling debris hit me and all around. I lay there, the wind knocked out of my body. Disappointment fills me. Colin set this up. Whoever was in this cabin, it wasn't him. Not this time.

But I will get him.

Chapter 6
SKULL
ONE WEEK LATER

It's been one week. One week since I've had Beth back under my roof. One full week and I've barely spoken to her. One full week of having her close. That should make me feel better. Instead, I feel dead. So cold and empty, I wonder sometimes how I'm breathing. How I'm existing. I'm pulled to her, even as I never want to see her again. My head is so fucked up, it may never be right again. I can't figure out how I can be so fucking mad at a woman and yet want her at the same time.

And I do want her. Sometimes I wake up at night in a cold sweat after dreaming of having her. It's ridiculous. I can't stand to look at her, but yet every night I sneak in her fucking room after I'm sure she's sleeping and I watch her like some fucking stalker.

Tonight is no exception. She's lying in the bed. The sheet has fallen down around her stomach exposing the soft, white, cotton gown she's wearing. The *V* of the neck has been pulled while she tossed and turned and it exposes the soft swell of her right breast. I fist my hands at my side to prevent myself from reaching out and ripping the gown away from her body. A body I remember like the back of my hand. A body I fucking yearn for.

A body that haunts me.

How could she have done this to us? To me? How can you say you love someone when you nearly destroy them with your lies—with not trusting them? I've told her I hated her, and she thinks I truly do. It would be so much easier if I could. *I want to.* I'm spending my time fucking pounding the life out of Pistol because if I don't, I wouldn't be able to contain my anger. I'm barely doing it now. What would Beth think if she knew just how much of an animal her coming back has turned me into?

And if I'm honest, that's why I'm so mad at her. I was starting to put my life back together. Pick up the pieces I was left in when she... *died.* Seeing Dragon and Nicole together, watching how they are both willing to give up their lives for each other... it reminded me that love is real. It reminded me what it was like to share a connection with someone above all others. I miss it. I was actively searching for it. I was starting to live again.

Then, in the blink of an eye, Beth set my world upside down again.

The fucking Donahues have come close to destroying me, and I've still been unable to find Colin. After the messed-up search for them in Georgia, I drove straight back home and continued searching them out. I'm getting nowhere. They've picked a mighty big rock to crawl under, but I won't stop. I will get them and I will have my revenge. Until then, however, I'm here watching Beth and just remembering.

I'm back to where I was the day that boat exploded. I'm back in this fucking hole, feeling like the world is closing in on me and there's not a fucking thing I can do about it. Having Beth back should have brought me joy. Instead, it makes me wish I was dead because I don't want any more pain. It might make me a fucking pussy, but that's the simple truth. Losing her once destroyed me. Finding out she lives and it's all been some fucking... *lie?*

It's killed me.

I back out of the room and close the door, calming my heart and breathing. *Breathing.* For so long, I don't think I was breathing at all, at least not consciously. Now, every breath is labored and each intake is filled with the scent of Beth's perfume, and it's painful.

It hurts to breathe. *That's her fault too.*

I want her gone. I need her gone.

And I can't let her go.

Chapter 7
Beth

I hear the door close and I turn on my back, letting the tears fall. I did this. I destroyed the love we had. He's right. Nicole's right. They all are. I should have tried harder to get back to him. He doesn't understand why I didn't. Some days I don't, myself. I was nineteen basically, scared, tired, and emotionally scarred. I just had a baby and almost died. Getting that damn note, seeing those pictures, it was like some giant cosmic sign that I needed to just… give it up. I never should have been with Skull. I knew better, I just couldn't make myself stay away.

Did I quit because I was tired of fighting? I don't know. Maybe? I felt alone after that note. I felt completely alone after seeing those pictures. I made bad choices, I admit it. At the same time I'm so fucking tired of tears. I'm tired of being the bad guy. I might have made bad choices, but damn it, so did Skull. The only difference is, he is still making them.

I'm done. I sit up in bed and wipe my eyes. He wants to be a fucking asshole? Fine. I'm done. He scared me. He threatened to take my child, even if he didn't follow through with it. He looks at me like I'm dirt under his fingernails, or *worse*. I've seen that damn doctor here a couple of times alone this week. What does he do? Come stare at me in bed and then go to her? The idea makes me physically ill.

I'm done.

I can't keep going like this and I refuse to cry one more tear.

I use the back of my hand to wipe the tears away. Skull hates me? He wants to drive me away from him permanently?

I'll give him what he wants.

I need to figure out what I want out of life. Skull says he's intent on wiping Colin and Matthew from the face of the Earth. I'm more than okay with that. If he'd let me, I'd join in. It's time for me to start putting my life in order. The only way I can do that is to face Skull head-on. I might have been a terrified kid at the age of nineteen, but I can't be that person anymore. I can't. Gabby deserves more from me. I deserve more.

Decision made, I grab my robe and decide to find Skull now. It can't wait until morning. I've barely made it five steps away from my door when I see Skull standing in the hall talking to her. *Dr. Torres.* My stomach clenches and I feel acid churning in it. My first instinct is to go back in my room. Then, I remember my decision to be more adult. To face things head-on. I'm tired of running, and if I don't face this, that's all I'm doing again.

Running.

"Skull, could I have a word with you?" I ask, and I'm congratulating myself because I don't sound scared, which is the tone I normally have around him. I've got my hand wrapped around the belt of my robe and I hope he doesn't look, because I know I've pulled it so tight that my hand is deathly white because I'm cutting off circulation.

He whips around to see me, and it could be my imagination, but he looks almost ashamed. Was he not expecting me to find him talking to his mistress? Poor man. Okay, so she might not be his mistress, but she's sure not his wife. She might be someday, but that day is not right now.

He brings his hand up and rubs the back of his neck, his eyes going over me in that cold way that he's been using ever since I first got back.

"It's late, Beth."

"True, but you obviously aren't sleeping. Surely you can spend five minutes talking to me before you go do whatever you were getting ready to do?"

Did that sound accusatory? Did I sound jealous? Please, God, do not let me sound jealous. I'm steadfastly ignoring Dr. Torres. I wouldn't mind kicking her where it hurts. She'd probably swallow my foot whole though if I hit wrong. *The bitch.*

"Spill it, then."

"I'd rather not talk in front of your girlfriend, Skull."

"I don't have girlfriends."

"I'm all too familiar with that. I should have listened closer. Still, if it's all the same, I'd rather discuss this in private."

Skull exhales a large breath like I'm asking him to jump through hoops. He grabs me roughly and pulls me back to my room. I can't resist the urge to look over my shoulder at Dr. Torres. I don't know what I expected to see in the other woman's face, but it wasn't what I saw. There's annoyance there, but it seems like there's something else, something I can't describe, but it sets off warning bells.

I shrug it off. I'm probably just imagining it because I hate her and would like to see her die a horrible fiery death, or at least have to move to another country. One of those.

When we make it back to my room, Skull slams the door and then leans against it with his arms crossed. He seems to be waiting for me to talk. Too bad my brain seems to have short-circuited. I'm trying to remember my new resolve to face things head-on. Instead, I notice the changes in Skull. In the week since I've been back, I haven't really *looked* at him. He's gotten older. Sure, it *has* been two years, but he looks so much older. His eyes, which always sparkled with heat and humor, now look dull and cold. Another thing I did.

I shake it off. I can't go down that road.

"Well? Spit it out, Beth," he growls.

"So sorry I'm holding you up from getting lucky," I snarl back. I'm pretty fed up and, all of a sudden, it feels easier to stick to my new decision. I'm done letting him or anyone push me around.

I'm done.

CHAPTER 8
SKULL

Her response shocks me, but I'm not about to get into this with her. I need to stay away from her. I can't let her see just how much she gets to me.

"I don't have time for your bullshit, Beth. Just tell me what you wanted to say and get it over with. I have things to do," I tell her, keeping my voice cold.

"I want to leave."

"Not happening."

"Kidnapping is against the law, Skull, and I've had enough of men keeping me against my will. I want to take my daughter and leave," she growls.

That pulls my attention to her face instead of the way that damn robe is caressing her body.

"My daughter stays here. She's not leaving this compound, Beth."

"Bullshit. Living in a club with a bunch of horny bikers getting their rocks off is no place for a small child."

"I can remember a time you didn't mind it."

"I'm not that woman anymore, Skull."

"A pity. I actually liked that woman," I tell her, and I can see the exact moment my words hit her. She flinches. You would think that would bring me some sort of satisfaction. It doesn't. If anything, it bothers me that it hurt her. Which, in turn, just makes me mad for still being a fool when it comes to her.

"Something about being lied to, held captive, almost dying and killing someone, changes you. Go figure. You said you weren't turning me over to Colin," she states, waiting for me to answer. I want to yell at her, shake her and ask if she ever knew who the fuck I was. How could she even think I would do that? *How?* God, I wish I could hate her.

"I've had enough of this bullshit," I growl, turning to leave.

"I'm not staying, Skull. I'm going to leave, and I will take my daughter with me."

"If you think I will ever let you keep my daughter away from me again, Beth…"

"I don't want to keep her away from you," she says, and the shock in her voice is not fake. I study her face, looking for signs that she's taking me for a ride, but don't find any.

"Then she stays here. You need to be close to her, so you need to be here too, at least for now. Problem solved. Now, if you'll excuse me…"

"I'm not staying, and you're welcome to see and visit Gabby anytime."

"That doesn't work for me," I tell her, turning to face her fully.

"Too bad. Gabby and I can find a home close to your club. You can see her anytime and you can keep her and spend time with her within reason."

"Will you listen to yourself? *'Within reason'*? This is *my* child we're talking about. A child that you kept hidden from me. I'm not about to give you that chance again and no one, Beth, will *ever* keep my child from me again!"

"I'm not trying to keep you from her! But, I'm not about to give her up either. We have to learn to work this out, Skull! For Gabby!"

"She's here and you're here and that's it. It's worked out!"

"It's not worked out. You can't stand to look at me! Your girlfriend is outside waiting to…"

"To what, Beth? Go ahead say it! I dare you."

"It's none of my business what you choose to do with her," she growls, her face red and her hair scattered across her shoulder, rumpled from her being in bed. I shouldn't find her sexy in the midst of this fight. I shouldn't even notice it, but I do.

And my dick does. *Motherfucker.*

"You got that right. Christo! You lost the chance to care about who was in my bed when you lied to me and planned to leave me that day in Beast's hospital room! Anything that has happened since is on you, Beth. It's all on you."

"Bullshit! What would you have had me do, Skull? I was nineteen, scared of my father. I was ready to tell him to fuck off, to leave me alone. In fact, I had. But he had one last card to play. My sister. Did you expect me to just let him kill her? I couldn't do that. I still wouldn't, even if I could go back, I'd help Katie. I'd save Katie!"

"And that's the problem, isn't it Beth? You chose Katie over me. Over a life with me and my daughter. You turned your back on me. You didn't give me a chance to try and save Katie for you. You didn't trust me with anything!" I growl, her words wounding me, cutting open holes in my soul I thought scabbed over, creating pain where I had finally thought I was dead.

"How was I supposed to trust you could save Katie? Your own man was the one who helped my father. You couldn't even protect your own club! I did what I had to do to protect my family!"

Her words are truthful. She's just saying aloud the very thing that I have struggled the most with, the very reason Pistol is still drawing breath. I should have ended the fucking asshole way before he got the chance to betray me.

"*Me voy de aquí,*" I growl. I can't do this with her. I can't. I know my failures are the last thing I want to hear Beth throw in my face.

"Go, but it doesn't matter. I'm leaving, Skull. I'm not staying under the same roof with you."

I've turned so my back is to her. I take a breath. I don't want her here either. She's right. I can't go on like this. *Que así sea.*

"You won't leave until I've neutralized Colin and Matthew. Then, you can leave. I don't care where the fuck you go after that. I just want my daughter safe, but you better never keep me from Gabriella, Beth. If you do, you will not survive the hell I unleash on you."

"It can't be any worse than the hell I've survived, Skull. But don't worry. I wouldn't do that to Gabby. I want her to know the man I once loved."

"Sure doesn't seem like it," I snarl, opening the door.

"Yeah, well hearing you tell Matthew that you'll help hunt me down in exchange for your daughter has a way of changing a woman's mind," she says as I reach the outside.

Her words stop me and I turn around and face her. She's standing at the door now, her eyes glowing with unshed tears, but she's facing me head-on, her face set.

"*Me escuchaste?* What the fuck do you mean?"

"Matthew made sure I heard all about the deal the two of you agreed to."

Son of a fucking bitch. My mind immediately goes back to the phone conversation I had with Matthew. It replays every damning word. Clearly she didn't hear the whole conversation, but what the fuck does it matter? She had already succeeded in keeping my daughter away from me for way too fucking long. The only thing this information changes is the fact that Matthew will now reach the end of his life before Colin. That's all.

"You took my daughter from me for over a year by that time. You deserved whatever I decided to do. You still do."

"Poor Skull. Everyone around you always lets you down. It never has anything to do with your own choices, does it?"

"You seriously…"

"I told you we couldn't be together. All those years ago. I warned you. You made me believe you had it handled. People got killed because of our choice, because you wouldn't let me go! Pistol was able to manipulate me because of your choices! And I ran away because I thought that's what you wanted! Because that woman out there showed me things that made me believe Gabby and I had no place in your life anymore! Yet you're getting ready to take her to bed, and hating me all the while. So fuck you, Skull. I'm done being the scapegoat here. Everything, all this shit, it's not just on me. Look in the fucking mirror!" she growls, then goes to slam the door.

I put my hand up to stop her. Anger is vibrating through my body and I've had it.

"*Cuidadoso, mi esposa.* You are on thin ground. I still hold your life in my hands. You go too far."

"Like I said, do your worst. I've survived more than you can ever imagine. And I'm not your wife. I never was, but I'm definitely not now."

"You don't have to remind me of that. I give fucking thanks for it every day!" I lie. It's a bold-faced lie, but she'll never know it. *Ever.*

"You really are a bastard," she whispers, and I can see the hurt in her eyes, and for once, I take pleasure in it. Let her fucking hurt. *She's killing me.*

I'm not the one who gave up on us. You are.

"What? I am just giving you the truth. You should try it sometime. I realize it's new to you, but it actually is how most of the people in the world communicate! The only favor you ever did for me was refusing to marry me! But then, you were already planning on taking my child and leaving me, weren't you? *Maldita perra!*"

She blanches at my words. Does she understand Spanish, or is she just now realizing that I know she lied to me from the beginning? It doesn't matter. She knows what I think of her. That's enough.

"Whatever you want to think, Skull. Go ahead."

"No defense? Nothing to say for yourself, Beth? Have you finally ran out of lies?"

"It wouldn't matter. You'll believe what you want to. It doesn't matter what I say. Funny, how you can see all my faults but no one else's, not even the woman sharing your bed. Just go. We can avoid each other until you do whatever it is you need to do so Gabby and I can move out."

She closes the door and I immediately want to push it back open and yell at her some more. Fuck. She's right. I am a bastard because I feel more alive fighting with her than I've felt since the day I lost her.

"Skull? Is everything okay? Are you ready for that drink now?" Teena asks.

She's standing beside me and I just noticed her. What is she doing so close? Did she listen to the conversation Beth and I had? Most probably, since most of it was while we were screaming at each other.

"No, I don't want a fucking drink. Will you stop this, Teena? I told you I can't give you what you want. We've had this out before, and I'm tired of being nice about it. I've had enough of everything tonight," I growl, moving around her.

"*Mi amante*, surely you can see that she—"

"This isn't any of your concern, Teena. That's what I can see.

And stop calling me that. I haven't touched you in a year," I tell her as I'm walking away, giving her a view of my back.

Women. They're all fucking stupid.

I'm done with them all.

CHAPTER 9
SKULL

"Jesus, *amante*. You realize he's not going to survive this forever," Teena says, looking over the unconscious Pistol.

After the blow up with Beth last night, I had too much frustration built up. I came down here to beat the shit out of Pistol some more. I'll admit, I probably went overboard. I'm hoping she can fix the fucker, but I sure as hell won't cry if she can't. Besides, my mind is made up. I'll have Matthew here to torture in a few days. There's no way that fucker will draw clean air anymore, not after feeding Beth some bullshit recording.

I have Pistol strung up in the basement of the club. No one is allowed in here but me right now. I'm keeping him under lock and key and only doing enough to prolong his misery. I'll have to end him soon. But hopefully not today.

"I don't need forever. Can you patch him up enough for now?" I ask her, annoyed she's still here. Annoyed I even called her the first time. Mostly, I'm just fucking pissed off that I can't seem to work through all of the shit in my head.

"*Si*. I can for now."

"Good. I'm out of here."

"You're going to leave me here?" Teena asks. The room is mostly dark, the florescent light above humming and only highlighting the area that Pistol hangs from, doing very little to brighten the rest of the room.

"He's tied up, Teena. I doubt you are in any danger. Besides,

I beat the fuck out of him so many times that I doubt anything works."

"You're still mad at me."

"You should have told me you delivered that package to Beth."

"I didn't know she was the woman you grieved after, *amante*. I didn't know any of this, not until you told me."

"Even when you knew, you didn't tell me. Not until Dragon said something. You mentioned none of it until Beth reminded me last night."

"It would have served no purpose. What is done is done."

Her words do nothing to kill the rage inside of me. She's not the object of it, however. No, that's reserved for the man in the mirror that stares back at me every morning.

"Lock the door when you leave," I order her. "I'll make sure Briar has the money for your trouble."

"I could swing by your room when I'm finished. Help you take the edge off?" she offers, trying to slide her body into mine, her fingers digging into my sides.

I haven't touched a woman since the night on the phone with Matthew over a year ago when I found out Beth was alive. I made an excuse to get Teena out the door and I've never taken her to my bed since. I've went over all this with Teena and fucking hell, if nothing else, you think she would have gotten the message loud and clear last night. I've had about all I can handle of *all* women. *Christo!* I would be better off as a monk having only my hand for pleasure.

"That's not happening. It hasn't happened for a long time. I told you, I am married."

"Not really. It wasn't a real marriage. And besides, she left you. She didn't believe in you," Teena says, moving her hand up the side of my face.

Her blonde hair and the color of her eyes once reminded me of Beth. She looks nothing like her. How did I convince myself of that? Did grief blind me so clearly? She's not Hispanic. She was married to a man who was. But even so, her skin is not the same tone as my Beth's. Her smile is a pale comparison. It's not fair, but when I measure them, Teena comes up short. I had to have been blinded by grief. Grief that was for… *nothing*.

I stop her hand, pulling it away from me. "It's real. I told you this is done, Teena."

"You'll change your mind. You two can barely look at each other now."

"It's been over a year. I told you, move on to someone else," I tell her, not commenting about me and Beth. There's nothing I can say to that. *Fuck*. There's not a damn thing I can say about it.

Chapter 10
Pistol

"Let me fucking die," I tell the bitch as she injects me more with her steroids and whatever else she puts in that fucking syringe that somehow keeps me going.

"But I cannot. You're helping to keep him distracted, giving him something to keep his mind on."

"If he knew what an evil bitch you were…"

"But he doesn't."

"I could tell him if you don't let me die," I tell her, wheezing.

"You haven't yet, and your time is almost done. You won't weaken now."

"I might," I bluff.

"No. You won't. To do so would mean the death of the one person you have ever cared about. You know, Pistol, that's kind of sad, if you think about it. A man living as long as you have and not having one thing to show for it. Would you like me to tell your sister how you suffered for her in the end? Would she hate you less then? I wonder…"

"Leave Hayden alone. You fuckers said you'd leave her out of this if I…"

"If you kept your mouth shut. Exactly. But don't piss me off, Pistol. You're helpless here. I could kill you and kill your sister and there's nothing you could do about it," the cold fucking bitch says. She's right. I've been swinging for weeks. Hell, maybe months now, and there's not a goddamn thing I can do about it. If

I told Skull about Hayden, he'd probably just kill her too.

I say nothing else. I let the evil bitch do what she does to keep me alive and be a slab of meat for Skull to torture longer. When I meet Torres in hell, I will make sure she pays. That's my last thought as unconsciousness claims me.

Chapter 11
Beth

"What are you doing hiding in here?" Katie asks when she opens the door to my room.

I'm sitting on the floor with Gabby playing with her blocks. I'm not actually hiding; I'd just rather not see Skull again for a day or, you know, maybe ten. I may have held onto my cool for the most part during our confrontation last night, but this resolution I've made to stop running is not coming easy.

"I'm not hiding. Your beautiful niece and I are playing blocks," I tell her.

"Kaydee!" Gabby cries out and pulls her wobbly little butt up to run to Katie, who bends down to scoop up Gabby and plant kisses all over her.

"I swear she gets bigger every day," she whispers. Sadly, I can't argue. The days are going by so quickly. I busy myself with picking up her blocks, trying to shake off this mood I seem to be stuck in ever since my run-in with Skull. "Are things not getting any better?"

"Not especially, though we did have a nice shouting match last night with that fucking Dr. Torres around to hear it all." I sigh, wincing as I curse in front of Gabby, but I can't help it. I swear I want to kill that woman. I don't know for sure she had anything to do with the package I got when I was in the hospital, but I feel like she did, and I just keep remembering that look on her face last night.

Dr. Torres is hiding shit. I'm almost positive ...

"That fucking bastard, he still has her here?"

"Sweetness, watch your language before my girl hears you," Torch says, coming into the room with his lazy grin. It's so strange to watch him and Katie together. I may have worried when she told me about him, but it was for nothing. He's completely in love with my sister. Gabby squeals when Torch takes her away from Katie. He blows on her stomach and she giggles, letting her little hands sink into his hair and pull. Torch doesn't seem to mind, blowing more raspberries against her stomach so she cackles even louder.

I set the container of blocks to the side and rise from the floor, coming to Katie's side. Torch settles Gabby in his arms and looks over at me with an easy smile.

"How are my favorite girls today?" he asks.

"I thought I was your favorite girl?" Katie speaks up.

"Greedy woman. You've had me in your bed last night and this morning and you got to ride on the back of my bike. I even flexed my muscles for you. I know you're good, Katy-did," he tells her, bending down to kiss her and seeming unaware of the way Gabby is tugging on his beard. "Come on, Beth. Time to get out of this room. Come with us into the kitchen and I'll cook breakfast for all three of my women," Torch says, and I'm not really hungry, but it sure would feel good to get out of here. Especially if I'm not alone.

Before I can respond, Katie grabs my arm and pulls me into her, linking our arms together. I guess I'm going to the kitchen, whether I want to or not. "Explain why I put up with your ass again?" Katie asks Torch with a smile on her face.

"That's easy," he says. "The size of my enormous, D-I-C-K," Torch says, spelling out the last word as he looks down at Gabby, grinning.

"Don't flatter yourself. Your dick isn't that big. I've seen bigger," Katie huffs, pulling me through the door as Torch opens it for us.

"I think Auntie Katie needs to be reminded of how lucky she is, don't you think, Gabby?"

"Kaydee!" Gabby calls out, still playing with Torch's beard.

"You, dear husband, are way too proud of your dick," Katie grumbles. "I swear he thinks he should have the fucker bronzed." She leans down to whisper in my ear where only I can here. "And he probably should, but I'll be damned if I'll admit that to him; he's already so full of himself."

"I think Auntie Katie has a potty-mouth. I'll have to find something large to stuff in it later to shut her up," Torch says to Gabby like he's talking about the latest cartoon on television.

"You two need therapy," I laugh, taking my daughter away from Torch. "Give her to me, and if her first words have anything to do with you-know-whats, I'm coming after both of you."

I think it's the first *real* smile I've had in days. I follow Katie and Torch down the hall, suddenly feeling hungry. We've only taken a few steps before the inevitable happens though: we run into Skull. It's much worse than I imagined, however, because not only is he there, but he's standing with—

"Dr. Torres," Katie growls, standing in front of me and Gabby as if to protect us. It's sweet, and there was a time I needed it. Not now. I'm not backing away anymore. It's amazing how much strength you find when your world is shattered.

"Sweetness, they're not…"

"If you dare tell me that Skull and her aren't fucking, that woman on your shirt is the only woman who will be sucking your dick," Katie growls. I cover Gabby's ears because I think my daughter might be hearing a little too much today. Still, even with my pain, I could almost laugh. Torch is wearing a shirt that has a woman on her knees in front of a man obviously diving down on his cock. She's got a ball and chain on her ankle and above the picture is the caption: "Off the market". At the bottom is another caption: "My wife makes me happy". I never thought I'd see Torch so crazy over a woman. The fact that it's my sister is even more surreal, but I love them together. They're good for each other in ways Skull and I could never manage, even when it was good.

"I was going to say Skull and Beth aren't together anymore," Torch says, bringing me out of my thoughts. His words are like a slap across the face.

"That…"

"Katie, stop," I tell her, walking around them to face the woman I might just hate more than anyone in the world right now. Since Matthew and Colin are still alive, that's saying something.

"Torch is right," Skull says, his face looking unmovable. It might be my imagination, but there's a hint of discomfort about him. I'm glad. I want to make him uncomfortable. Maybe he'll let me leave sooner. "We're not together. I'm not sure we ever were," he says, his eyes locking on mine. Okay, maybe I was wrong. He's not uncomfortable; just a fucking asshole.

"Gabby would seem to argue with that point," I remind him quietly.

"Mommy! Mommy!" Gabby yells, pulling on my hair.

I turn my attention to her. "That's right, baby. Let's go find you some food."

I start to walk around them, and Skull stops me. "You don't have a right to be upset."

"I never said I was upset, Skull. Why would I be? You're right. We're not together, we're nothing anymore."

I keep my face blank, even if inside I feel like I'm dying.

"I think I'll just go, *amante*," Teena says, and I want to scratch her eyes out. I can't stop myself—*even if I should*.

"Things are starting to get so clear. Tell me, *doctor*, when you delivered Skull's little package to me, did you really intercept it in admissions like you said? Or did he just give it to you after you two had fun in the bedroom?"

"I…"

"I bet you knew all along who I was. Right? I mean, why else would you even think to come to me? The envelope clearly said Beth Donahue, a name I would never use. And how could I have been the only Beth in the whole hospital?"

"You were the only Beth in the maternity wing," she defends, but she doesn't look in my eye.

The bitch is lying. "Sure, I was. And you, a person who has lived here forever, never realized who Skull was enough to tell me what he looked like?"

"What are you talking about?" Skull asks, but I ignore him.

"Listen, Beth, I realize that you're upset, but I don't have anything to do with this. What Skull and I share came along after you were gone."

"Sure it did. You're as fake as the blonde in your hair, *Dr. Torres*."

"Bitch." Teena makes to grab me, but Skull grabs her arm first.

"Don't touch her," his cold as steel voice says. My eyes go to him, but he's barely looking at me. "Get my daughter out of here if you're going, Beth."

"If you would let me move out, I would have her out of here already," I growl, starting to walk away.

"I told you, you could leave after your brothers have been found. Not before. I want my daughter safe."

I look over my shoulder at him. "Yes, sir. Whatever you say."

"If you had that attitude sooner, it might have saved us a lot of heartache."

"Do you even have a heart?" He shifts, and before he can answer, I shake my head. "No, don't answer that. Obviously your heart and other attributes belong to Dr. Torres now." I turn away so he can't see the pain that causes. I walk to the kitchen, not looking back even when I hear Katie behind me.

"Fucking asshole," she growls.

I love my sister.

Chapter 12
Skull

"You know you could just stop staring at her and breakdown and go talk to her," Sabre says, sitting down at my table.

We're in the compound. Beth, Katie, and a few of the club girls are in the corner planning Katie's bachelorette party along with Briar's old lady. In the past few days, Beth has settled in and made a place for herself here in the club in ways I never thought she would. We haven't talked since that day in the hall, not really. A few words here and there when I get Gabby or bring her back, but that's it. She asked me if I had any progress on finding Matthew and Colin. I lied. I know exactly where Matthew is. I could pick him up today. I'm fucking stalling getting revenge because that would make Beth's leaving one step closer. I don't want her here and I don't want her to leave.

Jesus, I'm fucked up.

"When I need your advice on women, I'll ask for it, *hermano*."

"Seems to me you need someone's."

"It doesn't matter. I'll have Matthew taken care of this week. Once we get Colin, Beth will no longer be here."

"Are you sure that's what you want?"

"*Totalmente*," I tell him, and I'm mostly telling the truth.

"When are we making the move on Donahue?"

My heart speeds up in rhythm. Do I keep putting it off? What is that really helping? This is done, right? I hear Beth's laugh ring out and I feel this phantom pain inside of me.

"Tomorrow morning. Call the boys in. We'll have church tonight and plan. I don't want anything to go wrong."

"I can do that," he says and leans back in his chair, tilting it so it's hung in the air as if in mid-rock, studying me.

When I get tired of him staring, I finally kick my foot out, causing the chair to scoot. He flails around a moment, looking ridiculous, before getting it back under control. *Fucker.*

"Out with it and then shut the fuck up," I growl, taking the last drink of my vodka.

"You're a fucking prick, you know that?"

I shrug. I'm an even bigger one since discovering Beth is breathing, so I can't really argue and I don't really give a fuck anyway.

"I was noticing that Dr. Torres left rather quickly this morning," he says and I frown into my glass, now empty of alcohol.

The ice clinks as I slam it down. "So?"

"Is it over?"

"It's been over for a while."

"She's here almost every other night," Sabre responds.

"Not for that. What are you being such a fucking busybody for, anyway? You want to tap it? I thought Annie had your dick sewn up, *hermano*."

"Fuck you. Annie is all I need. I'm just saying if you're so confused about Beth that you're giving Teena the shove, maybe you ought to get your head out of your ass."

"I gave Teena the shove way before Beth was back in the picture."

"So you consider her in the picture now?"

"Fuck no. I'm just saying Teena has nothing to do with Beth. *Christo*! Are we seriously talking about this shit? Next thing I know, you'll be asking me to make your cut pink."

"Fuck off. I'm just saying if you want Beth back, you better start figuring out how to make that happen instead of pushing her farther away."

"When I want your advice, I'll ask for it. Besides there's too much shit between us. Looking at her some days is hard enough. I sure as hell don't want to talk to her."

"So fuck her. Sex can work out a hell of a lot of anger."

"*Fuck no!* Women are too much fucking trouble. I think I'll stick to my hand," I tell him, grabbing the bottle on the table and pouring more into my glass.

"Funny how you decided on your hand and not a club whore. I mean, they're free, they have no strings. Seems to me a warm pussy is better than a calloused hand any fucking day of the week. Take my advice, Skull. If a woman has grabbed more than your dick, don't let it go easily," he says, getting up.

I let him leave without responding. When I want him to be my fucking therapist, I'll tell him. It doesn't matter if he is right. The thought of sinking between the legs of any woman right now leaves my cock as limp as if I just took a swim in an ice pond in the Arctic.

Any woman besides Beth.

Motherfucker.

Chapter 13
Beth

"If you stare at him any harder, your tongue will be hanging out," Briar's old lady, Stephanie Sakal, says. Everyone calls her Sacks. I don't know why and I'm kind of afraid to ask. I like her though. Her and Briar have just got together. Love at first sight. He literally saw her walking on the street, picked her up, put her on the back of his bike and then claimed her. I'm learning these Devil's Blaze men move hard and fast when it comes to women. Too bad I picked the one who didn't have staying power. Again, my eyes go to Skull, who is sitting over there talking to Sabre.

"He's planning something," I say mostly to myself.

"Men usually are, honey," Candy says. She's one of the club women, but she seems cool. She swore she never slept with Skull. Not that it should matter, but it does.

"Amen to that," Katie joins in, kissing a sleeping Gabby on her forehead. We should put her in her crib, but Katie loves holding her, so I haven't tried. It wouldn't surprise me if there's little Torches running around soon. Heaven help us all. I can't imagine the chaos they would cause. I almost smile, then I remember I won't be around to see it.

"I mean something about Matthew and Colin," I mumble, wishing I could read Skull's lips.

The girls go quiet. "What makes you say that?" Katie asks, suddenly studying Skull even more than I am.

"It's just a feeling, but it's a strong one."

"So? He needs to shut the fuckers down. Blow them off the map as far as I'm concerned," one of the other girls says. I can't remember her name. She's Annie's friend, kind of quiet, but I don't think it's because she's shy.

"Sabre says he's going to be leaving again sometime this week," Annie whispers like she's giving out state secrets, and I guess in a way she is.

"That means they've found Colin," Katie says.

"Or Matthew," I mumble.

"With any luck, both of them. We should party," Sacks says.

"I need to find out when they're going and where," I mutter to myself, then realize the others heard me. *Shit.*

"Why the fuck would you need to know that?" Katie asks, but she knows already; I see it in her eyes.

"Because I'm going to kill him."

"Bethie," she starts.

I cut her off. "Don't start, Katie. You above all people know what Matthew took from me… from us."

"You don't even know for sure it's Matthew. It could be Colin."

"Then he'll just be practice for the real target. They both deserve to die. You said that yourself."

"You can't risk yourself. Gabby needs you. I can do it."

"Hell no. You've given that monster enough. I will kill him. It's my right."

"I think that's my line," she mutters.

"You have Torch and you can't let anything stand in your way of that Katie. What you have is real and you get to live it out. You don't just give that up."

"You could have that," she mutters. The other girls go silent as we talk. They're hearing too much, but I trust them. I don't know why, but despite everything, I feel like we're all family.

"Skull can barely look at me. I'm not getting that."

"There's other men, honey," Candy says, and I give her a sad smile that I feel all the way into the depths of my soul.

"Not for me."

"So what do we do?" Annie asks. I look at her blue eyes, which shine extra bright. "I know all about having someone you need revenge on. I don't need to know what went down, but I'm in. So, what do we do?"

Wow... okay.

"Same here. I'm all in," Sacks says, and all eyes go to her.

"It could cause you problems with your men. This isn't your war, ladies. It's mine."

"Ours," Katie interjects. I frown at her.

"Bull hockey!" exclaims Annie. "We're the women of Devil's Blaze. The Donahues not only fucked with you girls, they fucked with our men. They've tried to kill each of them. I think that's reason enough. So, I repeat, what do we do?"

I smile despite myself. She doesn't curse but very seldom, and her sweet nature is directly at war with the look on her face right now. But, as I look around at all of these women, I realize I'm surrounded by fighters. It looks like I'm not alone. After all this time of being alone, and then my time with only Katie and Gabby, it's a strange feeling.

"We find out what the men are planning first, I guess," I tell them because I really have no clue on how to wage war. I just know I'm going to.

"Then what?"

"We find a way to foil their plans—or at least delay them—then strike ourselves." This comes from Katie. She looks at me with that kickass smile she used to get right before we'd strike out at our father or grandfather. That time was hell, but being a team with my twin? That part I definitely miss.

Looks like we're going to war.

Chapter 14
Beth

"They're meeting now," Sacks says, coming into my room where all the girls but Annie have gathered. She'll be here soon. I hope I'm not opening a can of worms. Skull already hates me. If I cause a war between the men and women of the club, Skull is going to kill me. I push those thoughts out of my head and pay attention to the here-and-now.

"We need to find out what's being said in the meeting."

"Already got that handled," Katie says.

I freeze. "What do you mean you already got it handled? Did Torch tell you what's going down?"

"Are you kidding? You know how close-lipped these men are about church. Nope, I didn't even try. I just remembered what I think you've forgotten, sister dear."

"What's that?" I question, almost afraid to ask.

"That I managed to survive our father and grandfather for a lot of fucking years and that we didn't do too bad for two women and a baby on the run for two years."

"If you don't count having a one-night-stand with a man tasked with bringing you back home at any cost to use as leverage, then sure, you were great. Oh, and we won't even get into the runaway eighteen-wheeler…"

"Sarcasm doesn't become you, sister dear. In any event, you know that little box of toys we took from our father's room at Hell?" I smirk. Hell is what we called my grandfather's mansion.

Sadly, it more than lived up to the name.

"Toys? Toenails and doughnuts, why are you carting around sex toys used by your father? That's just wrong on so many levels."

We all look up as Annie walks in and the laughter erupts almost simultaneously. It might be because of the comment about our father's toys, but more than likely it has to do with her aversion to cursing.

"Not *those* kind of toys, fruitcake," her friend Louise says.

"I swear, being with two men has fried your brain," Candy adds.

"I'm with *one*," Annie grumbles, though she blushes.

"Girl, please, you have both of them men jumping to your every command. They are pussy-whipped with a capital P," Candy says.

Annie's blush deepens, but she doesn't deny a thing. It's probably for the best; no one would believe her.

"Where's the baby?" Annie asks suddenly, looking around.

"Katie got Mattah to babysit," I tell her. Mattah is an older woman who works in the kitchen. She's great with Gabby and she's been really good to me since I got back.

"Actually, Mattah had to go home. Her daughter went into early labor."

"Then where is my daughter?" I ask, annoyed. I love Katie, but I just don't trust Gabby with very many people.

"Oddly enough, she wanted her Uncle Torch."

"He took Gabby into the meeting?" I asked, completely surprised.

"Yep. Along with something else…"

"What else?" I ask, knowing from that look on Katie's face that she's up to something. In answer, she takes out her cellphone and starts pushing buttons.

"Gather around, girls. We're about to attend our first church meeting."

"What did you do?"

"I slipped Father dear's mini nanny cam he used against us onto Gabby's hair bow."

"No fucking way. That will be way too big! You'll get us killed. They'll see it!"

"Relax, Louise. When I say mini, I mean *microscopic*. It's amazing what money and a twisted sick fuck can find when they want to spy on you," Katie says hatefully, and that same hate twists inside of me too. I hate my father for so many things. I thought I hated him before, especially the day I discovered Katie was alive. That was nothing compared to the hate that grew once I traveled back to France.

"But…" Louise starts.

"She's right. Trust me, I carried it around for months not even knowing it was there."

"Where did he hide it on you?" Annie asked, studying my face closely, almost like she understands what kind of monster that Katie and I called father. I doubt that's possible. My hand automatically goes to my upper arm, rubbing it through the cotton sleeve.

"It doesn't matter. Just trust me: Torch will never see it."

"Now let's see what the boys are up to, shall we?" Katie, says, drawing attention back to her.

When I look at her, she's looking me in the eye. Memories are there. The same ones I'm remembering. Nightmares even. She gives me a weak smile and I walk to her. I don't want to remember those. Not right now. It haunts me enough at night. Katie pulls up the camera feed on her phone. Time to get my mind on the task at hand. The past needs to stay in the past.

Maybe I can bury it with the cold dead bodies of Matthew

and Colin.

Chapter 15
Skull

"What are you doing with Gabby? Where's Beth?" I ask when Torch comes through the door carrying my daughter.

I immediately get up to take her from him. She's already fucked up enough about not knowing me. She's not going to get the chance to think of another man as her *papá*. That shit is not happening.

"Beth was sick. Katie was watching her, but she got a migraine. Mattah had to leave, so I volunteered to keep her."

I ignore the fear that's wrapped around my heart at the mention of Beth being sick. That's not my concern anymore. It doesn't stop the words that come out of my mouth, however.

"Is Beth okay?"

"Katie said the nightmares have been keeping Beth awake. She took the baby so she could sleep."

"Nightmares?"

"Yeah. Living with Redmond Jr. and Senior wasn't exactly a fun-filled ride. Katie gets them, too."

His words burrow down inside of me and I don't want to think about them—at least not right now. I'll think about them later after I take down Matthew.

"Call the club doctor and get Beth looked at," I grumble.

"No offense, boss, but if you get your girlfriend to check out your ex-wife, you're just inviting a murder," Briar says.

"True enough. My Annie is shy, but if I did that, she'd tear the doctor apart limb by limb."

"My money is on Beth," Latch speaks up. "She's quiet. Those quiet women can be hell on wheels."

"True story," Sabre says, bumping fists with Latch.

"I don't know. I think Dr. Torres might have the advantage, being a feisty Latina and all," teases Clutch.

"She's not Latina, you idiot," Shaft grumbles.

"I think she might take Beth, too. But it'd be a hell of a match," Torch chimes in.

"Will you fuckers shut up? I don't have a fucking girlfriend and I'm talking about Doc Patton. Get him to come out. He will help the club anytime we ask."

"Patton? Jesus Christ eating pancakes! Is that asshole still alive?" Torch asks. "How old is he now?"

"Shit, he has to be a hundred and twenty," Briar says.

"*Mierda!* Can we talk about what the fuck we're here for?"

"You know you need to watch the words you say in front of Gabby. Before you know it she's going to be running around telling everyone to fuck off."

"Good. Then they'll know not to mess with her," I grumble at T-Rex.

"Not so good," Beast objects, and his deep voice quiets the room down. "Little girls are supposed to be cherished and taken care of. They shouldn't need to tell anyone shit. That's our job." The room goes completely silent now. The man's eyes are glued on little Gabby and there's such pain coming off of him, it swamps the room. I haven't had Gabby long, but I swear I don't see how Beast does it. I don't know how the bastard still finds the courage to breathe.

I clear my throat over the lump I have in it and I hold a sleeping Gabby a little tighter. "Okay, let's talk business. Namely, Matthew. Do we know anything about this damn cabin he's holed up at?"

"It's a freaking cabin in Hurricane, Tennessee," Torch says.

"Tennessee? What's the asshole doing so fucking close? That's not even three hours away!" Briar growls.

"If I had to guess, I'd say he's staying close so he and Colin can attack easier," I answer.

"You think they're planning shit?" Latch asks.

"*Seguro*." I know they are. I can feel it.

"Then we should give them the fight they want," Beast murmurs, and I agree one hundred and fifty percent.

"What do we know about the cabin?" I prompt.

"They have it guarded like fucking Fort Knox," Torch says, and finally he is all business. Well, except for his t-shirt that has a giant rooster on it being whipped by a shadow figure which is obviously a very well-endowed female. Writing under the picture proclaims his wife is a giant cock tamer. *Christo*. I have no idea where he finds these motherfucking shirts.

"Any weaknesses?" I ask him, turning my mind back to the business at hand.

"The property butts up against the Green River. I think we can bring a boat in from the East and slip through the defenses there pretty easily. Plus, surveillance shows that bastard Matthew and about ten of his top henchmen. Sadly, there's no sign of that fucker Colin. I think it's pretty clear that word has gotten out we're hunting them."

"Good, I want them to fear what's coming," I tell him.

"Might make them harder to find," Sabre cautions.

"I'll find them," I tell him coldly. "Torch, what about explosives? I'm not about to walk into another fucking mess like last time," I growl.

"That's Colin's calling card, mostly," Beast says, and I know he's upset I didn't take Colin out and, instead, exacted all my revenge on Redmond. That's on me, too. I was too fucked up in the head to see what was going on.

"There's a supply building on the outskirts of the property line on the south side. Scans show that it contains explosives inside, but that's it. Of course, we can't be a hundred percent sure until we get in there, but it looks like it's mostly clear," Torch informs us.

"The cabin itself might be sketchy, but with the bastard inside it, I don't see it being rigged to blow," Clutch adds.

"Anything else pop up through surveillance that might help us?" I question the brothers, shifting Gabby in my arms. For being barely two, she's a chunk.

"Glad you asked, boss. Matthew and his men are randy motherfuckers. They have women delivered for a party every Friday," Torch says with a grin.

He knows as well as I do, this is our in.

"That's two days away. T-Rex, you're over the women. Do you think Clara and a few girls would be willing to help us out?"

Briar sits back with a calculating look. "You're thinking of intercepting their shipment with our own girls?" he asks.

"Damn straight," I answer without hesitation.

"I don't want the girls hurt," he says.

"Shit, man. We've trained our women in hand-to-hand so good they can take down any man. Plus, they can fire any gun on and off the market with pinpoint precision. Clara helped train them. Let her handpick the ones we should use," I answer.

The men around me seemingly grunt in approval. It wasn't an exaggeration. The first thing we do when we agree to take a woman on is to train her so she can take care of herself. If a john tries to rough her up, we'll send our own message, but she damn sure will make certain he doesn't take what she isn't willing to give.

"How many are we going to need?" T-Rex asks.

"Manny is their supplier. He usually brings seven girls."

"Fucking Manny. Does Diesel know Manny's tramping around in his territory?" I ask Torch.

"He does now. He wasn't exactly happy."

I nod in agreement. Diesel will nail his ass to the wall. Manny won't be an issue.

"Okay. Let's set it up. I want enough firepower to light up Afghanistan on a cloudy night," I order.

"How many men we talking?" Beast asks.

"Me, you, T-Rex, Latch, and Shaft."

"Boss," Sabre starts at about the same time Torch interjects.

"No fucking way!" Everything in him is ready for a fight.

Shit, why can't my men just listen to fucking orders?

Chapter 16
Beth

My nerves pick up as the meeting starts. It's so hard to even watch Skull, let alone hear his voice. I stand behind Katie and try to calm my nerves. I know what I'm planning on doing is crazy in the eyes of some. I don't care. I need to do this. Redmond and my grandfather took so much from me and Katie. I may have lived in hell for a little while, but Katie lived in it a lot longer. I need to do this for me, for Katie, and especially for Gabby. I owe it to all of us. They took so much from me and Katie, but Gabby? They took her chance to grow up in a happy home with both her parents, and I never want her to be used as a pawn in the family. They must be destroyed. Even as I'm justifying my reasons, I know the real truth. I know why I want to destroy Matthew and Colin. I rub my upper arms in memory… in just one memory of hundreds. If anyone needed to die, it would be my stepbrothers.

My attention is brought back to the meeting we're watching on Katie's phone when Skull starts talking. When he orders Torch to call the club doctor out here to check me out, I nearly lose it.

"What the fuck is he thinking? If that skank comes within two feet of me," I growl. I stop, however when the men start going over who they think will win in a fight. When Sabre brings up Annie, I laugh.

"Darn tootin' I would! No one is touching what's mine!" she says with a blush, and we all laugh. I stop when Torch thinks that whore Teena would take me.

"I'll kill him," Katie growls. "Kill him dead."

"I might help you," I tell her because that kind of hurts. None of the other members know me quite that well, but I expected Torch at least to have faith in me.

"Well, to be fair, he doesn't realize the training we've had," says Katie. "I haven't ever told him, or showed him for that matter... though that might change tonight, the damn bastard." That last part makes me smile.

As they continue the meeting, I'm still smarting over being discussed in the same breath as Teena. The only part that makes me feel marginally better is when Skull denies having a girlfriend. That's short-lived, however, when I remember back all those years when Skull told me he didn't have girlfriends. I guess old dogs keep the same old fucking tricks.

As they reveal more and more, my mind goes into planning mode. Nothing about this is going to be easy, but it can be done. The hardest part will be getting away from the club to attack. Plus, Skull is planning on attacking Friday, which only leaves us tomorrow to do it before he gets the chance. Not much breathing time for sure.

"I know where the lake is," Candy pipes up.

"I have a small john-boat we can load in the back of Briar's old truck. I've been on the Green River. It's pretty lazy, not a lot of current. We can put a trolling motor on there and be across the lake in no time," Sacks says.

"We need a diversion, really," Annie puts in. "Someone who can distract them and get all eyes on her while the rest of us make our move."

"Damsel in distress," Louise says, grabbing our attention.

"What do you mean?" asks Annie.

"She's saying one of us can pretend to be stranded and

distract them and get inside while the rest of us come up from the river," I answer, seeing the plan unfold in my mind. This could really work.

"Especially if the woman who's distracting has big boobs and a ready smile," Katie joins in with a wry grin.

All eyes go to Louise, who is easily a double D, possibly larger. She's pretty too, with dark black hair that falls in waves over her deep chocolate skin, which glistens. She could easily double for Sanaa Lathan.

"Do you know any self-defense? Can you shoot a gun?"

"And then some," she says confidently.

I don't like it. I wish I could be the one to do that part, but I'd be recognized immediately. This will have to be the way it is, I guess. My eyes go back to the phone when I hear Skull.

"Damn it, Torch!"

"Oh, shit," Katie says, and we all watch the screen again.

"Damn you, Skull. You don't know what Redmond did to Katie," he growls. Katie gasps, and I reach around to hold her hand. "You don't know what he let Matthew do to both of them!" Torch growls, and my heart stops.

"What does he know, Katie? What did you tell him?"

She looks over her shoulder at me with tears in her eyes.

"Almost everything," she whispers, and I feel a cold splash of dread fill me.

No...

Chapter 17
Skull

"Damn it, Torch!" I yell, distracted by the way Gabby is moving and shifting in my arms. She pulls herself up and immediately starts tugging on the gage in my ear.

"Damn you, Skull. You don't know what Redmond did to Katie. You don't know what he let Matthew do to both of them. I'm going, and the only way you can stop me is to put a bullet in me."

His words makes my blood run cold.

"Matthew tortured Beth?" I ask, not even recognizing my own voice.

"Daily," Torch growls. "Her and Katie both," he delivers in a deadly calm, but it's full of hate.

"Unka Torch!" Gabby squeals, pushing against me to try and get to him.

"Hey, kiddo," Torch smiles, even if it doesn't touch his eyes, and he reaches for her.

Bastard has no idea the knife he's twisting in my gut right now. The wound burns white hot. Knowing my child chooses Torch over me kills. I'm still a stranger to her, despite being around her just as much as he is. She's bonded with him. I want to scream at the unfairness of it. *I'm her father!* I should have been there for her first breath… her first tears, her first tooth, her first words… I'll never get any of it back. Never.

Hate, anger, and rage burn inside of me as I turn in my chair to lower Gabby onto the floor. Her legs kick out until I make sure she's standing strong, then she takes off running towards my brother. I watch as he scoops her up and her face explodes in happiness as she giggles. It destroys me. He blows on her stomach and makes noises, then kisses all over it. Gabby laughs louder and pulls on his hair when he stops.

"Uh-g-in! Unka Torch! Uh-g-in!" she shrieks, and he repeats. I watch until I can't handle it anymore. I need to know what happened to Beth.

"Did he rape her?" I growl, and the room goes still. Even Gabby picks up the anger in my voice and buries her face into Torch's neck.

"What do you care?" he asks. "You said you were through with Beth," the bastard cockily shoots back at me.

"Did. He. Rape. Her." I ask, punching each word singularly and with hardened anger. He's about two steps away from feeling a wrath that I have never given one of my brothers before. The only thing saving him from being thrown across the room right now is the fact that he's holding my daughter.

"Brother, you treat Beth like shit for the choices she made, but her choices saved my woman's life. For that, she has my thanks and my loyalty. So, I'm not telling you. It's Beth's story to tell, and if she wants to tell you, then she will."

"Everyone out!" I growl.

Silence rings through the room, except for little Gabby who whispers, "He mad." Regret fills me. I don't want her to see me as the monster I've become. I just can't seem to stop it. I have so much rage boiling inside of me that it's slowly killing me. Chairs begin scraping across the concrete floor as the men finally obey.

"Sabre, you take Gabby."

"Sure thing, boss."

Once everyone clears out and we're left with just the two of us, we stare at each other in a tense showdown.

"Tell me," I order, waiting.

Torch is silent and looks me over. I do my best to keep my face impassive, but I know I failed to lock down all of my emotion when he leans back and stares me in the eyes.

"You still love her."

"That doesn't concern you, motherfucker. Answer the question. *La violo?*"

He stares at me a few more minutes. Just when I'm about to go off, he answers, "No."

Relief floods through me and I stand up. I need some fresh air. Shit. I'm lying to myself. I know I need to let out some of the anger inside of me… let it run free where no one can see me. That's the only way I'm able to function these days. My thoughts immediately turn to Pistol. He may meet his end today like he's been begging me for.

I'm almost to the door when Torch stops me. "Skull?"

"*Si?*" My voice is hoarse, the monster inside of me too close to the surface.

"There can be things that a woman endures. Things that are worse than or at least just as bad as rape," he says, and any relief I felt earlier is gone in an instant. I'm left with a coldness that is deep and freezes me to the bone.

"What…" I clear my throat and try to breathe.

Before I can finish my question, Torch continues. "Whatever hell you blame Beth for putting you through, brother, believe me when I tell you that she paid for it over and over."

"I don't—"

"And her hell almost killed her, brother. It almost ended her. It was so bad that it caused the sweet innocent woman you fell in love with to take a man's life. Think about that."

I can't say anything to him. I couldn't if I wanted to. *Mierda!* Right now, I'm having trouble standing. It takes me a little bit to go over everything he's told me. When I finally do speak, my voice is thick with emotion.

"She should have told me," I growl, trying my best to hang on to my anger.

"Katie said Beth tried. She said Beth stood tall and faced the devil and told him to go straight to hell, even," Torch says.

"Then why?" I growl, frustrated.

"Redmond played his trump card. He showed her a video of you in the scopes of a rifle, telling Beth your life was in her hands."

Fucking Donahues and their stunts they pull. I'm so fucking tired of the way they have manipulated and ruined my life.

"It still doesn't mean shit. She should have…"

"Maybe so," Torch agrees, again interrupting me. Fucking asshole. I don't want logic—not right now. "But the asshole also dragged Katie out, bound up, crying, gagged, and having been badly beaten. A sister she loved. A sister that, up until that point, Beth believed was dead and lost to her forever. I think that might just tip the scales a little, don't you? Especially if you've lived the life that Beth has, sheltered and guarded from the world."

I want to scream at him or beat the fuck out of him. I don't want to talk or even work through my anger at Beth. I need it. I need the distance.

"I know what you're trying to do here, but…" I growl, but the bastard is not quite finished yet. He blasts me, yet again.

"She was nineteen, Skull. Nineteen. Fuck, man. Think about that, will you?" I growl an unintelligible sound and rake my hands through my hair. "Nineteen, man."

"Fine! She was right to make her choices. Doesn't mean she shouldn't have tried harder to see me when she had Gabby! She wasted *two years!* Two years that I can never have back, Torch."

"I get it. I do. I can't say I fully understand that, myself. Except if you get told you're worthless and garbage to be thrown away often enough, you start to believe it."

The fucker is pissing me off. He's trying to clear Beth of any wrongdoing. He's acting like I don't have a right to be fucking pissed. That's easy for him to say. He isn't me. He hasn't lived my life since Beth left. *He wasn't betrayed by the woman he loved.*

"You weren't robbed of two fucking years with your *niña*, left thinking you killed the woman you loved!"

Torch sighs and gets up. He slaps me hard on the shoulder.

"True, brother," he agrees. "But if you aren't careful, it won't be Beth robbing you of more time with your daughter and the woman you love. It will be the bastard staring back at you in the mirror."

Having delivered that nice little dagger, he walks around me. He goes out into the hall and closes the door. When he's gone, I'm left… alone. Alone as I have been for years. I tear the clock down off the wall beside me and slam it into the wall across the room. It explodes on impact and shatters into a hundred pieces. That does nothing to make me feel better. Nothing.

Time to visit Pistol.

Chapter 18
Beth

"What did you tell him, Katie?!" I yell when Sabre leaves the meeting and I can no longer hear. I don't want Skull to know. I don't... I can't... "What did you tell him?!?"

"Beth, calm down. You didn't do anything wrong. Maybe it will be good if Skull finally knows the fucking hell you lived through. Maybe that will help him understand!"

"No! I don't want *anyone* to know! That's mine! No one gets to know what I lived through! You had no right to tell Torch!"

"I had every right! He's my man! This shit didn't just happen to you. It happened to me too, and it happened for a hell of a lot longer! I get to share that with Torch. I need to share that with Torch. Sometimes, it gets to me so much that it fucking chokes me at night. I can't keep it in any longer! It's destroying me!" she cries and I close my eyes.

"We'll leave and let you guys talk about things. Do you want to meet later tonight? Sabre and Latch tell me we're staying at the club for the next few days while they try and take care of any threats. So we'll all be here," Annie whispers.

"That'd be good. We can meet in the game room in the basement. We'll tell them we're planning for my bachelorette party again. About nine tonight?" Katie says, her voice broken.

When everyone has finally gone, I sink to the floor, wrapping my arms around my legs. I refuse to give in to the tears. I've done too much of that. I look at Katie. I know she can see the tears gathered in my eyes because I see them in hers.

"I don't want Skull to know."

"Maybe if he knew…"

"It would what? Magically erase all the hateful words? The fact that I kept his child from him? The fact that he sleeps with another woman now? There's no going back, Katie. It's much too late."

"You're scared," she says and I don't bother denying it. "Is that why you didn't want to push when you first got the pictures of Skull in the hospital? Are you afraid to show him, Beth?"

"You've seen Dr. Torres and Nicole. You saw the girl in the picture, Katie."

"So? They can't hold a candle to you, Beth. Besides, it wouldn't matter, not if Skull loves you. Torch didn't even blink at my scars. Not once."

"He might have loved the Beth he knew, but it's been too long. And we both know we might have the same scars on the inside, but on the outside…"

"If they bother you that much, why don't you see a surgeon?"

"Money? Time away from Gabby? Fear? Pick a reason, any reason."

"So we're really going to go through with this? We're going to kill Matthew?"

"I'm going to. For you, for me… for Gabby and…"

"Our real mother," she whispers.

"For her," I whisper. We just stare at each other for what seems like hours, but in reality is just minutes. Each of us lost in our own thoughts and what might have been… if things had only been different.

If only…

Chapter 19
Skull

Tortured. Worse than rape. Nightmares.

I'm slamming my fist into the meat slab that hangs from the hook suspended from the ceiling. I'm zoned out, completely in my own head as Torch's words play over and over. I want to march into Beth's room and demand that she tell me exactly what the fuck went on while she was gone. Doing that feels like being weak. It feels like opening myself up to the woman who turned her back on me.

Everything Torch said was valid. I can't even deny it. I'm left in the end with the same question I always have. The same question I always come back to.

Why couldn't she choose me?

It's selfish and, in her position, I most likely would have chosen the same path... except I would have come back to her. Nothing would have stopped me from finding my way back. Especially photos or some damned recording.

"Let me die," a fading voice pleads, pulling me out of my head. I look up and see Pistol and even I wince. *Joder.* I may have gone too far this time. I may not have a choice but to grant him his wish.

"I'll call the doctor to come knock you out," I mumble. It's more than he fucking deserves. I'll have her give enough to make sure he doesn't wake up again.

"I have...a...sis...sister," he manages to say. I stop. Does he think he'll gain sympathy from me after all of his betrayals?

"Why do I care? You took from me the thing that is most important above all. You planned to…"

"I know… things."

"Anything you know, I will discover eventually."

"About..."

"You're dead. Nothing you tell me will save you," I respond, just to make sure he knows I'm not playing his damn game.

"Not asking for that," he tells me, surprising clear. His swollen eyes start to shut and I know he's fading. That can't happen. I walk over to the wall by the entrance and flip a button. The chain and hook slowly lower and, inch by inch, the body descends.

When Pistol's legs buckle under him, I click off the button and walk over to him. I take the metal chain that's been used to shackle him and slip it off the hook. His body immediately falls to the ground in a flat thud. He groans. I look over him, surveying what I've done to him. Moments like this are fleeting, but they're when I know I have a little bit of sanity left in me. Moments of clarity when I look at the monster I've become behind closed doors and know I can never find my way back. I'm too far gone—too close to the edge.

Pistol's body is just a huge lump. So many bones have been broken, so many cuts have been made that most of him doesn't resemble anything close to the man he was before—most notably, his face. I can't slam my fists into it as often as I want. It takes too long to recover and the satisfaction isn't there anymore. As a result, his nose is broken, swollen, and there's a grotesque shade of black that slowly blends into purple around his eyes… eyes that don't see anymore, or if they do, it's through a small slit that the swelling allows. I'm pretty sure his jaw has been broken too. His fingers and hands are shattered; that was done prior to me putting him in chains. The most telling area is his ribs and stomach. Bruised over and over, swollen and cut so the red of the blood has dried and mingled into the bruised skin. The beating I gave him tonight hasn't added to the rainbow just yet. I have a feeling he's not going to live until it does. Pity.

"What could you tell me that I want to hear? That could possibly make it worth me not hearing you draw your last breath, *hijo de puta*?" I spit on him with that last insult.

"I have… a sister… who needs protection…"

"Why in the fuck would I care?"

"Most… of what I did…" He wheezes and coughs for a few seconds before he can continue. "I did to protect her."

"Blackmailed?" I ask, not believing him.

"Not at first." I wait for him to finish, his breathing growing ragged, much more so than before. Maybe a rib punctured a lung. "Got in too deep… You… You protect her…"

"Protect the sister of my enemy? Why would I ever do that, *cabron*? You're shit out of luck."

"She's innocent," he moans and coughs. Blood drips from his lips. I definitely went too far this time. "Chrome Saints have someone in your club," he says, coughing again.

Well, now. It looks like the motherfucker has my attention.

"Who?" I ask, kneeling down to hear his words because he's barely whispering now.

"Promise you will protect my sister. They'll kill her…"

"I promise," I tell him easily. If the information is right, I might send a man out to get her. She might make a good club whore. That's protection—mostly.

"I need your promise," he whispers coughing up more blood, and there's a rattle in his chest. *Mierda!*

"I want everything. You stay alive until I have it all or I'll kill your sister myself," I growl. Betrayal burns in my gut, adding to the misery inside of me, feeding the monster beneath the surface.

"Need… sister…" Pistol wheezes in between each word. His body shaking with the force it takes to get them out.

"Tell me!"

"Viper sent his…"

"His what?" I yell, slapping Pistol's face to try and bring him around.

It doesn't help. I've gone too far. He's dead. Motherfucker! He's dead! Who the fuck is the mole? I have someone in my club betraying me besides Pistol. How could I have been so motherfucking blind? Who is it? Briar? Latch? One of the newer recruits?

How much can a man take before he breaks? I lock it down for now. I need to figure how to deal with this. I'm fucking tired of everything. The only thing I know for sure is that now I have more than just the Donahue Brothers to destroy.

Chapter 20
Beth

"I'm Doctor Patton. The club called and asked me to come down. Your brother-in-law said you were sick?"

I'm standing at the door of my room, a little in shock. I just came back from meeting with the ladies. We planned everything out for tomorrow and I'm exhausted. Annie, due to her being pregnant, will be watching Gabby tomorrow and helping distract the men. She'll enlist a few of the club girls to help, too. The one main concern is Torch. Katie says she can handle it though, so I'm going to trust in her. It's decided that me, Katie, Sacks, Louise, and Candy will all go. We'll meet at Sack's and Briar's home, and from there, take the truck and boat. Briar told her he'll be gone most of the day on club business, so that part should work out okay. Louise is in charge of firepower. Her brother runs a pawnshop. Katie gave her a list of what we are looking for. If there's one thing that Katie and I have done in the last two years, it's train ourselves in weapons and self-defense.

We will never be helpless again. That's one promise we made ourselves and made to Gabby.

So after all that, what I really want to do is go see my daughter who is spending the night with Annie and tell her goodnight. The last thing I wanted was to deal with a doctor. No matter how good-looking he is. *And he is.* He stands even taller than Skull. I'd say he's six foot five, maybe more. He's built in ways that makes you feel small and womanly in comparison. Broad shoulders with a defined body that are definitely pleasing to the eye. He's not quite as built as Skull, but still dang good. He's got on jeans and a sweater and looks so refined with his blonde hair, which is cut short around the head. The top is a little longer, but perfectly fixed. He's got sparkling blue eyes and a nice smile. He should be everything that makes my heart speed up, plus he's the complete opposite of Skull.

Over the years, I've had men flirt with me, but I've ignored them. Skull was occupying my heart and there was no reason to look elsewhere. Plus, there are things about my body now that I never want to show another person. I've realized that I will forever be alone, and for the most part, I am okay with that. Still, I know a good-looking man when I see one, and Dr. Patton is all that and more.

It surprises me. I didn't figure this would be the kind of doctor he would pick to examine me. I thought they were getting some older man. Still, this is probably one more sign that Skull really is done with me. That shouldn't bother me; I've known that and accepted it.

Still, it *does* bother me somehow.

"I'm fine. I'm sorry they wasted your time," I tell him with a smile as I open the door to my room. I was hoping to get a shower before I go see Gabby.

"Maybe I should just do a quick exam to be sure? This is my first call for the Devil's. They usually get my dad to do everything. I don't want to take a chance on making anyone unhappy."

I stop and look up at him. "I'll tell them I made you leave."

"From what I know of the club, I don't think that would be enough to save my job," he returns.

I sigh. He's probably right.

"This is ridiculous," I grumble. "Come on in, but can we try and make it quick? I need to go check on my daughter."

"Sure thing. You have a child?" he asks, following me in.

"A little girl. She just turned two. Gabby. She's my reason for living." He probably thinks those are just pretty words, but for me, it's the total truth.

"I have a son myself. He just turned three. They sure make life better."

"That, they do," I agree, looking around and finally sitting at the foot of the bed. "I'm not sure what you're supposed to examine. I had a headache earlier, but I'm fine now."

He puts his bag on the nightstand and pulls out a stethoscope and a few other items from it, arranging them.

"Do you get a lot of headaches?" he asks while using an instrument to check my temperature by clicking it in my ear.

"Occasionally I get migraines. I don't sleep well. Old ghosts…"

"I understand. I had the same problem when I first got divorced. Hard to get used to an empty bed and a quiet house."

"You don't have custody of your son?"

"Joint. I get him every second week of the month. It works for now, but we will have to work something out when Chase starts school. Helen and I have talked about it. I'm sure we will sort it out eventually."

"You get along well with your ex? That's good. Skull and I barely talk to each other," I admit with a sigh, feeling tired.

"Your ex's name is Skull? A lady who lives on the wild side." He laughs. "Tell me where your headaches start."

He's standing over me. If I reach a certain way, my hand will hit him. So I reach up over my shoulder to show him the place at the back of my neck where the pain usually starts. I jump when his cold hand touches the back of my neck, partly because it's cold and partly because it's been so long since any man has touched me, no matter how innocently. Single mothers rarely have time to go to the doctor; we usually work through being sick.

"That's me. Wild Beth." I laugh, trying to get comfortable, but he does something with his hand around my neck and it pops. There's a moment of pain, but then he pushes down with his hand and I swear I think my toes actually curl. "Oh my God, whatever you're doing, don't stop." I laugh again and he joins in this time.

Then, the door slams.

"Who the fuck are you and why do you have your hands on my wife?"

I tense up when I see Skull, who looks like he'd like to tear the doctor's head from his body. When his eyes move down to meet mine, I wonder if he wouldn't like to do the same to me.

Then I recall his words.

His wife?

CHAPTER 21
SKULL

I'm fucked up after everything Pistol told me—and didn't tell me. I got Beast and Torch to help drag the body into a truck and we buried him where no one but the crows will find him. We threw in some lime and a few other things to help make sure the dead stay dead, so to speak. Out of all of my men, I figure the safest two to lean on are Beast and Torch, but who the hell knows anymore. It's clear that I have lost my edge when it comes to judging a man.

For that reason alone, I haven't told any of the men yet what the bastard Pistol told me, though I can tell Torch knows something is up. If they were shocked by the shape Pistol was in, they didn't tell me. Torch kept giving me strange looks all the way back. I don't know what the motherfucker is thinking, but I'm sure the fact that Pistol just tipped me further into madness shows somehow.

Fuck, I feel as if there's something under my skin crawling to get out. I'm so consumed by anger inside, I don't think I'll ever find my way out. I'm starting to think the darkness will claim me. I reach up and scratch the back of my shoulder, digging my fingers in so there's pain. Fuck, I might have even drawn blood. I hope I did. I need to mark or scar myself somehow. That way, the outside will match the inside.

I need to figure out what I'm going to do with… everything. The club, the traitors, Beth… fuck, even Teena. I may not have fucked her for a year, but I keep calling on her to help me. That's not right. Especially with Beth around now. I don't know what I'm going to do with Beth, but the thought of her being tortured while she was in France... She made some fucked up choices, but she's right: I did in the beginning, too. Jesus. I need to cut Teena out completely if I keep Beth here.

Teena. *Christo!* She came along at a weak moment and at one time, I for some reason thought she reminded me of Beth. Her hair, though dyed, had the same blonde hue. She wore the type of dresses Beth used to wear. She made me stop feeling dead inside, but she never took away the emptiness. Even as far gone as I am right now, I have to acknowledge that the emptiness is gone now that Beth is here at the club.

As I go over everything, my mind pictures Beth on the street that day. Her blonde hair shining in the sun, that white dress flowing in the wind. Such innocence and beauty and it was mine. All mine... for a time. Can I get that back? Does it still exist? She's not the same. She never wears those dresses now. In fact, she wears nothing but long sleeves and pants that cover almost all of her body.

Could Torch have lied? Did they actually rape Beth?

Mierda! I'm so damned tired. There's just too many *games,* so many fucking *games* that it's no wonder I'm being pulled into the darkness. It's always been there, calling me. Beth pulled me out of it once... With her, I felt alive in ways I never have before.

So, it's sheer madness that brings me to her door. I hesitate before I knock on the door. You can't go back, and there's too much between Beth and I for what we have to ever be good again. I'm about to turn away when I hear it.

Her laughter.

So sweet and free that listening to it warms something inside of me—a spot that has probably been frozen over since she left. I turn the knob carefully. It's unlocked. I have a key that I've been using at night, but still, maybe this is a sign that I should talk to her? Can she save me once again?

I don't fully open the door. I just hold it there, cracked enough so I can hear her easily. Her vanilla and strawberry scent hits me and I close my eyes and drink it in. I imagine her in my mind. She's probably laughing at Gabby while they play with those blocks that Gabby loves so much. She's probably helping her build a tower just to watch Gabby knock it over. My wife and my child... together... under my roof...

I allow myself to live in the fantasy for a minute, maybe two... It's been so long, but there's a ghost of a feeling inside of me. Not happiness, but... close. Satisfaction. I'm about to close the door again and leave before this small moment in time can be ruined—when I hear Beth's voice.

"That's me. Wild Beth..."

Maybe she's laughing with Katie? What's she talking about, "wild"? She had a wild streak in her once, one she reserved for only me. Has another man had her since she left me?

Can I believe anything she says?

"Oh my God! Whatever you're doing, don't stop," she moans again. My body tenses with her words.

Then, I hear a fucking man laughing with her.

She is not fucking one of my brothers while she's here. Who's with her? Is it Beast? That motherfucker always had a soft spot for her. Shit, it's probably Shaft, that damn asshole can't keep his *polla* in his damn pants! I'll make sure he doesn't have one to worry about after this.

I shove the door open with such force that it slams against the wall when it flings open. Beth's sitting on the bed and some fucker is rubbing the back of her neck. The only thing that stops me from going to him and immediately snapping his neck is the fact that they're both still fully dressed.

"Who the fuck are you and why do you have your hands on my wife?" I growl before I can stop myself.

Chapter 22
Skull

"Skull! What on Earth?" Beth starts, but she's drowned out by the man. He's holding his hands up in defense.

As if that would keep me away. I'll fucking end him.

"Hey man, nothing's going on. I was just checking Beth out and—"

"I saw that, motherfucker. I'm asking you what the hell you're doing in my wife's room and why you have your fucking hands on her."

"We're not married!" Beth growls, standing up and stomping her foot. I ignore her.

"You got about one minute to start talking and then, trust me when I tell you, you won't be able to talk when I'm through."

"This must be your ex, Skull?"

That's it. I go to him and grab him around the neck, literally pulling him over to the wall. I slam him up against the wall so hard that the pictures on it rattle.

"That's right, *el cabrón*, it's good you know the name of the man who's going to—Ow! Beth, goddamn it, what in the hell are you doing?" I growl, keeping my hand around the neck of the man while turning to look at Beth.

She's taken a fucking stuffed animal and continues to slap me up the side of the head with it. I look at it and then her. She's continuing to hit me with it: a giant, stuffed pony with rainbow colored hair. *Christo!*

"Will you let him go? That's the doctor that you sent here!"

"The fuck he is. I sent Doctor Patton!"

"That's his son!"

"Well, I didn't know that, now did I? The *gilipollas* should have spoken up!"

"Quit calling him a dickhead and maybe he would have spoken up if you would quit choking him! You're killing him! He's turning blue for Christ's sake! Will you let him go?"

I drop my hand from the asshole's neck, ignoring his gasping and coughing beside me.

"Tell your father he will be dealing with me later. When I ask for him to come out, I mean *him*. Now, get out," I order him, but I'm looking at Beth. Her gray eyes are watching me. There's something shining in them and the only word I can think of to describe it is excitement.

For the first time in years, ever since Beth left my life, I'm feeling the same. My blood is thrumming through my system. My heart is beating hard against my chest. My dick is jerking against my pants and I feel… *alive.*

"Listen, Mr… errr… Skull. Dad retired last month. When your men called my office, I just assumed—"

"That was your first mistake. One I will be bringing up with your father. Now. Get. The. Fuck. Out."

"Maybe if you hadn't had Dr. Torres tending to your needs so often, you would have known," Beth snips.

I haven't taken my eyes off of her. I couldn't if my life depended on it. She's enjoying challenging me. *She's baiting me.* She's breathing heavy and her breasts are heaving against the tight black turtleneck she's wearing. Breasts that I remember vividly. Breasts that are larger now that she's had our daughter. Breasts that I want to bury my face in and just… breathe.

The doctor finally leaves, which should make me happy.

Instead, I want to growl because Beth is hugging that damned stuffed pony against her chest like some kind of fucking lifeline, blocking herself from me.

"When did you learn to speak Spanish?" I ask because she knew what I called the asshole. That's new. What other secrets is Beth keeping?

"I thought it would be useful. I figured you would want... I mean, I wanted to teach Gabby to speak Spanish, and they say it's best to start them young... and I, well..."

She trails off, but her slip didn't escape me. She thought I would want Gabby to know Spanish. She started to say that before she changed her mind. Did she plan for me to become part of Gabby's life before that damn package in the hospital? Is this just another game? Another lie in a line of many that I seem to keep falling for?

"You shouldn't have done that," she whispers when she gets tired of my silence. Her cheeks blush a pale pink from me continuously staring at her.

"He had his hands on you."

"He was examining me," she says.

"I don't give a fuck," I tell her, taking a step toward her and closing the distance between us.

I reach out and pull her to me, keeping each of my hands on the cheeks of her ass. Those damn gray eyes of hers go large.

"Skull? What are you doing?" she asks, bringing her hands up to my arms and holding on, maybe to push me away, but she doesn't do it.

"It's both of us here, Beth," I tell her, wanting her to admit that she feels this fucking pull between us.

"What are we doing?" she asks, and I could almost smile.

Instead, I bring my head down closer. "We're learning, *mi cielo*, learning..." The old nickname slips out and I regret it instantly, but I can't call it back. She gasps against my lips and her nails bite into my hands.

I know she's made note of it. It makes me feel weak, but I can't stop.

I take her mouth with mine. My tongue slips through her lips and finds... *home*. Her taste, the feel of her... It's like a spark to the ashes that have been lying dormant, just waiting. I curve my tongue around hers, demanding she join me for this ride. She hums, and it's all I can do to hold back. I want this kiss to be different. Slow and gentle. Reconnecting... remembering... reclaiming something I lost. I ignore the voice in my head calling me a stupid fool and instead I lose myself in the taste of the woman who nearly destroyed me years ago.

When we break apart, I keep my eyes closed and hold my forehead against hers, trying to regroup.

"What are we learning?" she asks, her voice thick and soft. How do I tell her I was trying to see if she could pull me from the darkness again?

I can't.

I pull away and clear my throat, retreating to the door. I'm confused as hell... and horny. I want to push Beth onto the bed and fuck her until the voices in my head are gone, until the anger and the darkness are obliterated. I can do neither.

Distance... *I need distance.*

"Where are you going?" she asks, sounding confused. She should be. I'm confused as hell, too.

"It's late. I'll talk to you tomorrow," I tell her without looking back. I can't look back. I can't go back. I can't. I can't survive Beth a second time.

Distance. I need distance, I repeat over and over in my head. But, with her taste on my tongue, I wonder if that's even possible now.

Chapter 23
Beth

"You okay Beth?" Katie asks for like the tenth time today.

She's really starting to irritate me, and I shouldn't be that way. Because of her, we have more time than ever before the club discovers we're gone. She convinced Torch that we all needed a day to ourselves to relax before starting in on all of the wedding chores. As a result, he had three prospects follow him to the day spa in town. He left them to monitor the place and kissed Katie, telling her he'd see her this evening. I know she's feeling guilty about lying to him, but then again, she wants to be responsible for Matthew's death as much as I do. The only difference is she doesn't have anything to prove.

Torch looks at her and sees this strong woman who could take on the world. No one sees that in me. I don't even see it in myself, but that's changing. Yesterday changes nothing. If anything, it proves to me that what Skull and I had is gone. The kiss was good, so much of it that I remember, but it didn't have the emotion that was between us before. It was almost as if he was proving to himself that he doesn't want me anymore.

Learning... he said we were learning. For a brief moment, especially after he called me "*my sky*", I thought maybe... but I was wrong. So wrong. Having him walk away from me proved that more than anything else could have.

So I have one path before me. I'm going to end Matthew and Colin. I will make things safe for me and my sister, but most importantly, my daughter. Then I will get the fuck away from Skull and try to live again and hopefully gain some respect along the way, not only from the men in Skull's crew, but from myself. Matthew and Colin took so much from me, I need to claim this back. It doesn't matter if I'll never see Skull's men again. Knowing they don't see me as the weak woman that I was will mean something to me.

"I told you I'm fine," I insist with a sigh, looking out the window of the truck as we drive down an old backroad.

Sacks is in the front driving with Louise and Candy, leaving me and Katie in the back. *Alone.* Katie wants to talk, and I want to do anything but.

"You don't act fine, Bethie. Talk to me. We don't have to do this if you're not ready to face them."

"I'm not worried about facing them. This needs to be done and you more than anyone knows why it should be us that do it," I whisper.

"Then what's going on? And don't you dare tell me you're fine again."

"Aren't you worried about lying to Torch?" I ask, trying to divert her attention.

"Don't change the subject. Spill it, Bethie."

"Skull kissed me last night," I mutter, knowing I'm not going to get her to drop it.

"He kissed you?!" That screech ensures that everyone in the truck and probably anyone standing within a three mile radius knows now.

"Katie, it's no big deal..."

"Girl, don't even!" Sacks interjects from the front, slapping her hands on the steering wheel. "He kissed you! As mad as he's been, that's freaking monumental!"

"You know, come to think of it, I didn't see that fancy

smancy Dr. Torres around yesterday or this morning either," Candy adds in.

"Who cares? Beth should have kicked him in the balls. Did you kick him in the balls?" Louise asks. "I would have kicked him in the balls."

"I didn't kick him in the balls. I should have," I grumble. "I think I was in shock."

"Or lust."

"Shut it, Katie."

"What? I'm just saying it's been a long time since you got a little something-something, sister dear."

"How long we talking?" Sacks asks.

"We're closer to three years than we are over two now," Katie blabs.

"Jesus, Mary, and Joseph," Candy says.

"Talk about blue lady balls," Sacks joins in.

"There's probably cobwebs up in your shit," Louise commiserates.

"Are we saying that Skull was the last baloney-pony you took a ride on?" Sacks asks.

"Can we please quit discussing my sex life?" I mutter, feeling the heat scorch my face.

"Or lack of," Katie mutters. "I tried to get her to spread her wings…"

"You mean her legs," Louise mentions and Candy snorts.

"I was married…"

"The fuck you were. Besides, that didn't stop *him* from getting some strange," Katie gripes.

"Men are assholes," Louise states.

"That they are, and they think with their dicks," Sacks grumbles.

"Well, the first thing we're going to do after we take care of business today is get you laid," Sacks declares.

"I don't want—"

"Bullshit. Your hormones have been on lockdown for so long, you don't know what you want," Candy says.

"I really can't even think about being with another man. Skull is…"

"Is what?" Sacks asks.

"I don't think any man could live up to him," I tell them honestly.

"Fuck," Sacks mutters.

"Damn," Candy joins in.

"Was he that big? Wait, don't tell me. If I know what size Skull's cock is, having to see him every day would just be weird," Katie realizes.

"How big's his cock?" Sacks asks. "I don't care if it's weird."

"Yeah, me too. C'mon, tell us how big Skull junior is."

"Uh… I'm not sure Skull would want me talking about *that*," I stutter. I'm new to having friends. *Do women really talk about this stuff?*

"I bet it hangs down his leg like a damn anaconda," Candy mutters.

"Candy!" Katie growls. She's looking at me and she knows I'm not comfortable with this conversation.

"What? A man like that walking around with the attitude he has, you just know he's got the tools to back it up," she reasons.

"It doesn't matter because I'm not going there, ever again," I announce, going back to looking out the window.

"Damn! I bet it was so big it scared you, right? I heard talk you were a teenager when you were with him. Jesus, were you, like, sixteen? That kind of shit can scar you if the man ain't gentle," Candy says.

"Skull don't seem the gentle type," Louise agrees.

"Fuck gentle. I'm more of a pull-my-hair-and-make-me-beg type," Sacks says. "Briar knows exactly how I like it, or I probably wouldn't put up with his ass."

"You could always try women," Louise offers.

"That's not for me."

"Never know it 'til you try it," she counters.

"I kissed a girl once. Did nothing for me," I tell them, glad we've stopped talking about Skull's dick.

"No way," Katie says, and I could almost laugh at the stricken look on her face.

"All-girl school, remember?"

"Oh fuck."

"Yeah, we're going to get you laid after this, Beth," Louise says and all the women are nodding their heads in agreement.

As we pull up to the lake and I look at all the women's faces who are bravely serious… all I can think is, if I survive this, I might want to run away.

Chapter 24
Skull

What the fuck was I thinking, kissing Beth? Now, I can do nothing but remember the feel of my tongue in her mouth, her taste, and the whispery soft feel of her breath against my skin. *Christo!* I thought I was haunted before; it's clear that I was stupid. *Now*, all I can think about is kissing her and wanting more. I thought she could save me from the darkness, but becoming obsessed with her might be worse.

I forced myself to stay away from her last night. It wasn't easy, but I knew if I saw her lying in bed, I'd fall on her like a man condemned to die enjoying his last meal on earth. *Mierda!*

I'm obsessed with her.

I need to think about shit, especially the latest shit storm dealt to me by Pistol. I need to plan. I'm not sure how to find the mole in my club without alerting him. Whatever I do, I need to be careful. First, I need to kill the Donahues. Getting rid of them will be two less threats hanging over my head, threats that I know for sure are there. They aren't hiding in the shadows, so they come first.

If I was the man I used to be, I would talk things out with my closest brothers. That's not an option for me right now. I'm pretty sure I'm just done. Being president of the Devil's Blaze has cost me so much and I'm fucking tired of it. I've given my life and I have nothing to show for it. Nothing.

I'll use the club to kill the Donahues and then... I'll find the mole and exact my revenge personally. It could be stupid and it may be the fucking end of me, but then again, I'm tired of breathing anyways.

There's a meeting planned for tonight to go over our strike. Until then, I need a fucking break. I need to get away from Beth. I throw some clothes on, a plan forming in my mind.

I walk out of the room and down the hall. The first thing I do is hesitate at Beth's door. I should check on Gabby before I leave. It wouldn't be to see Beth again; it's just that Gabby already sees me as a stranger. If I'm going to leave for the day, I should see her. *That's all.*

I turn to go in when I see Sabre walking down the hall with Gabby on his hip. *God, she is a beautiful baby. I should have been there for her. I should have been the first to hold her...*

"What are you doing with *mi hija*?"

"Annie's supposed to be watching Gabby for Beth, but she's had a bad time with morning sickness today. So, I took Gabby when Annie fell back asleep. Jesus, 'morning' sickness... that's a bunch of shit. She stayed sick all night long. Daytime is the only time she rests at all."

"I'll take her back to Beth," I tell him, already reaching for Gabby. Thankfully, she comes to me with a smile. Those are fucking rare, and I know in my gut that it wouldn't have happened if Torch was around.

"She's not here," Sabre says so casually he has no idea I'm resisting the urge to slap the shit out of him.

"Where the hell is she?"

"Torch got a few prospects and took the girls into town to the day spa. Supposed to last all day. Some kind of pre-wedding gift."

"Pre-wedding gift? Jesus, that man is whipped," I growl, hating him a little bit more.

RELEASED

"And proud of it," the bastard says, coming up behind us.

"Who's watching the girls?" I growl, instantly worried. I don't want Beth left on her own at all until I neutralize the Donahues—or whoever the fuck else is in the wings.

Jesus, and now I need to take care of the Chrome Saints and Viper. Yeah, he's going down separate from his fucking club. The world will be a better place without him.

Christo, my list just keeps growing.

"I've got three of our prospects watching over them. They're good. I'll go back and pick them up this evening."

"See that you do," I growl, and when he goes to reach for Gabby and she starts twisting in my arms to get to him, I shut that shit down. "Gabby and I are going to see Diesel. I'm taking the wagon," I tell him, talking about my SUV.

"You going to get Diesel and his men to help on the raid?" Sabre asks.

"Shit no. If the ones that are going can't take down Matthew and those sorry bodyguards he keeps, we don't deserve to wear cuts. No, I'm just getting out for the day. Going to show my daughter off."

"We'll follow you down," Torch tells me. "I got some of the specs that Crusher wanted for the computer setup that Diesel's wanting to install."

"You have to make sure the girls are safe."

"Latch and I will be here, and our best prospects are on them. They'll be fine. Honestly, I'd prefer the two of you travel together. Can't be too careful these days. There's safety in numbers," Sabre says, and I want to beat the hell out of him. I want to be alone. The last fucking thing I need is Torch tagging along.

"I want Beast standing over the girls," I growl, not knowing who I can trust, but knowing Beast is my best bet. If Sabre looks put-off, he doesn't saying anything, though he does watch me carefully. Could *he* be the fucking mole?

"Sounds good," Torch says, and just like that I'm trapped with the fucker.

"You'll drive so I can pay attention to Gabby," I grumble. There's no way that I'm going to let him bond with my daughter any further. No way.

As we load up, I'm left with one thought. *What in the hell else is going to fuck up today?*

Somehow I know something will.

Chapter 25
Beth

"Shit! Any word from Louise?" I ask for the tenth time.

We made it here fine. Matthew's men were such morons that the backside of the lake wasn't even being monitored. Of course, the cabin and land around it were being guarded like freaking Fort Knox on a day when more gold was being delivered. Louise went on around towards the front perimeter and was going to try walking down the graveled road saying her car had broken down a few miles back and she was stranded. It was sketchy at best, and there was a chance she might need to blast her way out if it went south. Sacks and Candy were waiting just beyond the road so that when a couple of men went to check out the vehicle, they could take them out. They were also close enough that if Louise got in trouble and had to call for a mayday, they would be right there.

Katie and I are still on the backside of the property searching the defenses and waiting to see if our diversion would give us a small crack, a weakness to let us slide through. If not, we have a bigger diversion planned. I just hope it doesn't come to that.

"Why do you keep asking that? You can hear them if they use the radio, the same as me," Katie grumbles, the tension coming off from her in waves, too. *What on earth possessed us to do this?* I should have kept my mouth quiet and tried it on my own. I don't want to be responsible for these women losing their lives and I know Matthew won't hesitate to end them.

"Stop it, Bethie," Katie murmurs, looking out over the cabin and waiting.

"Stop what?" I ask, playing dumb.

"They chose to help us. They knew the risks, you didn't twist their arms."

"They don't know Matthew like we do, either," I remind her.

"Still…"

"Guys, Louise has made contact," Candy whispers over the two-way radios that Louise picked up from her brother.

"Are they going for the bait?"

"Are you kidding? Hell, I'm only into dick and even I almost swooned at those jugs she was flashing. How does someone with double-Ds manage to still be perky?"

Katie snorts and I smile despite the gravity of the situation.

"Okay, we'll let you know when they get her to the cabin from our line of sight. Then when she gets in, we'll give her the ten minutes she asked for and storm," Katie says.

"I still say ten minutes is too damn much," I complain.

"I agree," Sacks whispers.

"We'll be able to tell if it goes the wrong direction. Let's sit tight and stick to the damn game plan," Katie counters.

We all go radio silent after that. I can't tell if it's because everyone is nervous or if my own nerves are so on-edge that something feels off. I just don't have a good feeling. I suck air in and hold it as I watch Louise walking up to the front porch of the small cabin. She stumbles slightly on the second step. I think that was by design because she bends over to adjust her sandal and one of her boobs almost pops out. She braces her hand on one of Matthew's goons and smiles up at him, laughing and flirting. She seems like a different person compared to the hard-nosed woman that I know.

When the door closes behind her, my eyes go to my watch

and I don't move as I start counting down the time. With each minute that passes, my heart kicks up in speed. At nine minutes, Katie and I look at each other and nod.

"Okay, girls. Let's kick some ass and take some names," Katie tells them.

We cock our weapons and nod at each other. I know we're both nervous as hell and I'm second-guessing myself like crazy. I figure Katie is, too.

The only bright side to all of this is that I snuck into Skull's office last night and started looking around his desk. He didn't leave anything out, but there was a locked drawer. Skull hasn't met this side of me, the side that grew up with a need to learn so I could defend. I picked the lock in no time and found their plans. They had surveillance of the cabin. They planned to enter through the back mudroom. There was a window with a torn screen. I had decided to go first and secure the room before the other girls enter. That way when we go into war we'll be unified, with Louise being our surprise. And it *will* be a war. Matthew might be stupid, but he's evil. *Pure evil, all the way through.*

We wait at the back of the house. It's about three minutes before the other two show up. I go in first. Since having Gabby and living life on the run, I've lost so much weight it makes getting into the small window pretty easy. I can't hear anything from the other rooms, but the main living room and kitchen are down a hall, so that's not a big surprise. I keep the door closed and go back to helping pull the others through. Everyone slips in easily, but it takes me and Candy to pull Katie through.

"Your ass was not made for this window," I joke quietly.

"No, but Hunter likes a little cushion for the pushing, so I'm keeping it," she whispers and grins. "Besides, I got a feeling I'm going to be glad for the extra padding tonight if he finds out about this."

"Let's hope they don't. I love everything about Briar, but when he's mad, I feel it for weeks."

I don't respond. There's not much I can add to this conversation and it's probably best we don't talk like a bunch of nervous idiots. I crack the door open and, when I see nothing, open it a little wider. I look at the girls and all signs of the joking we shared a little bit ago are gone.

It's show time.

I want to ask if they're sure they want to do this, but it's too late for that. Louise is out there and, everything else aside, we cannot leave her here with these men. It's too late to turn back.

Please, God, let us pull this off.

Chapter 26
Skull

"I don't want you here," I tell Torch like a damn kid. I sound childish even to my own ears, but I'm tired of him asking why I'm so fucking quiet.

"Why the hell not?"

"You wouldn't understand."

"I understand that you're pushing your club away when you need us the most."

"The thing I need the most is to be left the fuck alone. *Estúpido*," I grumble under my breath but loud enough so he can hear me. We're in the truck driving in Tennessee. My nerves are shot. I feel this sense of fucking doom, and I feel like I'm just driving around waiting for a damned shoe to drop on my head.

"That's the last thing you need. You need to get out of your head. You've been holding yourself apart from us for far too fucking long. Shit, most of us didn't even know you were sticking your dick in the doctor."

"It's not your business to know where I stick my *polla*."

"Maybe not, but if I had known, I would have told you to steer away from the damn piranha."

My hands clench the armrest at his words. "What do you have against her?" I'm already wishing she wasn't around for Beth to see. The last thing I want to do is talk about this shit.

"Can't put my finger on it, but she's just… calculating. She set her sights on you from the beginning. We all saw it," Torch says while driving, looking over at me briefly as he talks.

"*I* chased *her*," I argue, hating myself for it now, but admitting it.

"Bullshit in July, you did. She spotted you at Dragon's funeral. All the boys talked about how she made sure to sit in your line of sight and kept smiling at you, so shy-like. At first we thought it was cute, but the more you get to know the good doctor, she doesn't seem shy at all, does she?"

"You and the men are fucking busybodies. If you honestly thought she was making a play, why didn't you say something before now?"

"Like I said, until she started coming to the club every couple of days, we didn't know you were fucking her, so it didn't matter."

Ironically, I haven't been fucking her since she started coming to the club. She's only been around to help keep Pistol alive. I'm not confessing that, though. I don't know if it's worse they think I got taken for a ride or if they know that I haven't touched a woman in over a year, not since the moment I knew Beth was alive. I haven't even had an interest in any woman. Fuck, the only time my dick seems to react is with Beth. The most action I've had in a year came last night when I was whacking off to a memory of the fucking kiss I shared with her.

I turn the radio up to drown him out, but just a little since Gabby is sleeping in the back. I turn to watch her. *Mi hija.* Her dark hair and skin look so much like me, but she has a softness about her that is all her mother. And those eyes... I once vowed as a child to have a woman with blue eyes. I was stupid. It's gray. The color of the blue sky and white clouds as they roll above—dusky gray. That's the color that claims your soul. Now, I have two women in my life with those eyes. Can I manage to keep them both?

The rest of the trip is silent as we make it down to Diesel's. We've pulled in and I'm unlatching Gabby's car seat from the back when Diesel and Crusher come running out.

"Why the fuck haven't you answered your phones?"

"It didn't ring," Torch says, looking at his cell.

"What's up?" I ask, knowing that look on Diesel's face.

"Your girls have flown the coop. Latch and Sabre couldn't find them at that spa. He's been tearing the place apart and been trying to call you for the last hour."

"What the fuck do you mean they can't find them?" Torch growls, dialing his phone.

I know why I didn't hear my phone. I didn't even bring the son of a bitch. I didn't want to hear from the motherfuckers for a while. I knew I'd be here, and if anything was urgent they'd know where to find me. Foolishly, I knew I'd have Gabby and Beast would watch Beth… I was a fucking stupid *tonto*.

"Katie's phone just rings," Torch says and the man is panicking like I've never seen him do before. If I'm honest, I'm feeling it too. My mind may say I'm done with Beth, but the rest of me sure as fuck isn't.

I grab Torch's phone out of his hand after handing Gabby, car seat and all, over to Crusher. "Sabre, I need you to—"

"Boss, the girls…"

"Yeah, I know. Diesel told us. Question your woman, find out where the other women are."

"Boss, we've asked Annie. She doesn't know and she wasn't with them…"

"The fuck she doesn't. She agreed to babysit for Beth. I'd bet the club that she knows exactly where the women are. You question her hard. If you can't do it, get one of the other men to do it," I order him, not about to tell him right now that betting the club isn't a big deal. I'm so damned tired.

"I can do it, but I'm telling you, she doesn't know."

"Whatever, just do it! Call me back. I'm going to get Gabby settled with Dani. Then Torch and I will head back."

I don't give him time to respond. I'm going to beat Beth when I find her because somehow I know this is all her doing. The woman just isn't happy unless she's making me miserable.

Chapter 27
Skull

"What the fuck were you thinking, letting the women go into town when I've declared war on the Donahues?" I growl at Torch.

I'm driving down the road at a ridiculous amount of speed. The wheels are squealing as I turn the curves. I don't give a fuck. I want to get back to the club, find the women, and then I'm... *What?* What the fuck am I going to do? I can't leave, not yet, not until I've killed the Donahues and found the threat. I need to make it safe for all of the club. Make up for my past mistakes and make sure there aren't people out there who will hurt Gabby... *or Beth.* Then I'm completely done. I owe nothing to no one else and my decisions won't get people I care about killed.

"Fuck, I know. It was just one day though, and Katie's been through so much. Jesus, Skull, I just wanted to give her and Bethie one day to feel like queens. They deserve that."

His words cut another layer inside of me, leaving me to bleed. How many wounds can a man sustain and still draw breath? Apparently a fucking lot. I grunt; there's not an answer left inside of me.

My phone rings about twenty minutes later.

"Tell me," I order, my mind busy going over all of the shit that Matthew and Colin could be doing to Beth. We checked when we were at Diesels and there's no new intel to suggest

Colin and Matthew are moving, but who the fuck knows with those two.

"You were right. Annie knew." There's a gut punch, but that's good. If the girls left on their own, it's probably some fucking thing they are planning for Katie's bachelorette party. My foot eases up on the gas, and I calm a little.

Before I can picture the male stripper parties and what other craziness women can get up to, Sabre stops me cold. "It's bad man. They went after Matthew."

I slam the brakes, causing Torch to lurch, almost hitting his head into the windshield.

"What the fuck do you mean they went after Donahue?"

"What the fucking hell are you talking about, Skull?" Torch yells in the background.

"They heard us talking and Beth somehow got our plans and copy of the photos of the cabin. Her, Briar's old lady, Katie, Candy, and that fucking Louise all headed out after the son of a bitch, like they were fucking comic book heroes man."

"Jesús Cristo de mierda! Where are you?"

"We're at a gas station off the interstate. We're about to head out on our bikes. Beast got a boat off Dragon, since the girls took Briars, and he's following in the pickup. We're about an hour out, man."

"Torch and I are about forty, make sure you're there at the same time. I don't give a fuck what you have to do. You got the firepower?"

"Yeah, boss. That shit was already loaded in the truck for tomorrow."

"Good," I growl, hanging the phone up.

"What the fucking hell is going on?" Torch yells.

"You ignoring my lockdown is biting us in the fucking ass," I tell him.

RELEASED

Then, I tell him exactly what his woman, Beth, and the others have planned. He goes white. That would make me happy if this fucking shit wasn't about to blow up. There's no way of knowing how big of a head start the women have. I'm just hoping we're not too late…

Chapter 28
Beth

We walk through the tiny hallway as quietly as we can. I'm afraid to breathe. I don't want to do anything that might give us away. We need every advantage we can get, especially the element of surprise. I can feel the tension from the other girls. Katie is right behind me and even if we weren't twins, I could read the strain on her face.

I look at the other girls. We nod at each other in silent support. I take a breath, then step out into the open with my gun drawn.

I would have liked to fire first and ask questions later, but I can't take the chance that Louise will get caught in the gunfire. That might have been a hole in our plan. I planned on saying something cool, like *"Drop to the ground, you dirty pig!"* I think I could've pulled it off, especially when I shot out his kneecaps.

I don't get the chance, though. When I come out from around the door frame with my gun drawn, the first thing I see is Matthew standing there. He's got a gun shoved up against Louise's neck. He's holding her by the hair of her head, pulling so her neck is at an awkward angle. Her shirt has been ripped open and her lip is bleeding. She doesn't look that scared though. Instead, she looks majorly pissed. Her eyes are locked on mine. I glance briefly, but my eyes go to Matthew's and I keep him in the sights on my gun. The other ladies behind me fan out, each with a gun drawn and aimed at the men. Mexican standoff. *How great.*

Fuck, I should have never let the women know what I wanted to do.

"What a surprise. It's nice of you to come see me, Beth. I knew you missed me," Matthew says in his cold voice that reminds me of a snake slithering in the winter. Cold, slimy, creepy and completely against the natural order of life. *Wrong.* That sums up Matthew. So completely wrong that nothing about him could ever be right. He deserves to die—for so many things.

"It looks like you were expecting me," I tell him, not relaxing the hold on my gun at all.

"Well sis, I wasn't, but can I share a small tidbit of advice, sister dear?" Him calling me sis makes my stomach turn. It'd be so easy to just shoot him between the eyes.

"By all means," I invite, hoping I sound bored and in-control and betray none of the panic and sheer terror I'm feeling.

"Two-way radios went out with the last decade. They're picked up so easily."

Bastard.

"You're smarter than I gave you credit for," I tell him, again trying to sound bored. "I'll remember that for next time, though it won't matter for you, because you won't survive this," I tell him. *God, please don't let him survive this.*

"You might want to look around. You're outnumbered, Beth. My men are stronger and better-trained. And your friend here is about two seconds from never breathing again, unless you and your band of female counterparts drop your weapons."

"I'm not so much concerned about your men. I came into this knowing I was probably going to die. After what you did to me, the risk was worth it. The only thing I need to accomplish to win here today is plant a bullet between your eyes, and I do plan on doing exactly that," I tell him boldly, hoping against hope that

I'm bluffing the shit out of him.

His eyes go hard at my words. He pulls tighter on Louise's hair, causing her to gasp. My eyes go to hers, second-guessing myself. I know my hand is trembling. I watch as Louise's hand goes up the arm that Matthew has wrapped around her, holding her in place, so he can hide behind her like the scared little coward he is. He's real good at inflicting pain on anyone helpless. I know that lesson all too well. I'm about to put my gun down. If I give myself over to Matthew, there's a chance the others can get away. Maybe not Katie, but we survived this idiot before and we can do it again, and even if not… Gabby is safe now. She's the reason we got the courage up to kill grandfather in the first place.

Just as I start to lower my gun, I see Louise's hand she's counting with her fingers. She holds one up. *One…*

Are you sure? I ask without words, hoping she can read the message in my eyes. In response, I see a flash of silver in her hand. A knife, not big, but it might just be enough if she knows what she is doing. She holds up a second finger.

Two.

I tighten my hold back on my gun, strengthen my finger on the trigger.

Three.

"Now!" I shout just as Louise jabs the knife low on Matthew's leg. He screams out and Louise gets clear enough to deliver a head-butt into the back of his face, blood smearing instantly. I hope she broke his fucking nose.

The pain must be severe enough, because he lets go of Louise and she dives for cover as we all fan out. Bullets start flying. I dive behind a recliner, shooting. Katie is somehow on the other side of me shooting out. I look around as best as I can since bullets are flying. As covers go, the chair sucks, but it's better than being out in the open. I find Louise beside Candy; they've retreated back to the hallway, trying to get what cover they can from the small space along the door frame. Sacks, I've lost sight of, and as a bullet almost grazes me, I pull back in and look at Katie. I don't see reassurance in her face.

We're in trouble.

Chapter 29
Skull

"I'm going to chain her to the fucking bed and spank her raw for weeks. Motherfucking-son-of-a-bitching-flying-monkeys-up-the-ass weeks," Torch is muttering under his breath. The rest of us aren't talking. There's not much to fucking say. In fact, except for Torch, not another man is talking. Briar is stone, his face a cold mask of fury. Sabre and Latch may not have a woman in there, but you can tell they feel responsible. Beast... well fuck, who the hell knows what Beast is these days. *Hermano* is one messed up fucking pile.

Then there's me. I have so much rage boiling inside of me on a daily basis that I can't tell a huge difference, except... fear. I feel fear. If something happens to Beth because I failed to take out her stepbrothers, that's just one more black mark against me. History repeating itself.

Tan jodidamente cansado—so fucking tired.

As we get out of the boat and fall in line heading towards the old fishing cabin, the fear inside me increases. I hate the bitter taste of it, and frustration bubbles up from inside yet again. This is Beth's fault too. She's trying to destroy me. Fuck that shit. She's *already* destroyed me. Now, she's just adding to the destruction, breaking me in so many ways I won't ever find daylight.

At the back of the building, the bedroom window we had planned to use is wide open—a testament to what the women did.

A testament to the fact that Beth did, in fact, steal plans from my desk. *Christo!* Who the fuck does she think she is? She has a child to worry about. It is not her place to handle these assholes.

Then again, I failed to take care of them before, didn't I? I look over at Beast. Everything that's happened from the day my brother lost his family rests on my shoulders. No one else's.

Mine.

It's a testament to how fucking stupid Matthew is that the damn room is not being monitored and the window is not at least closed. Then again, from the screaming in the next room, he may have his hands a little busy. Three of us are going through the window. Me, Torch, and Briar. It's our old ladies... or rather, *their* old ladies, since Beth is not mine. She's just the mother of my child. Sabre, Latch, and Beast are storming from around front. It'll be a blitz attack, which will only happen when they hear me call for them. I'm not about to let them storm in and get the women killed. I just pray we're not too late to keep that from happening. I know I have to be careful with my approach, but hell, too much fucking time has passed as it is. I don't think the girls had that big of a head start on us, but it has definitely been long enough.

I wait at the opening of the hall, hiding in the shadows, to take stock of the situation. The first thing I see are the women. Katie, Candy, Sacks, and Louise are on the floor in a corner with some motherfucker standing over them with a gun pointed at them. Each one is bloody. Katie looks like she's taken a bullet in the leg. There's a torn piece of black cloth fashioned as a homemade tourniquet over it. The blood doesn't seem excessive, but there's enough there to worry about.

I know the moment Torch sees it because I can feel the anger radiating off of him and a low rumbling growl escapes him. He starts to charge forward and Briar claps his hand on the man's shoulder, pulling him back.

I scan the area looking for Beth. When I see her, my heart turns over. She's sitting on the ground in front of Matthew. She's got a busted lip and I can see the red whelp of being hit evident on her cheek, even from this distance.

I'm going to fucking kill the S.O.B.

"You dress so boring these days, Beth. Why is that, do you wonder? Are you ashamed of the little love tracks I left on your body?"

"Fuck you!" she growls, her face looking so hard, her words so harsh that I can hardly reconcile her with the woman that I know.

Matthew bends down and grabs her by the hair, pulling it taut in his hand. "I'd keep a civil tongue in your head when you talk to me, sister dear."

In response, Beth spits on him.

"I'll make you regret that," he promises, wiping the spittle from his chin. He backhands her hard, letting her fall to the floor with the force of the hit when he lets go of her hair.

"You asshole! Leave her alone! Haven't you done enough damage to her?" Katie yells, pain in her voice. Beth turns so that her side is to Matthew, wiping the blood off her lip. When he hauls off and kicks her hard in the ribs sending her back down on the ground, I've had enough.

"Kick her again and I'll cut your fucking leg off and feed it to you," I growl, storming in.

He's got his gun down because he's been torturing Beth, so I point my gun straight at him, daring him to move. Torch screams and takes the butt of his gun to the man's head who stands over the women, sending him flying. I watch out of the corner of my vision as Torch slams his steel-toed boot into the man's junk over and over. The final time, he shifts his foot around, making sure the damage is permanent. Briar sends off two quick shots to Matthew's other men, burying a bullet in each of their brains and effectively taking them out. Now the odds are much better. Though, this is clearly not all of Matthew's men.

Beast and the other two storm in when they hear Briar's shots, surveying the damage. I'm momentarily distracted and Matthew makes a move for his gun. I fire a shot into his arm. Fucking asshole! Who exactly does he think he is fooling with?

"Told you not to move, *gilipollas*," I tell him, enjoying the way the red flow of blood oozes from his three-thousand-dollar suit. I don't think that can be dry-cleaned. "Beast, take the men and secure the perimeter. We need to know where Matthew's other men are."

He doesn't answer, but they head out.

"How's Katie?" Beth asks, trying to look around me to see her sister.

"Get up and see for yourself so I can clean up the fucking mess you've made," I growl, my anger at her starting to bubble over. *Mierda!* Even now, she's sitting on the floor in front of him like she stupidly has all day.

"I had things under control," she argues, and the anger in her face when she looks at me pisses me off even more. *Who the fuck does she think she is?*

"It sure looked like it. Were you trying to wear his fists out with your face? Real great plan, Beth. *Christo*," I mutter, disgusted.

"I had a plan!" she argues.

I snap. "Briar, watch the fucker," I tell him, talking about Matthew. I'm not going to get distracted by Beth and let the son of a bitch get away. He will die before I leave this damn cabin.

"What kind of plan? You *que mujer estúpida!*"

"This!" she growls, thrusting her hand up towards Matthew's

balls. At first I think she's just going to punch them, which I'm okay with. She's crazier than I thought if she assumed that move would save the day. Then, I hear Matthew scream out, and when I look to see where her hand connects, there is a small blade sticking out of his crotch. She stabbed at least one of his balls. Interesting. *My Beth has developed claws.* She twists the knife for good measure before pulling it out. Matthew drops to the floor and Beth wipes the blade on the jacket of his suit. "Call me stupid again, Skull, and I'll give you the same as I did Matthew, and honest to God, I might enjoy it even more," she warns, her eyes spitting fire at me.

Damn. She does have claws, and the twisted fucked-up mess that I am, I apparently love it because my cock is rock hard.

Cagar!

Chapter 30
Beth

I'm totally lying out of my ass. I, in no way, had things under control. Once Katie was shot, I folded like a damn cheap pair of pants. I was going to kill Matthew, but I knew I'd end up dying in the process too. I accepted it. Doesn't mean that I didn't still worry over Gabby and wish things would be different, but there comes a time in your life where you quit running, a time when you reach the end of what you can take. I had been there for a while, but being under the same roof with Skull and having to face his anger and hate has pushed me beyond that point. I've had it. I'm done, and when I say that, I mean completely and utterly done. He gave me a taste of him in a kiss and walked away. I hate him for that—for reminding me of what I don't have anymore.

"Did you honestly believe that what you just did would have saved you? Did you not see the men with guns before we got here?"

"You asshole! Of course I saw them! They shot my sister!" she huffs, walking around him to get to Katie. "Are you okay?" I ask her, dismissing Skull. He's not important. *Not anymore*.

"I'm..."

"No, you're not fucking fine," Torch interrupts. "You're shot. In your fucking bad leg. What in the hell did you think you were doing, Katie?" Torch rips open Katie's pants to better inspect the wound.

"Gee, I don't know, Hunter. I was thinking, *wow*, it's a beautiful day today. I wonder what a fucking bullet would feel like in my leg!"

"I would watch your tone with me, Katydid, because I'm a man on the fucking edge right now."

"I'm not exactly happy-go-lucky myself, and quit yelling at me! I'm in pain!"

"Get used to it, sweetheart, because when I get you home, your ass will be sore for a fucking year."

I stand back as they go at each other. I rake my hand through my hair, feeling my adrenaline start to ebb. I didn't think I would live past this point. I should be thankful that I am. It might be easier if Skull wasn't breathing down my neck. *Literally.* He grabs my arm and spins me around, looking only slightly less intimidating now that he's put his gun up. I look over to see that Latch has come back and helped Briar subdue the men inside.

"Eyes on me, Beth," Skull growls, instantly pushing me back to the edge.

"What is your problem?"

"My problem? You did something incredibly stupid here! You could have been killed!"

"What do you care? You don't even like me! What I choose to do is none of your damn business now, Skull!"

"Maybe not, but you almost got the others killed, and they are a part of my club. They *are* my concern."

His words couldn't have hurt me more if he had slapped me across the face. His face is full of hate—all for me. I'm so sick of being the one to blame. I might have been stupid when I was younger, but *this*... this is not on me!

"I tried to get them to stay behind!" I scream, so sick of him blaming me for everything. Next thing you know, it will be my fault for the drought in Bum-Fuck Egypt.

"Lay off Beth. We made our own decisions," Candy says.

"Damn straight. We wanted in on this," Sacks chimes in.

"Woman," Briar warns.

"It's the truth," Louise adds. "We didn't really give her a choice."

"You know what, Skull? You can just go to hell. This war isn't yours. It's my sister's and mine," Katie says, but her voice is full of pain.

"Katydid, you need to…"

"Just drop it, you guys. Torch, get her to the doctor," I tell him. In response, all I get are glares. *Perfect.* I just sigh, wanting this night over with.

"You were planning on doing this alone?" Skull asks and his eyes are appraising me.

"Yes."

"You would have been killed. You almost were!" I don't say anything to that. There's nothing to say. "That's what you planned all along, wasn't it, Beth? You were just going to walk in and risk your life without a thought to…"

"All I do is *think*, Skull. Every damn minute I *think*. I think about all I lost. I think about all my father and grandfather stole not only from me, but from Katie. I think of how they hunted my mother. I think about how they lied over and over. I think of all the hell I lived through. I think about losing you. I think about denying Gabby a home with two parents. All I do is think and I'm tired of it. I'm so tired, Skull. So sure, I would have probably died tonight, but by God, I would have taken Matthew into hell with me and I would have made sure his filth never touched my daughter. And you know what, Skull? That was a win for me, at this point!"

His eyes are locked onto me and I can't read anything from him. I turn away from him. It's time I go.

"What are you doing?" I cry when Skull's hand wraps around my arm and pulls me back around to face him.

"Everybody, get the fuck out. Right now!" Skull growls, and there's so much anger in his face, alarm bells are starting to go off.

"Hold on," Katie protests. "You can't just…"

Torch ignores her argument and picks her up, carrying her outside. I can hear all the ladies arguing, but I can't take my eyes off Skull.

I think it would be dangerous to at this point if I did.

Chapter 31
Skull

I wait while Briar and Latch drag Matthew and his henchmen from the room while Torch carries a screaming Katie and makes the other women walk in front of him. It takes a few minutes, but the room is completely empty now. Beth doesn't speak during all this time. Her gray eyes are locked on mine.

Me, I'm seeing red. Rational thought has fled and let's face it, it's never too close around when Beth is, regardless. *She was walking to her death.* She was walking to her death, *again*. She was trying to handle it all by herself—again. Moving ahead, not counting the people she had around her.

I'm not letting her get away with it this time.

"What do you think you are…?"

I'm tired of hearing her talk. I'm tired of her not thinking I can't handle whatever is thrown at her. I'm tired of accepting that she doesn't have faith in me. Fuck, I don't have faith in me. *How can I expect her to?* So, I do the only thing I can at this point. I shut her the hell up with my mouth.

She's rigid in my arms at first. Holding herself so taut that it pisses me off. My hand moves up to her breast, cupping it in my hand. I squeeze it through the black sweater she wears, loving the way it overflows in my hand. Larger than before, but fitting in it, feeling like a lost piece of me. I groan, because I can feel her nipple pushing against the palm of my hand even through her sweater.

Beth still hasn't opened her mouth to me, though her hands have moved up to my shoulder and her fingers are biting into my arms. I suck on her bottom lip. Instantly, the taste of sugar sweet vanilla hits my taste buds along with another flavor that is all woman, but even more. It's all Beth. A taste that I had forgotten over the years. A taste I barely experienced with our last kiss and a taste that hits my system like a fucking drug.

I can feel the shift in her body and I know it's hitting her, too. Frustration fills me that she won't give in to it. I bite her lip. Not hard, but definitely not gentle. She gasps, her hands tightening on my arms to push me away. It pisses me off. She doesn't want to kiss me? *Fine.*

I break away, holding one side of her neck tight in my hand. I run my lips along the opposite side, tasting the skin and letting my tongue trail up the path my lips make. When I reach her ear, I suck the lobe into my mouth, biting on it with the same exertion I expended before. Beth breathes out, the sound loud, ragged, and loaded with want. It calls to the need clawing inside of me.

My fingers wrap in her hair. *How could I have forgotten the feel of that over the years?* How right it felt when each strand grazes against my skin.

"You never learn, *querida*. Always pushing ahead with what you think is best. Never considering your options," I growl against her ear before moving my lips back down to the inside of her neck and biting into the tender skin and sucking on it, marking her in ways I've never been able to mark her on the inside.

"I do what I have to do," she whispers breathlessly, but her voice is stubborn.

"I got this. I got *you*. This is not your fight alone, *querida*, it never was," I tell her, my voice hoarse with anger, regret, and pain. Always where Beth is concerned, there is pain.

"Maybe once you were right, Skull. *Not anymore*. I'm not yours," she responds, and maybe it's wishful thinking, or maybe it's just plain stupidity, but I think I hear regret laced in her words.

I want to concentrate on that, but the anger inside, the raging monster that has been festering inside of me since the day I watched that ship explode, is there. It claws inside, wanting out, and her words are just a reminder of what I have been denied. A reminder that she doesn't realize what I did that first day when she was standing on the street. I knew the moment I saw her. How did she miss it? Maybe it's time to remind her.

"You'll always be mine, Beth," I growl, pinching the hardened nipple of her breast and tugging on it.

"Skull, no," she cries, but her hips thrust into me.

"You'll always be mine, *querida*," I tell her again. "Your body knows it. Maybe it's time I remind you," I growl, my hand sliding down to the waistband of her pants. Her skin is soft and warm, searing me.

"We shouldn't do this," she whispers, but she's pushing my t-shirt up and scoring my stomach with her nails.

I pop open the button on her pants. I don't bother unzipping them, choosing to just thrust my hand inside. The heat of her pussy wraps around my palm, warming it instantly and making my dick throb out of control. My fingers immediately go to pull the lips of her pussy apart and rake against the swollen clit. Beth whimpers and shifts her body, whether to try and get away for more, I don't know, nor do I care. I slide my fingers apart in her pussy and work them like scissors to pinch and hold her clit so it plumps out over the top of my fingers. The pressure teases her, giving her a taste of what she needs. The muscles in her thighs tighten and she pushes into my hand, craving what only I am giving her. What only *I* should ever give her.

Mine. *Motherfucking mine*. If I can never have her heart, I will tie her body to me. She's wet, but not like my Beth used to be for me. She's trying foolishly to hold herself away from me, to not give in to what her body is craving.

"Do you want my cock, *mi cielo*?" I whisper into her ear, biting down on the lobe as my fingers continue to work her clit.

"I shouldn't," she breathes, as her nails continue to bite into me, holding me close to her.

Mierda! I could come now, but that's not how this is going to end.

"Maybe you should, querida. Maybe this is the only thing that's ever made sense between us," I tell her, spinning her around and pushing her into the wall. Her hands go up to brace herself and I put my much larger ones over them. Pushing my fingers in between hers and clenching my hand so she's forced to do the same. I grab her clothes pushing them down off her hips in one quick movement. Revealing that beautiful ass of hers that used to keep me up at night. I squeeze the cheeks, letting my thumbs push into the crevice and push against her entrance there.

"Tell me, Beth do you still want my cock in your ass? We never got to experience that did we mi cielo? I was taking my time with you. Maybe I should fuck you right here, forcing you to take my cock, without even preparing you."

"Just give me your cock. God Skull, quit teasing me, if you're going to fuck me! Fuck me!" she demands and I slap her ass hard for daring me. She cries out, pushing her ass hard against me and I spank it again.

"I ought to make you wait until we get back just because I can," I groan. "I just fucking can't," I tell her, unzipping my pants. My dick is killing me, dying to get free. My breath is lodged in my chest at just the thought of getting back inside of her. It can't be as good as I remember. There's no way that could be possible.

"Skull!" she cries and for a minute I let my mind drift back, back before the pain, the heartache, the distrust. Back to a time when it was just me and her and our bodies. My hands bite into her hips as I pull her out from the wall, pushing her legs apart. I push down on her back—getting her into the position I need.

"Hold on, mi cielo, hold on," I warn her, grabbing my dick and rubbing my shaft against her pussy, letting it push through her lips and glide in her sweet juices. "You're so wet and eager for me aren't you, Beth? Dying for me to fuck you," I groan, as my tip grazes against her clit. She's so hot and warm.

"Quit talking about it and just do it already!" she demands.

"Greedy little puta," her hunger turning me on like nothing else could. I push my cock up, feeling my way by instinct and sliding into her sweet depths. Her walls instantly close in on my cock, sucking him in. I pull back out and then plunge back in, deeper, not stopping until my body is pressed tight against her and her sweet creamy juices are dripping onto my balls.

"You feel so good," Beth gasps. I reach around, cupping her breasts in my hand as I thrust back into her, grinding myself deep inside. I massage them with my hand, kneading them and working my cock in and out of her. She thrusts back into me, each time I withdraw. We work together in perfect time and I can feel her cunt tightening against me, the muscles fluttering as she nears her climax.

"Skull, baby," she whimpers and hearing her voice so close to the edge, full of need, nearly destroys me. Emotions that I don't want to feel right now come close to the surface. I fight to lock them down and instead concentrate on pounding her pussy, on driving myself so deep inside of her she can taste me…on fucking…

One of my hands moves from her breast to her hair and I grab it, fisting it as I fuck her harder.

"Take it, Beth. Take what I give you. God, mujer, you're so fucking tight…"

"I told you," she gasps, working my cock like a fucking pro. "I haven't had anyone but you. It's been so long….." she cries as the first ripple of her orgasm starts to take hold. I feel every contraction, every slick, wet, flutter of her walls and when she squeezes tight, trying to choke my dick I know I'm going to blow. I take my hand, grab hers and move both them down the front of her body until I hit her center. I brace my fingers against hers and search out her clit. She cries out my name as our fingers work together to find her clit and move over the swollen, pulsing nub. I work it harder, and faster in tandem with my thrusts.

"Skull! I'm coming!" she screams, as I push our fingers hard against her clit. I make one final thrust deep inside of her, and I can feel my cum jet out rocking me and her with the force of my release.

Mine! My brain cries and as much as I want to fight against it, I know in my soul that she is. She always has been. That's the thought that keeps echoing in my brain and we both slide to the floor, our pants around our legs like some fucking teenagers too eager to get undressed.

CHAPTER 32
BETH

When Skull rolls off of me, I slowly open my eyes. What did we just do? *What did I just do?* I spread my legs for him like I was in heat. *Okay, so I know what I did.* I just have no idea what to do now. It was good. *It* was fucking good. It was definite proof that vibrators are no substitute for the real thing, and Skull is definitely real.

It's also proof that I'm never going to get this man out of my system.

"Motherfucker," he mutters, throwing his hand over his face as he lets go. Then he lays on his back, looking up at the ceiling. Regret is thick in his voice, making my stomach turn. Yeah, he's real alright. *Too damned real.*

I go to get up, inwardly cursing myself. I've gone without a man since that night years ago in Skull's bed. I'd like to blame my weakness on that. Trouble is, I'd be lying. It's because it was him. *Skull.* If this were the movies, the man would be my kryptonite. He always has been.

His big hand grabs my hip, stopping me from standing. It flexes, squeezing me. It sends chills through my body, small electrical currents that travel from the base of my neck and spreads through my body right until it reaches my clit, which should be dead after the workout I just received.

"*Kryptonite,*" I mutter to myself.

"*Querida,*" he whispers close to me, so close I can feel his breath against my back. Having that and hearing his voice all deep and gravelly from his orgasm kills me. "We should talk," he prompts again.

Totally fucking kills me.

"There's not much to say, Skull," I tell him. *Except I'm a dirty whore who screamed for your dick while a bunch of men were outside—including the asshole who tried to destroy me,* I mentally add in my head. I disgust myself. All that doesn't even include the fact that I did this even knowing my sister was shot.

The only good news is that finally someone hates me more than Skull does now. *Myself.*

"Beth, we just had sex," he says, like he's explaining himself to a small child. *Had sex*, not made love. *Could he hurt me any further?*

I stand up quickly, pulling my pants up. At least he didn't see my scars. I adjust my shirt and bra, glad I managed to keep those on. I might have worked up the courage to reveal them to him before. *Not now.* Would he compare me to Dr. Torres? Would I measure up? After all, my experience is limited to just him. All of these thoughts hit me all at once—all at the same time. I want to throw up, but instead I swallow down the bile.

"I need to go check on Katie and make sure they get her to the hospital. It's just a graze, but it bled a lot at first."

"Beth, we had sex," he repeats with a groan as he pushes up off the floor.

"I know that," I tell him, turning away from him. "I think it's best if we just forget that ever happened."

"Forget it?" he growls, grabbing me and making me face him. He's mad, but then—but then that's all I've seen of him since I've been back.

"Yes—*forget it.* It was a momentary lapse in judgment."

"A lapse in judgment?" he asks incredulously.

I drag my eyes up to him. Hmm... I think I hurt his feelings. *That thought brings me joy.*

"Exactly," I tell him. "It's not something we'll ever repeat. We'll just forget all about it."

"Got it all planned out, do you, *cariño*?"

"There's no planning! It was a mistake, one not to be repeated. In fact, we should never speak of it again. I'm going to check on Katie and then we can discuss what we're going to do with Matthew."

"*We're?*"

"We're," I insist, finally looking at him. He's buttoning his pants and, except for his hair being mussed up, you can't tell that moments before he was fucking me to within an inch of my life.

Shit! I can't think of that. The way the muscles of my pussy clench at the memory is proof that I cannot go there.

"*I'll* tell you exactly what *I'm* going to do, *querida*. I'm going to kill him," Skull announces calmly.

"You can't!" I yell in a panic.

"The fuck I can't."

"You can't, Skull. I mean, sure that's what I was going to do to him, but that was before."

"Before what? You mean before when you were planning on dying here?" he growls, showing me he is still upset.

"Whatever. Surely, you can see that now that we have Matthew, we can use him to smoke out Colin."

"Smoke out? You've watched too many police dramas. Besides, I don't need him to find Colin."

"You do. We have to find both of them, Skull, so that this *ends.*"

"I'll find Colin. I don't need that sad fuck-bag outside to do it."

"You're sure?"

"Positive," he confirms.

"Good," I tell him, walking towards the door.

"Where are you going?" he asks, following me.

"I'm going to go kill Matthew," I tell him, deadly serious.

Chapter 33
Beth

"I don't quite remember you being so bloodthirsty," Skull says.

I stop and take a breath. "There are things that change you forever," I tell him, trying to blot out the memories. "The girl you knew had to grow up fast."

I expect him to say something in response to that, but he doesn't. I'm almost to the door, congratulating myself. I extricated myself out of that relatively easily, and now we'll be one step closer to me getting away from the club. And away from Skull. I may not want that, but it's needed. I wonder if hypnosis can really make people forget things? Maybe there's someone in town that does that.

"What are you doing?" I gasp when Skull grabs me from behind and brings me around to face him. I hold onto his hand to try and steady myself. "Skull! Stop!" I cry in outrage as he lifts me up and throws me over his shoulders.

"I'm saving you from yourself this time, *querida*," Skull mutters.

"What does that even mean? Let me down right now!"

"Afraid not, *cariño*."

"If you don't let me down right now, I'll make sure your girlfriend knows all about what we did back there!" I threaten him.

"I don't have a girlfriend, but be my guest to tell anyone you want, Beth. I doubt it will be much of a secret since my men had to have heard you screaming for me," he calmly tells me. If blood wasn't already rushing to my face from being held upside down, I know I would be blushing bright red right now. Then... *it hits me.* I go completely still.

"Beth?" Skull asks, noticing the change at once.

"Skull, let me down," I order him and I can tell from the surroundings that we're practically at the back door.

"I don't think so, we..."

"Let me down!" I scream, close to the edge.

"What's wrong with you?" he asks.

"Please, put me down," I beg, my voice broken.

He does so, but barely in time. I cap my hand over my mouth and rush outside, barely making it there before I throw up. Skull is right behind me. He even holds my damn hair. As soon as I'm able, I pull away from him. He whisks his shirt off to hand it to me. I use it to wipe my mouth, trying to ignore that it smells like him. I mostly achieve this. I have a harder time ignoring his chest. The designs of the ink he wears and the way the skulls are intricately woven together... *I always loved that.* Then there's the tiny barbells in his nipples... the ones I just had in my mouth... *Shit!* What the hell is wrong with me? This is Skull's fault. All his fault. He's done something to me.

I look around and all of the men are there. Candy, Louise, and Sacks are all there, too. But I don't see Katie and Torch anywhere. Beast is standing over Matthew with a gun. I look at him briefly. Sadly, there's very little blood visible on his pants. That's Skull's fault, too. When I planned it out in my head, I was going to thrust my knife into his jugular. That would have killed him. All of this is Skull's fault.

Skull—who has destroyed my life. Skull—who threatened to take my child away from me. Skull—who fucked me even though he had a girlfriend. Skull—who has ruined me for other men. Skull—with the perfect fucking pierced nipples.

"Where's Katie?" I ask the men, still thinking of all the reasons I should hate him.

"Beth, are you sick again?" Skull asks, concern and worry laced in his growly-He-Man voice, which feels good. Which, in turn, pisses me off.

"I just threw up!" I hiss at him. "I'm done. I'm pretty sure there's nothing left in there to be sick with again. Trust me, if there was, I'd probably still be barfing! Now can we get your…"

"What the hell is wrong with you that you're throwing up?" Skull yells, jarring me. His face is tight and I could swear he's trying to keep himself from shaking me.

"I want to know where my sister is!" I yell back.

"Torch took her to the club doctor," Skull says.

"You took her to your whore?" I screech.

His men starting laughing, and I'm pretty sure that if I could get away with it, I'd slap them all.

Skull has a strange look on his face. "No, to that damn doctor who tried to examine *you*," he finally says. Then, his mouth twists into a *grin*. "Are you jealous, *querida*?" he asks cockily.

"Shut up," I growl. "I want to go see Katie now."

"No."

"*No?*" I screech again. *What is he turning me into, a banshee?*

"Tell me why you got sick," Skull says calmly.

My head goes back in disbelief. Is he insane? Fine. He wants me to lay it out? I will.

"Because, *estúpido*, I had sex with a man who sleeps with a she-bitch from hell!"

"You threw up because you had sex with me?" he growls, his face going tight with anger again, and all trace of the cocky, worrying asshole is erased. Now he looks normal again. I almost wince because I didn't mean it like that—not exactly. I want to explain, but then I remember what an asshole he is, what an asshole he's been—especially the part where he slept with me *while having a girlfriend.*

"Exactly!" I growl.

The men are laughing. Shit! I forgot about them. Something about Skull always makes everything and everyone else disappear for me. At least they are making an effort to be quiet.

"Don't worry, Skull. Beth has a weak stomach. Don't you, *Bethie?*" Matthew goads me. "I used to use that to my advantage quite often. Those were good times, weren't they, Beth? Have you shared them with Skull yet?" he asks. "I wonder how he'll see you when he knows about them."

His words. The memories… they slam into me like a sledgehammer. I know my face goes white because I am cold all the way to the tips of my toes. It's made even worse because the men have all gone quiet now. I feel their eyes on me and it takes all I have not to buckle under the pressure and take off running.

Instead, I walk over to Beast and reach my hand out. "Give me your gun."

Beast looks down at my outstretched hand and I hate that it's shaking.

"Beth, maybe you…" he starts, his voice dark.

He's not looking at me though. He's looking over my head at Skull. Skull's face is unreadable—which is probably a good thing.

"Give me your gun," I repeat.

Skull must have okayed it, because Beast tears his eyes away from him and he carefully hands me the gun. He looks at me with understanding and something I completely loathe: *pity.*

I turn my attention to Matthew. The bastard isn't pleading for his life. If anything, he looks satisfied. I spit on him.

"I'll see you in hell, brother dear."

"You could let me live long enough to see Skull's face when he discovers all your new secrets. I mean really, I think…"

I shoot him before he can taunt me further. I aim between his eyes and it hits dead center. I'm standing so close, blood splatters against my skin. It's okay, I already feel dirty. After my time in France, I may never feel clean again.

I wipe the spray of blood I felt that hit my face with the back of my hand. In this case, it doesn't bother me to see the smearing red against my skin. I feel no need whatsoever to get sick. I hand the gun back to Beast.

"Can one of your men take me to see my sister now?" I ask Skull.

"You played into his hands," Skull says. "You gave him an easy death."

"I know I did. I also know that he needed to die. He's not breathing my air anymore. He can't touch my daughter. I'm okay with it."

"Briar do we have the keys to Donahue's vehicles?" Skull asks.

"Got keys to an SUV and one to that fancy Mercedes thing he was so proud of," Briar answers.

"Give me the keys to his. I'll set it on fire for fun later," Skull says, catching the keys when Briar tosses them. "Come on, *querida*," he says, turning his attention back to me. "I'll take you to your sister."

"Your girlfriend won't mind?" I ask, hoping I can annoy him enough that he'll send me with someone else.

"You've been through enough today, Beth. Don't make me paddle your ass too," he says. I don't respond. I'm too busy trying to keep myself from shaking, as reality starts setting in.

Chapter 34
Skull

There are things that change you forever. The girl you knew had to grow up fast.

I'm lying in bed with my eyes closed and I just can't get Beth and those words out of my head. It's true, too. There are traces of my Beth—*the old Beth*.

I sit up, knowing I'm too tense to rest. So much of today was a revelation. Least of all, there is this new side of Beth that seems to be emerging, completely different at times from the girl I knew. The thing is, I think I want this version more than the old one, and that's bad. She's still the woman who cut my heart out. The same woman who went head first into a decision that left me twisting in the wind in pieces. I can't allow myself to forget that.

I'm getting a damn headache. I rub the tension out of my forehead, willing the pain that's setting in to leave. It doesn't help, but then I didn't really expect it to.

The biggest thing from today was the discovery that Beth is definitely hiding something from me. Scars? Maybe worse, knowing the twisted fucks she's dealt with. I should have taken my time with her body, gotten to know it all over again. I didn't because I was in too much of a damn hurry, and fuck, she was even better than I remembered. Just thinking about it makes my dick hard, and that's bad because I know there's no way in hell that Beth is going to let me back in there without a fight. I shouldn't even want back in—*but I do*. Even with the shit that went down, even having to deal with Donahue at all... today was the first day that I felt truly alive. I was ready to give up, push it all away and say fuck it. Now... I'm not so sure.

Jesus. I should have known she would have the power to tie me in fucking knots again.

I might have been able to keep away from her the night before, but that's not happening today. I get up with a sigh, going back to her room like some sick-fuck lunatic stalker. It's playing with fire. Eventually, Beth will catch me. What will I say then? *"Oh, sorry, I was just standing here over your bed with a hard-on thinking about the weather?"*

Even as I'm berating myself, I go to her room and use my key to open her damn door. I enter slowly at first to see if she's awake. She's lying on dark brown sheets, her blonde hair fanning out over her pillow and her hand under her cheek. She looks almost angelic. You certainly would never guess that she took a man's life today. She did it with deadly accuracy, too. That didn't escape my notice. Torch had mentioned the girls had been training themselves while they were on the run. I mostly wrote it off, but it's clear that now it was *serious* fucking training. You don't get that fucking accurate even close-up without hours put in. Add in the fact that Beth was shaking when she did it, and... *well, hell...* it makes you wonder exactly what she can do.

I walk over to the corner where she keeps Gabby's crib. She's outgrowing it. Soon, she'll be in a toddler bed. I missed so much with her. My eyes immediately go back to Beth. I didn't use a condom when I fucked her. She's the only woman I've ever fucked without a condom. It's like second nature with her. I don't think she realizes it yet and I'm sure as hell not going to tell her... at least not yet.

I might be crazy as fuck, but I'm tying her to me again, and this time she's not getting the chance to get away. This time no one is coming between me and what is mine. Not fucking Viper or his club, and definitely not my own. This time, things will be different. Beth will accept it. She won't have a fucking choice. Beth is going nowhere—*unless I'm right beside her*.

She's mine. Nothing else matters.

Chapter 35
Beth

"Are you ready?"

I look up from putting some more Cheerios in Gabby's plate to see Skull standing there looking at me expectantly.

"Ready for what?" I ask him, confused.

"We're going for a ride today," he announces, as if it's something I should have known already.

"I can't go for a ride, Skull," I tell him, half-tempted to say yes—and I can't do that. What happened yesterday can never be repeated. *Never*.

"Yes, you can," he says, but instead of sounding put-off or frustrated because I'm refusing, he's… smiling. How long has it been since I've seen him smile? How tempting it would be to feed that smile and get lost in him…

"I can't. I don't have a sitter. And don't you have a girlfriend to take for a ride? Or does she only ride on her broom or your…"

"Ah…ah…ah…" Skull interrupts me, shaking his finger. "Better watch your words in front of our daughter. I'm not asking anyone but you, Beth."

God, how tempting. Asshole. I need to remember he's an asshole.

"I suppose I should be flattered, but that doesn't change the fact that I don't have a sitter."

"That's why we're taking Gabby with us," he explains.

I freeze. "We are?" I ask confused.

"It's time I start spending more time with my daughter."

"Oh. Actually… that sounds great. Doesn't it, Gabby? Would you like to go bye-bye with daddy?" I ask her, getting her up out of the chair.

"Ice cream!" she yells excitedly, moving her hands up and down with her happiness. I laugh.

"Uncle Torch has her a little spoiled. She thinks going bye-bye means ice cream automatically," I tell him when I stand beside him with a wiggling Gabby.

"Then daddy needs to take her for ice cream, 'cause daddy is more fun than Uncle Torch," Skull tells her, and she giggles.

"Daddy more fun," she says, though I'm positive she doesn't know what she's saying. Still, I know what Skull is doing and I can't stop from laughing. I watch as he pulls her in to kiss her forehead. Gabby wraps her arms around him like she's been holding him her whole life. The picture makes my heart squeeze in pain of what might have been. I close my eyes briefly against the weight of the regrets swamping me.

"Beth."

Skull's voice grabs me and pulls me from my thoughts. I slowly open my eyes to find him and my daughter staring at me. *Our daughter.*

How often have I wanted that? How often have I needed this very thing? How is it fair that I'm getting it now when it's much too late?

"Sorry. I'm just a little tired. I didn't get much sleep," I tell him, not a lie exactly. "What time will you be back with her?"

"You're not understanding me, Beth. The three of us are going. You, me, and Gabby."

"Why?"

"Do I need a reason to spend the day with my family?" he asks, like none of the hate and anger exists between us anymore.

"Skull, you don't need me to spend time with your daughter."

"I know that. I *want* you... with me."

I don't think it was my imagination that there was a pause between his words.

"I don't think that would be a good idea," I tell him.

"Too bad. I do. Now get what you need to be gone for the day and let's get hopping. My baby needs some ice cream."

"Ice cream!" Gabby agrees.

"Skull, after yesterday... I mean, I think it would be best if we stay away from each other, at least for a little while."

"You're cute," he says, bending down to kiss my cheek. *Kiss. My. Cheek.*

"I'm *cute*? Who are you and what have you done with the man who hates me?" He laughs. *Laughs.* I've obviously entered into the Twilight Zone without realizing it. "Seriously, Skull. What has gotten into you?"

He looks me over and the heat in his eyes makes me want to melt into a puddle right where I'm standing. He leans down and whispers into my ear.

"It's not what has gotten in me, *cariño,* and everything to do with *me* getting inside of *you.* In fact, I can still feel you squeezing my cock, begging me to go deeper."

His voice scrapes against my ear, the low vibration teasing every nerve ending I have. His words bring back memories, memories I already spent the night reliving. I moisten my lips and bite against the bottom one to keep from moaning. This is where alarms bells should be going off like crazy. I'd have to be blind, deaf, and dumb to go with him today. Stupid. I'd definitely have to be stupid.

"C'mon, *mi cielo, vivir peligrosamente,*" he says, watching me while holding our daughter and offering something I've dreamed of having. Something that can't be real, but I don't want to turn it down. Standing there, daring me.

Live dangerously, he says…

"Okay," I whisper, my heart hammering until the moment it stops completely and the breath lodges in my chest—because in that moment, I get Skull smiling and happy in a way I haven't seen since the first time we pledged our love to each other.

I hope I don't wake up from this dream.

Chapter 36
Skull

"Is she out?"

"Yeah, definitely down for the count," Beth whispers, laying Gabby back down in her portable play pen that we brought. I realize I'm new to this baby thing, but I never dreamed there would be so much stuff associated with spending the day out with a kid. She's so little, who knew you would need to bring everything along but the kitchen sink?

I'm not lying when I say I was pretty sure I was making a huge mistake planning this day out with Beth and Gabby. I might have made up my mind to keep Beth, but that didn't mean I was ready to dive back in. Still, the more I thought on it, the more a plan began to form in my mind. I'll reel her back in. I can make her crave me and my body, giving her so much pleasure that she never wants loose, and play to the girl I once knew, the one who wanted dates and flowers. I can do that shit. Just because I never have before doesn't mean I can't. I'll give her that shit while cleaning house and getting rid of all of the threats.

Things could be different this time. I could make it so it was just the three of us...

If today is any indication, I'm completely right. It's been a good day. No. That's wrong. It's been a *great* fucking day, and it's not over yet. I took Beth and Gabby to my houseboat. I just bought it a couple months ago. I needed a place to get away from the club. I've been so close to telling the club to fuck off for so long, but I just couldn't, not until I make sure the Saints and Donahues have all been neutralized. I was going to forge ahead and do it all on my own. I still will when it comes to the Saints, but I need the club resources to track down Colin.

The houseboat gives me peace, a peace I've been unable to recapture since my days back in Georgia. I have it docked at Holly Bay on Laurel Lake. It's peaceful and, not counting Dragon, there isn't anyone in the world who knows I own it—except Beth, now. I got them onboard and took them out into the middle of the lake and dropped anchor. I played with my daughter, spent time flirting with Beth, and imagined this might be what life could be if I didn't have the weight of the club on my shoulders—the life I need to make sure those I love stay safe.

Now the sun is starting to wane. Its golden rays are reflecting on the lake still, but now have shadows chasing them. Once Beth gets Gabby settled, I grab the little portable monitor she brought and take her hand. She looks down as my fingers join with hers slowly. When she looks back up, I see the questions in her eyes, but she doesn't say anything to ruin the moment. I lead her back to the top deck, letting her sit on the sofa that's there while I go to prepare the grill.

"Hungry?" I ask her, igniting the gas once I have the chips arranged to give it that applewood flavor.

"Famished. What's for dinner?"

"I'm going all out, *querida*," I tell her, then wink. "Burgers."

She studies my face before giving me a soft smile. "Can I help?"

"You are. You're giving me a fucking great view while I cook." She shakes her head in disagreement, but turns away to look out over the water.

"Do you like Kentucky?" she asks.

"Never really thought about it. At first it was just a place to get away from the memories. Slowly, it became home," I tell her, trying to tread carefully. "Tell me about your life while you were away, *querida*."

"Skull," she starts, her voice tight.

"Nothing heavy. When you're ready to tell me that, you can. Tell me about life with you, Gabby, and your sister."

"What's caused this change in you? It can't be the sex. You obviously haven't been lacking in that department," she says.

My face goes tight. I don't want to talk about that shit, especially not right now.

"Beth, *cariño*, how about we make a deal? Let's try moving forward without looking at what we've left behind."

"No looking back?" she asks, studying me.

"We can't change the past. There's never a choice of going back. All we can do is look to the future."

"I don't think I've quite figured out why you want to look to the future," she says as I busy myself with dinner.

"Our daughter is a good enough reason for both of us, don't you think?" I ask, and when I look up to gage her response, I can swear I see disappointment in her eyes.

"So we learn to be friends for Gabby's sake?"

"Is that so wrong?"

She shakes her head and gives me a smile, but this one seems lacking. "It sounds great, Skull. I don't want to constantly be at war with you. Gabby needs both of us."

"I'm glad we can agree," I tell her, going back to working on the food. When I get the hamburger meat on the grill, I go to the small compartment behind me and pull out the folded throw that the previous owner kept there. I bring it out and wrap it over Beth's shoulders while standing behind her. She looks over her shoulder at me, surprised. "I should warn you though, *mi cielo*. I plan on being much more than your friend," I whisper against her neck. I let my tongue glide along the pulse point, which jumps erratically. I press my lips along the same path. "Much fucking more," I promise her and get rewarded with her intake of breath.

"Skull..."

"One day at a time, *querida*. We both have old wounds that need to heal."

She looks at me and nods her head in agreement. I see the fear and distrust there, but she's pushing through. It's enough for now.

But soon...

Chapter 37
Beth

"Has he nailed you again, yet?" Katie asks.

We're outside sitting at the tables across from the garage. Skull, Torch, and Briar are all around Torch's bike trying to figure out what's wrong with it. Annie asked to keep Gabby for the day, as her and Sabre were going fishing. I think Sabre is just trying to keep Annie busy because Latch reported for duty yesterday. I don't understand the dynamic there. It surprised me that he would want to reenlist, considering the obvious bond Sabre, he, and Annie have. Then again, I don't know much about how that type of relationship works.

"Katie," I grumble, feeling the heat rise in my face.

"What? I mean, you fucked him in Matthew's cabin, for heaven's sake. *Ewww*, by the way. And girl, I was in pain and didn't even stay long and even *I* heard the moaning from outside. So you can't be embarrassed about my question now."

"How is your leg?"

"It's fine. Or, well, as fine as it ever has been. Now quit changing the subject! Give me the dirty—and I mean the *dirty*."

"There's nothing to say. We've shared a few kisses, he's flirted a little. That's about it."

"That's it? What do you mean that's it? Oh, fuck! You're giving him the cold shoulder after he blew your cobwebs out? Damn, that's cold. Mad props, sis. I didn't know you had it in you."

"What? No. It's not like that."

"What do you mean?"

"I just mean, I think, we're... *friends*."

"*Friends*? Are you insane? You've mooned over the man for years. He's the father of your child. The seal has already been broken, so why not ride that pony every night?"

I shift uncomfortably in my seat as she keeps asking about Skull. I glance over to see if they're watching us. He's not; he's busy working on the bike, but almost as if he can feel my eyes on him, he looks up at that exact moment. He gives me a smile, one like I've gotten every day for a week since we went out on our first date. *God*. He's in an old white shirt that has grease on it. He's not wearing his club vest, and yet standing there in old blue jeans and that greasy white shirt, I have never seen a sexier man in my life.

"*Kryptonite*," I mutter.

"What?" Katie asks.

I have to shake myself. "Nothing," I mumble. "It's just..."

"Bethie..." Katie's voice changes, and I know she's finally getting it.

"I don't know if I can, Katie," I say, turning away from Skull.

"But you have. You two went at it at the cabin, right? Did I misunderstand..."

"No, we did, but well... mostly the clothes were in place."

"Damn. He couldn't even wait to get undressed?"

I sigh. "Neither of us could."

"Bethie, you have to know... I mean..."

"Know *what* Katie? You remember how Skull was when he found us."

"Yeah, but he's done a complete one-eighty here, Bethie."

"But why? Am I just supposed to trust that everything is fine between us now? Hell, it was just a little over a week ago that damned Dr. Torres was making nightly visits here."

"Torch swears that cow hasn't been around since, Bethie. I think you're going to have to decide what you want here."

"What do you mean?"

"I mean, sweetheart, and I know this is hard to hear, but you were gone for over two years."

"I know, but—"

"This is why I tried to get you to see other men. *Over two years*, Bethie."

"But…"

"No buts. He thought you were dead. He thought he killed you, and who knows what shit Matthew and Colin fed to him later. It sucks he slept with someone else, but it's not like he did it with the intent of being unfaithful to you."

"When did you become such a Skull supporter?" I ask her, annoyed.

"It's not that I'm a big Skull supporter. I still want to kick him in the balls, but I know you love him."

"I don't…"

"Bethie, you've always loved him. You've grieved him nonstop ever since our fuck-face of a father blackmailed you into leaving."

"It's just because he was my first…"

"Really? So you would be okay with opening your legs for someone else, now?"

"What is it you used to tell me? Sex is sex."

"I was a stupid fool. You were the one who was right."

"Get real."

"I'm serious. I don't regret my past, but I will tell you there's not a man I remember since the very moment I laid eyes on Torch. He's it. When you find the one you're meant to be with, you know it."

"You're just all drugged up. You're talking out of your head," I joke, praying I'm right.

"Laugh. It doesn't change things. Sometimes I hate myself because I'm the reason you had to give him up," she says and my stomach tightens in reaction. I reach out and hold her hand in mine.

"Neither one of us can change what went on, Katie. It's not your fault. It's *theirs*. Besides, there's so much we didn't know. I mean, hell, *we* didn't even know our real mother."

"If there are things the Donahues are good at, it is definitely secrets. The thing is, Bethie, you have a second chance. You need to decide what you want to do with it."

I sigh. "I'm just not sure I can let myself go with him now, Katie. I just… it's all different."

"Then you have to be prepared to let him go."

"I know…"

"And you need to be sure that's what you want, because you can be sure Dr. Torres or some other skank will be waiting in the wings." She squeezes my hand. I don't say anything else. She's right. I just don't know what to do. "But if you do take him back, for God's sake, don't make it easy for him."

"I thought you were a Skull supporter now?"

"I'm a Bethie supporter, and I think Skull might be the only man to make you happy. It still doesn't change the fact he was a horse's ass. Make him work for it," she adds with a wink.

I try to smile in response. I just wish I knew what I was going to do.

Chapter 38
Skull

"Wanna go for a ride on my bike?" I ask the woman who has been haunting my thoughts for the last week. This dating thing is not made for a weak man. It's been fucking hard not to just push her up against the wall and fuck her until she agrees to everything I want. I know Annie is watching Gabby today since Sabre was trying to distract her from Latch signing back up on duty and heading out. I'm glad he's going. That's one less man to suspect at this point. Shit, I'm even worrying about Sabre watching Gabby, but I know Beast, Torch, and Sabre should be the three men I can count on… but fuck, I thought they all were. Regardless, I know Annie would die before anything happens to Gabby. I have to go with that right now. It's all I have.

Beth looks up from where she is talking with Katie. Her eyes go wide for a minute, and then I get that tentative smile she's been giving me lately, one that says she's happy… but cautious. I'm okay with it. Fuck, I'm feeling the exact same way.

"Aww, look! Skull's asking a girl on a date. Where's the candy and flowers?" Katie grins.

"Quit being a pain in my ass, pipsqueak," I grumble. I'd never admit it, but I kind of like her. I don't get that her and Beth are twins. I guess if Katie's hair was blonde, they would look alike, but where it counts, they are as different as night and day.

"I need to change," Beth says. She's wearing jeans and a long sleeve sweater. Her hair is tied back in a ponytail. She's beautiful, but I still mourn the dresses and the way she used to let her hair free so the wind could slide through it.

"Unless you're going to put on one of those dresses you used to wear all the time, *mi cielo*, you look beautiful."

Her eyes go soft with my term of endearment. I can't stop myself from using them; I gave up trying.

"Well, you can't wear a dress on a bike."

"I seem to remember a time when you did."

"You didn't really give me much of a choice, if I remember correctly."

"Come ride with me, *mi cielo*."

I watch the muscles in her throat work as she swallows nervously, then she puts her hand in mine and I pull her up from her seat. Our hands clasped, her fingers wrapped around mine, feels like perfection. We're walking towards my bike without talking when Katie hollers out, making me stop and turn to face her.

"Hey Skull, how many girls you had on the back of your bike?"

"Is there a reason you're asking?" I know why; I just want to see if she will admit it. Beth's grip tightens, but I don't let her pull away.

"Call it mild curiosity," Katie says.

"Curiosity killed the cat."

"I think I'll risk it, Señor Asshole."

"Torch doesn't spank you enough."

"I'll tell him that after you man up here."

"Two," I tell her, and her lips curl in dislike. I feel Beth's hand trying to leave mine, but I don't let it.

"Then I guess you are dumber than you look," Katie says.

"Katie, let it go. Are you ready, Skull?"

"Yes." I turn to walk with Beth to my bike again. I take three steps and the tension is still making Beth tense beside me. It's coming off of her in waves.

"Hey, Pipsqueak," I call out, still giving Katie my back and making sure to give her the nickname that she hates.

"Yeah?"

"My mom."

"What?" she asks, and Beth comes to a complete stop beside me. I half turn so I'm looking at Beth when I tell her.

"My mom. She's the only other woman who has been on my bike," I tell Katie, but I'm looking at Beth the whole time. Beth stares at me and then she gives me her own surprise. She reaches up on her tip-toes, slides her tongue along the ring in my lip, tugging, and then she kisses me. It's a brief kiss and she doesn't deepen it, giving me her tongue like I want. But her lips on mine, in any way, is good. We break apart when I feel a slap on my back, startling me.

"I might grow to like you yet, Skull. I just might," Katie says, limping around us on her crutches after slapping me hard on the back. The girl has some strength in her.

"I live for the moment," I tell her sarcastically, winking at Beth.

Beth laughs. It's soft, but it's sincere and I gave it to her.

That's all that matters.

CHAPTER 39
SKULL

"This is beautiful," she says.

We're not on my houseboat, but close. I took her out to a small piece of land that's close to the lake. There's no dock, but there's water close to the bank, and it's a place that I've visited a lot over the years and for only one reason...

"It is," I tell her, looking out over the water.

"It reminds me of..." She trails off, and I look over at her. Her face is red and I don't think it's a trick of the sun that's starting to set over the water.

"Of the place in Georgia where you and I made love?"

She looks away from me, and I think I might have pushed too far.

"Yes," she finally whispers, her chin resting on her knees as she gathers her legs up against her chest, watching the sunset.

"That's the reason I started coming here," I tell her, knowing what I'm giving away, but unable to stop myself. "When I missed you the most, I could come out here and try to calm my thoughts."

I expected her to ask me more about that, but she doesn't. I'm almost disappointed. Doesn't she want to know more about how I've missed her?

"Did your mom actually ride on the back of your bike?" she asks instead, and I take a breath, remembering the first woman I loved; it only seems right that I give that title to Beth.

"Only once. She was sick. She wanted to feel free. She asked me to take her to the lake so she could breathe the air. She swore you could smell the fish in the water."

Beth takes a deep breath with her eyes closed. I smile, knowing what she's doing, but my eyes are glued to the way her sweater clings to her breasts and how they move with her breath.

"Why did you name Gabby after her?" I ask, wondering if she'll tell me the real reason.

"Skull, our time together might have been short, but I knew how much you adored your mother, and she was a strong woman. I want Gabby to have that to lean on. I never did."

"How did your mom get messed up with the Donahues?"

I watch her face, and something moves over it that I can't read. Instinctively, I know that there's yet another secret Beth is keeping.

"With my family, nothing is ever what it seems," she says cryptically.

"No offense, but I believe I know that already, *mi cielo*."

"My sky…"

"Beth…"

"I used to lie in bed at night and remember your voice whispering those words as you made love to me. I ached to hear them. Now that you're saying it… I'm not sure I trust it."

"I'm trying, Beth. That's all I can do," I tell her, aggravated that it might not be enough.

"There's so much between us. Maybe there's just too much water under the bridge," she says, looking out over the water.

"I don't believe that."

"Are you really over all of the anger you have towards me? That day in the hotel, and then the plane ride home… No one talked to me. There was so much anger inside of you. You threatened to take my daughter from me. Am I just supposed to believe you've let all of that go, Skull? For no reason?"

"I believe we proved that there's still something between us that day in the cabin," I grumble, not wanting to be reminded of the pain between us.

"My sister once told me that sex is just sex, an elemental need that proves we're alive."

"Well, she's right and she's wrong," I tell her, watching her closely. "Sex is natural, and when two people are attracted to each other, it's good… or can be. But until you, Beth, it never involved more than my dick. When you have feelings for someone, it changes the ballgame, *querida*."

"Maybe someday I'll be able to tell the difference," she says with a sad sigh, and I freeze. *What the fuck?* What does she think I'm doing here? *Mierda!* I know I've been going slow, but she has to know what I have on my mind here.

"That is not fucking happening," I growl, and it's a growl. Fuck, it's a growl that might rival a bear. What the hell does she think we're doing here?

She turns towards me. "Skull…"

"Do not *'Skull'* me. Do not try feeding me some bullshit about how that day in the cabin was a mistake. Do not tell me how we need to be friends for Gabby's sake. *Jesucristo!* What the hell do you think we've been doing for the last week, Beth?"

Her eyes go wide. *Could she really be this clueless?*

"Becoming friends?" she whispers.

Friends? Fuck me.

"I've got friends. I don't see me taking Torch out every night, fixing him dinner, and trying to get him to talk to me," I tell her, sounding like a pouting child because, hell, how can she *not* know what has been going on here?

"Well, if you spent that much time with Torch, you'd probably kill each other," she says with a smile.

"Cute, *querida*, but I'm being serious here. You cannot tell me that you didn't know that I want more from you, from us."

"Skull, what happened in that cabin was—"

"Fucking phenomenal."

"It doesn't change the fact that barely two weeks ago, you hated to even look at me. It doesn't change the fact that a week ago, you had another woman in your bed, and it doesn't change the fact that the past will always be between us."

I take a breath, rubbing the back of my neck. Hell, why do women have to complicate shit?

"I was angry at you," I start, the words lodging in my throat.

"You're still angry with me, Skull. You might be trying to hide it, but it's still there."

"What do you want me to say, Beth? Do you want me to tell you that it didn't rip my heart out to think you were dead? Do you want me to tell you that I thought about swallowing a bullet when I thought I had killed you? Do you want me to tell you that when I found out over two years later that you were not only alive, but that you had my child out there somewhere, that I didn't want to…?"

"Want to what, Skull? See, now you're being honest! Stop hiding behind whatever this is and tell me. Stop hiding from me!" she insists, and she doesn't know what she's asking. If I let this anger out, this monster that keeps clawing its way to the surface, I'm not sure either of us will survive.

"Beth," I start, my voice hoarse.

"Give me the truth, Skull. You want to put the past behind us? Then let's get it all out. Let's finally have it out," she insists.

Shit…

Chapter 40
Beth

I hope I know what I'm doing. I just can't take this nice Skull. It's good, getting to know him all over again and spending time with him. That's all great. But he's not the man I fell in love with. He's trying to be someone else, and it's driving me crazy. *Worse...* I don't know why he's trying.

He gets up, raking his hands through his hair, then walks towards the lake, giving me his back. I stay where I'm at, afraid to move.

"Beth. Fuck, I don't want to do this." He turns around and there's anguish all over his face. I hate it. *I despise it* because, I played a part in putting it there. "Why can't we just go forward?"

I swallow. "Skull..."

"You want the truth?" he asks, and at this point, I'm not sure, but instinctively I know I have to hear it.

"Tell me," I whisper, wondering if he can tell how hoarse my voice is, if he can hear the fear contained in it.

"Losing you destroyed me. It felt like someone cut my motherfucking heart out. I wanted to swallow a fucking bullet and follow you. Jesus Christ, there were so many nights I almost did, but I just couldn't make myself pull the trigger! I was weak and couldn't just... end it."

I thought I was prepared. *I wasn't.* To picture him holding a gun even thinking about taking his life... To picture this alpha male, who is so larger than life, being that low... knowing it was my fault… it *kills* me. I feel the tears leaking from my eyes. I can't stop them. My eyes are glued to Skull's face, to the anguish so real it's like a living thing.

"I thought nothing could be worse than that, *querida*. I thought that was the worst fucking thing I would ever live through. Then I find out almost two years later that you're alive. That you have my daughter and you're out there somewhere. I hated you, Beth. I wanted to make you suffer. I wanted to destroy you, just like you… destroyed me…"

"Skull…"

"Do you know how I found out you were alive?"

"Skull, maybe…" I start, wanting him to stop, not sure I can take what comes next.

"I was in bed with another woman. With Teena. I had been alone for a year and a half, and I just wanted to feel… alive again. I was starting to feel normal, and then I get this call, and once again, you singlehandedly destroyed my world."

And I thought I was crying before. His words rip what's left of my heart out. I get up and take off running back the way we came. I don't know where I'm going; I only know that I need to get away, that I have to get away from his words, from what they mean, from the… *pain*.

He grabs me from behind, not letting me escape. I yank my body away from him, taking a few steps away. His face is right there in front of me and I can see his own pain and he has tears shining in his eyes.

"You can't run away from me! You wanted me to tell you the truth!" he growls.

"I was wrong!" I scream. "I don't want to hear about you with her. I don't want to hear this! I don't want to hear how you fell in love with someone else! I can't hear that!"

"It's been almost three years, Beth! Our daughter is two

years old! What did you expect from me?"

"I don't know!" I scream again, so loud that the frogs that had been croaking in the hot Kentucky air go silent. "I don't know," I cry out, quieter this time, but so much more broken. "Not once in that time did I ever look at another man. You were it for me. You were... *it*," I cry at the unfairness of it all.

"I thought you were dead! You knew I was out there! You can't be mad because you started this whole series of events! *Christo!* You think I don't hate myself, Beth? You think that I don't despise myself for ever touching Teena when you were out there somewhere? She isn't a bad woman. She tried to bring me comfort even knowing I was in love with another woman. And yet after one phone call, I push her away and set about trying to find you... even while hating you, even while wishing you had fucking stayed dead!" he yells, and what was left of my heart breaks with those words.

There's nothing left to say... *That says it all.*

Chapter 41
Skull

The words leave before I can stop them. I see her visibly jerk with them. See the exact moment they cut her open, just like they were meant to. The monster is loose. He got to strike out, except it doesn't bring satisfaction. Seeing her tears, feeling the pain between us, it doesn't help the scars from the past; it's just making new ones. *What the fuck am I doing?*

"You need to let me go, Skull. When we get back to the club, just let me go. Put me and Gabby in one of your safe houses until you find Colin. I don't care, just please set me free."

"I can't. Don't you even get it, Beth? I can't release you even if I wanted to. You're in my blood, buried in the fucking bones of me. Jesus, cutting out my heart would be easier than releasing you."

"You have Teena…"

"I have no one! I don't want anyone. *Mierda!*" I growl.

"Then what do you want, Skull?"

"To go back. Go back to the night we pledged our love to each other. The night I was sure I had slipped inside of you as deep as you are rooted in me. The night I thought I got through to you…"

She looks up at me, her tears still flowing down her cheeks unchecked.

"I lie in bed and think of that night. I want that too, Skull. I do. I want to go back and never have to make the decision I made. I tried every way I could not to. I didn't have a choice, Skull. If I hadn't gone with him, he would have killed Katie. He wouldn't have stopped. I had already cost your club so much. Poor Beast... I couldn't risk more happening. I couldn't let my sister die. But, if it had just been me, Skull... If it had just been the two of us, I would have taken my last breath never leaving your side. Even if that breath was just a moment more, I would have chosen you. You have to know that," she whispers sadly.

If it was just the two of us.

"It's just us here, now."

"But there's more involved when we leave here."

"Torch would die before he let anything happen to your sister, and Gabby can only be happier if the two of us are together."

"There's more involved now," I repeated. "There's your club. I have nightmares about what happened with Jan and that sweet baby... and Beast... That's all *my* fault..."

I walk to her now and cup the side of her face. "*Mi cielo*, no one is responsible for that except the Donahues and Jan. You did not have any control with her stealing the keys from Bull. You could not control the actions of your father or any of the other *culos* in that family."

Her hand trembles as it comes up and lies over mine. She squeezes gently as my thumb absently brushes the silent tears still falling from her face.

"Skull, it's not that simple. There are other things... There's..."

I instinctively know what she's going to say, and I don't want those words to pass her lips or even exist in her head.

"I didn't love her, Beth. She knew that, and she knows it even more now. Since the moment I found out you were alive, I haven't touched another woman."

"You don't have to tell me that, Skull, I don't have a right to know who has been in your bed since I left. I knew that when I gave birth to Gabby, me staying away didn't have to do with that."

"Then why the fuck didn't you come back to me, Beth?" I ask, forgetting to tread lightly.

"I was scared. God, Skull, I was *weak*. I was *pathetic*. I don't have Katie's courage and I'm not sure I ever will…"

"*Las tonterías.*"

"Okay, I've learned Spanish as much as I could, but that one…"

"Bullshit," I translate for her, and for the first time since this conversation started, I find a smile. "You're standing here, Beth. You put your life on the line to save your sister. You faced Matthew and ended him without blinking. That's not someone who is weak."

"But…"

"And you survived your grandfather and father," I tell her, pulling her face closer into mine. Something flashes across her face and I know there are more things to be uncovered, but I can't tackle those tonight. Right now, I need her. "You're strong, *mi cielo*. Even steel bends… when the fire forges it," I whisper against her lips.

"Skull," she breathes, and the taste of her lips is right there and I can't fight it anymore.

"Give me your lips, sweet Beth. *Los Necesito mas que necesito respirar,*" I whisper before I claim them.

CHAPTER 42
BETH

I whimper as he deepens the kiss, unable to fight it anymore. I'm tired of fighting. My hands go up, digging my fingers into his hair. I had forgotten the soft feel of his dark locks slipping against my skin. I had forgotten the taste of him, and after that night in the cabin, it has been haunting me.

He reaches behind me and undoes my hair, letting it fall around my face. I look into his eyes and they glow, so dark and demanding. This feels big. Before, it was just in the heat of the moment, and this... this can't be explained away. This is opening ourselves back up. *Can we really make it work?*

His hand moves under the bottom of my shirt, his callused fingers teasing the sensitive skin on my stomach. It feels good, but makes me nervous at the same time. I'm not ready for him to see... *me*. I need to distract him.

I reach up to push his cut from his shoulders, letting the heavy leather material fall to the ground.

He breaks away from our kiss, staring at me. The desire in his look threatens to burn me alive.

"*Mi mujer*," he whispers, *my woman*... Does he know how true those words are? I have been his from the first moment he looked at me. I fell fast and hard and there hasn't been a moment since that first meeting that I didn't want him—didn't *need* him.

I drop down to my knees, using my hands on his legs to brace myself.

"Beth…"

"I used to lie awake at night and remember how it felt to hold your cock in my hands. The heat, the feel… as I wrapped my hand around it and stroked you," I tell him while reaching up to unzip his pants and push them down his hips.

His cock springs out, as if it's pointing right at me. His dick, dark in color, is wet from the way his pre-cum has risen to the top and spilled out, painting the head in a clear gloss that makes me lick my lips.

"It'd drive me crazy because I could remember everything from the way you heated in my hands, to the texture when I would squeeze your cock tight, and even the way you stretched my mouth. I dreamed of the way it felt to slide my tongue along your shaft as I took you to the back of my throat," I tell him, my voice a little more than a whisper, my body tense with need.

"*Christo*, Beth, *mi cielo*, let me…" he exhales.

I hold his cock tight in my hand and stroke him once slowly and deliberately before bringing him to my mouth. I run my tongue over the tip, moaning as the taste of his pre-cum blooms on my tongue. I watch him as I swirl my tongue across the head.

"I wanted to cry each time because, as much as I could remember, I couldn't taste you. I wanted to taste you again, just once… one more time…" I tell him, right before I inch my mouth down on his cock, slowly taking him in, using my tongue to brush along his shaft. I slide him in until he reaches the back of my throat. I hollow my cheeks out, sucking him hard. Slowly, I let him go, withdrawing him from my mouth.

"Beth, *mi cielo*, I need inside you…"

"And I need this… Skull. I need it more than I could tell you."

That part, at least, is honest. I do need him like this. I need him in so many ways.

His hand comes around to pull on my hair, holding me still. His thumb brushes along my jawline, as he studies me.

"I will see your body soon, *querida*," he tells me, so I know now that he has me figured out. I know I will show him eventually, but I can't deal with it right now. *I just can't.*

"I'll show you... I just..."

"It's okay, *mi cielo*. We'll take this slow," he tells me, his face tender. This side of Skull, I've missed.

I rub the side of my face against his cock, pushing down so his pants are out of the way. I let my tongue slide along his balls. They're warm and tight, and I feel moisture slide along the inside of my thighs. I flatten my tongue, then curl it under his balls before licking slowly up his cock, gathering the pre-cum which is running down the sides.

"*Tan bueno,*" he groans, his hands moving back to my hair and tightening into it to the point of pain, sending tingles through my body. *So good...* and it is. I had missed him like he was a piece of me, but I had forgotten just how good being together was.

Skull holds the base of his cock with one hand and my face with the other. He moves his dick along my lips, painting them. I can't resist letting my tongue come up and lick more of his taste. He yanks my hair harder, forcing my head back.

"I'll give it to you, *mi cielo*, and you're going to drink down every drop." Shivers of need roll through my body, especially when his voice drops a notch. "Open for me," he demands, putting pressure on the side of my face. I open and he guides his cock into my mouth. I close my lips around it, humming against his shaft as he pushes my head down. He fills my mouth so full it's hard to close my lips around him because of the way he stretches me.

He pushes me down and hits the back of my throat. I pull

from his hold, but he doesn't let me go. I try to relax my throat, swallowing in my nervousness. Skull moans and pushes even farther, holding me tight so that my face rests against his fine nest of hair at the base of his cock. I whimper, feeling both submissive and powerful at the same time. He slowly backs out of my mouth, and then sets a pace that has me moving up and down on his cock so hard and fast I'm forced to hold onto him and take what he does.

I'm helpless—and I love every second of it.

My fingers bite into the cheeks of his ass, my nails scoring the skin as he fucks my mouth hard. He's murmuring Spanish above me, but I'm so caught up in what I'm doing I can't grasp the words. I know they're dirty, filthy-hot, and that does nothing but make me more excited.

"I'm getting ready to blow, Beth, and you're going to swallow every drop."

I can't talk. My mouth is too full of cock, but I hum my approval. *I want it.*

One more thrust in my mouth, and pulling back out... then another... and another... then I feel the first spray of his cum hit the back of my throat just before he thrusts back in, hard, not giving me a chance to catch my breath. I swallow it down.

He withdraws and roughly pushes back in, then more cum bathes my mouth. I swallow it all... and then more... and then impossibly more. Slowly, he begins to fade, his cock never completely soft, but enough so that my mouth isn't as full, and I can breathe in through my nose and try to calm my heartrate.

He pulls me off of him by the hold on my hair.

"*Mierda! Mi cielo...* you undo me." I don't answer, I can't. All I can do is lick my lips and see what he does next. I don't have long to wait. "*Christo!* I hope you're ready for round two because I need back in your pussy now."

I look up at the sky, glad that night has started to fall, because I want everything he gives me and for once, I don't want to worry about the scars on my body.

Chapter 43
Beth

"Good morning, *mi cielo*," Skull whispers and I tense up, thinking I'm just dreaming again.

"If you disappear, I don't think I can't handle it."

"Disappear?"

"I can't count the number of times I've dreamed of us like this… in your arms with that look in your eyes, and you calling me 'your sky'… all of it. Only to wake up and find it was all a dream."

"It's not a dream, Beth. It is a promise."

"A promise?" I ask him, my fingers trailing over the ink on his chest, unable to drag my eyes away from it. *God, everything about him is just as beautiful as I remember.* His hand moves up my shoulder, trailing a path along my neck, then arriving at my jawline and chin. Carefully, he adds the slightest bit of pressure so that he pulls my head up. I look at him in question.

"Last night was our beginning, *mi cielo*. There is no looking back, no forgetting that no matter what is at stake, it is the two of us and Gabby—"

"Against the world," I finish, kissing the inside of his hand. His response is a warm smile, which looks amazing on him. "I love you, Skull. I always have, but I love you so much more now. I'll never take having you in my life for granted."

"What do you say we pick our daughter up from Sabre's and drive out to Natural Bridge for the day? I feel the need to spend the day with my two favorite girls."

"You can take the day off from the club?" I ask, greedy to spend more time with him, but not wanting him to be lax. I can't let anything happen to him—not now. *Not ever.*

"I can do anything I want and I most definitely want this," he whispers. He's leaning over me, his hand still holding the side of my neck. He buries his face in the other side, letting his teeth rake against the skin. My hips thrust up against his. He groans.

When we got home last night, he took me straight to his room. He let me get ready for bed on my own, giving me one of his long-sleeved shirts that fell to my knees. I thought he would pressure me to show him what I've been hiding. He hasn't, and I'm glad, but as his hand moves up under the shirt and the pads of his fingers trail up my leg, I wish I'd just let him...

When he gets to my hip, I tense up. I know he feels it because his eyes go to me and he squeezes my hip gently.

"*Mi cielo*, nothing you are hiding could bother me. You are beautiful to me no matter what," he whispers, and I want to believe him. I want that so much. I swallow and it's on the tip of my tongue to tell him it's okay.

"Skull," I start, but I stop when there's a pounding on the door.

"Boss, you in there?" Sabre asks.

"*Hijo de puta*," Skull mutters, holding his head down. He slowly brings it back up, his eyes holding mine. "This better be good, Sabre," he growls, much louder, still looking at me.

"We've found Colin," Sabre says.

Both of us tense at the same time.

"I'll be right there. Tell everyone to meet me in my office," Skull tells him, and we hear Sabre walk away.

"When this is over, Beth, I am loading you and Gabby up and we're hitting the road and only stopping when we want, and only answering the fucking phone if we feel like it."

"I'm not sure I like that idea," I tell him honestly.

"Why's that?"

"Our bed isn't on the road."

"But you haven't experienced the joys of hotel sex yet, *querida*. Trust me, I'll make you like it."

"I'll hold you to that," I tell him with a half-smile.

"I better go to work," he says. I nod my head in agreement and regret. I don't want to lose the connection the two of us have finally made. "Hey, I got this," he says, correctly reading the worry on my face.

"I know, I just… things are so good right now…"

"I'm going to kill him, Beth. Then, when he's no longer polluting the air we breathe, you and I are going on our trip with our daughter. That's my promise to you."

"Do I get to…"

He puts his finger on my lips. "You killed Matthew. You have to save one for me, *querida*. They destroyed my life, too."

"You'll let me know what's going on? You won't hide it from me?" I ask him, knowing that if I at least know what he's doing, that will be enough.

"I promise. You and me against the world, remember?"

"And Gabby," I answer.

"Always Gabby," he confirms.

"Then get off of me. It's time we get this day started." I smile, trying to shake off this bad feeling I have. He reaches down to kiss me, and I take it with gratitude. His tongue pushes inside my mouth, moving against my own as we slowly taste and enjoy one another. I bring my fingers up to my lips when we pull apart. Five minutes later when Skull has dressed and left the room, I'm still holding my fingers to my lips and wishing I was on the road with my family.

Chapter 44
Skull

"You're looking awfully satisfied there, boss," Briar says when I come through the door.

I look him over. *Could he be the mole?* A man could drive himself fucking insane trying to figure this shit out.

"This mean you're finally boning your wife again?" Torch asks. I slap him on the back of his head, harder than is warranted, but that shit feels good.

"Respect, *estúpido*," I warn him. Bastard doesn't even blink an eye. He laughs. I could almost hate him.

"'Bout damn time. Hell, my balls were turning blue watching you two pussyfoot around each other," Sabre says.

"Pussyfoot? What the fuck, man? What the hell does that even mean?" Briar asks.

"That means your old lady's been broke by a foot-long dick," Shaft says.

"Fuck you motherfucker," Briar grumbles, flipping Shaft the bird.

"Can you fuckwads tell me what we've found out about Colin or are you just going to gossip like a bunch of old ladies all night?"

"Damn, I don't remember you getting so bitchy when you get sex. Someone pass the boss a candy bar."

"Torch," I growl.

"You're not yourself when you're hungry, boss."

"*Christo!*" The men laugh, but eventually settle down. When the serious face comes over Torch, I know I need to be worried. "Spill it," I tell him, my hand tightening into a fist while I wait.

"Boss, the Chrome Saints have moved into that textiles factory that went out of business last year."

"What the fuck? They moved less than two hundred miles from us and I'm just finding out about this shit now?" I yell, standing up and knocking the chair behind me to the floor.

"Shit, boss, I don't know. Dragon had no idea either."

"Dragon doesn't have the fucking history with these sons of bitches like we do! Does Diesel know they're this fucking close?"

"He does now, but in his defense, his club's been handling some of their own shit. Some fruitcake bitch kidnapped his Ry," Torch says, and my stomach clenches. Diesel's son was kidnapped? *Mierda*, what would I have done if that was Gabby?

"How am I just hearing of this? Why didn't we help him?"

"He didn't reach out, boss. He locked it down and dealt with it in-house. I guess he knew the bitch," Torch says.

I rake my hand through my hair. "Everything around me is going nuts. Do we think Colin is making his move with Viper and the Saints as his muscle?" I ask, because the Saints have always been the Donahue's lackeys.

"That was our first thought, boss, but that's not the reports we're getting."

"What reports?"

"Word is that Viper's old man, Tucker, stripped him of the gavel and took the club back over."

"*Christo!* Really?" I'm almost grinning. I hate that rat-bastard Viper.

"It gets even more interesting, boss. The old bastard has declared war on the Donahues."

"Que diablos esta pasando?"

"The old bastard wants to talk to you, boss. He says he'll make it worth your while."

"Son of a bitch doesn't have one thing I want," I tell him with certainty.

"He says he knows where Colin Donahue is and he will deliver the man's head on a silver platter for you."

"So why doesn't he?"

"He wants something."

"Don't they always. What the fuck does he want?"

"He won't tell me. He says he'll only talk to you. He requested you meet him at Psychotic Ruby's."

"*Jesús.*" I think it over. Ruby's is a fucking hole-in-the-wall bar. We don't do a lot of business there because Ruby is truly psychotic and she owns that shit. "When?" I growl, wondering if it's not a trap, but I need to do anything I can to get my hands on Colin.

"Tomorrow night," Torch tells me.

I rub the tension between my eyes and think it over. "Beast, you and Torch are going with me. Sabre, you're here watching over the club and my family." He wants to argue, I can see it, but he wisely shuts that shit down. "The rest of you will be Sabre's backup."

"Just the three of us, boss? You sure you can trust Tucker enough that we aren't walking into a trap?"

"You don't have enough balls to think the three of us can handle whatever they dish?" I challenge him.

"Fuck you," Torch gripes, and I flip him off. I should tell him, Sabre, and Beast about the fact that there's a plant in the club, but I just can't yet. I'll get Colin taken care of, then I'll handle that shit before I just tell them all to fuck it.

"Arrange it. Set it up for six that evening, though. I'm not about to drive through that damn town after dark, not with Colin out there somewhere."

"Got it."

"Good. Now if you bitches will excuse me, I'm taking my daughter and wife out for the rest of the day," I tell them, and I give them my back as the assholes are saying shit to me. It's the closest thing I've been to happy in fucking years.

I've got Beth back; the mere thought makes me smile.

Chapter 45
Beth

"Did I tell you what a great fucking day I had with you and Gabby, *mi cielo?*"

"I can't remember," I tell him jokingly.

"Best fucking day ever," he tells me, letting his finger drift through my hair. We're lying in bed and it's late, but I don't want to go to sleep. I want to capture this whole day and not let go of it.

"I think so too," I whisper shyly. "I'm almost afraid to go to sleep."

"Afraid it is a dream?" he asks me.

"Yeah. I've wanted this for so long," I tell him, capturing his hand and following the lines on his palm with my finger.

"So have I, *mi cielo*. More than you know."

"I don't want to lose you again, Skull. I don't think I could handle it a second time," I whisper, letting my fingers slide in between his, loving the way his large hand swallows mine, and the dark ink of his tattoos stands out holding my pale white skin.

"I'm going nowhere, Beth. We're going to get it right this time. There's no other alternative," he tells me, squeezing my hand.

"You promise?" I ask, looking up at his face for reassurance.

"*Lo prometo,*" he tells me, bending down to kiss me. As his tongue pushes into my mouth, I suck on it, humming with happiness. Skull has a taste that is all him. Elemental, sweet, spicy, and delicious *man*. I'm addicted to it.

His hand moves down to my gown, which falls to just below my knee. He lets his callused fingers brush against my leg.

"What do you say we get rid of this gown, and I prove to you I'm here and I'm not going anywhere?"

Nervousness pushes through my system hard and fast. Fear. The same fear that has crippled me. The same fear that made me swallow the lies Pistol organized when I gave birth to Gabby. The same fear that kept me away from Skull for years. The same fear that deep down inside makes me hear the voice that says Skull is too beautiful, too amazing to settle for someone scarred, ugly, and dirty. *Shame...* shame is a powerful force.

"Skull..." I whisper, holding his hand tight and keeping him from pushing my nightgown up my body.

"Beth, you have to know that I love you. *Christo!* Have I not shown you that since we have started over?"

"I'm just not ready, Skull. I need time."

His eyes bore into me and I know he wants to demand I give in. Part of me wants him to, because if he did, then he could see it and the fear of the unknown would be over.

It's on the tip of my tongue to tell him to just go ahead when he lets out a tired sigh. "If I turn the lights out?"

"Can I keep the gown on? It makes me feel... safer," I tell him, knowing what those words reveal.

"Mi dulce tortura, you can have anything you want."

My sweet torture. His words make tears in my eyes. Why can't I give myself to him without worry? Why do I keep holding onto this fear? *Why can't I be stronger?*

"Skull..."

He bends down and kisses the tears that are escaping. "Do not cry, *mi cielo*. This is just another hurdle. We will clear it together when you're ready to fight it," he tells me, right before he reaches over and hits the ceiling fan remote, making the room go dark. I know he can feel the scars on my stomach and thighs, but feeling small marks is nothing like seeing them. I'm going to have to give in soon and let him see it all.

I worry about it, but when Skull's fingers move between my legs, I give up worrying all together.

He drags his fingers through my wetness, slowly pushing inside of me. I'm so wet, you can hear his fingers thrusting in and out of me. I spread my legs, accepting his weight as he crawls over me.

"How do you want me, *mi cielo?* Tonight, you tell me exactly what you want." His breath is against my skin, warm.

I open my eyes slowly, mourning that I can't see him in the darkness. I see the shadow of his face, and his dark eyes glow down at me, inky and intense.

"Love me, Skull," I whisper, asking for more than just sex. I just need to know he's here with me and he's not going anywhere.

In response, he does the last thing I expect. He reaches over and turns the light back on. I cry out and tense up, but Skull instantly brushes my hair with his large hand.

"Shh… be calm, *mi cielo*. This is all we'll do," he tells me, pulling the covers over his body so they shield us both. Then, he reaches under them, pushing my gown up to my hips. My body is still tight. Fear causes my blood to rush in my ears. A sick feeling curls in my stomach because I feel so weak and stupid, but I can't get the words or actions out to show him my body. Skull seems to understand though, because he commands me to look at him.

"Look at me, *mi cielo*. Let me be your anchor. Don't get lost in the memories. They're gone."

"Skull…"

"I love you, Beth. I've always loved you. I always will. Nothing else matters. I know that's hard for you to understand, but it's true. Look at my eyes. Watch me as I claim you," he says, his voice gravelly and full of need.

I swallow and keep our eyes locked as he slowly slides inside of me. I pull my legs up to cradle him as he sinks all the way inside. When he's gone as deep as he can, he doesn't move. He just stays there, his eyes boring into mine.

"Skull…"

"Do you feel that, Beth? Do you feel how we fit? How everything stills around us when we connect? You are everything I have ever wanted," he tells me, and the tears begin again, but for a different reason this time.

He kisses them away one by one as his body slowly starts moving. I angle my body to the right, trying to get more friction, but it doesn't make him go faster. If anything, he goes slower, more deliberate. I bring my legs up, wanting him deeper, unable to get it.

"Skull," I cry because he's smiling and I know he's enjoying torturing me. He reaches beside me, grabbing his pillow. He uses his hold on my hip to lift me up and slide the pillow underneath me. I gasp as he sinks deeper inside, filling me almost to the point of pain.

"Do you feel that, *querida?* Feel how hard I am? How I'm so fucking hard I stretch your tight pussy, marking it, stretching it so that it's made only for me, only for my cock?"

I whimper. I can't get words out. I squeeze him tight inside of me and I can literally feel how his dick shudders with the action.

"Mierda!" Skull groans, bracing his hands on the mattress, on either side of me. "Wrap your legs around me, *mi cielo.* This is going to go faster than I wanted."

I do as he said, wrapping my legs above his hips, locking them together and pushing up to meet his thrusts. I pull myself up so I can run my tongue over his nipple. My tongue pushes down hard on the small barbell he has there before I suck it into my mouth, worrying it.

He slams into me so hard, I wouldn't be surprised if the entire bed scraped across the floor with the force of his thrusts. When he reaches down with his fingers and manipulates my clit in time with his thrusts, I know I'm done. I cry out as my orgasm tears through me. I lock my body into place, tensing up, unable to do anything but moan. Then, I plunge over the cliff and I come so hard, I literally feel my cum streaming out of me, bathing his cock and leaving me weak.

Skull keeps fucking me harder and harder, pushing into me, then pulling out only to slam back in. It only takes a little bit though, and he's yelling out his pleasure as he finally joins me.

"*Te amo, mi cielo. Te amo,*" he groans, as the last of his cum leaves his body, scalding me and branding me as his.

Chapter 46
Skull

Our bikes pull in together to Ruby's. The place is dead. Then again, I expected that. Tucker most likely made sure of it. We switch off our bikes and stare at the place for a minute. Neither one of us are in a hurry to see what is on the other side of that door.

As much bad blood as there is between the Saints and the Blaze, it's kind of hard to judge what it might be. I never really dealt much with Tucker, but if Viper took after his old man, I definitely have problems coming my way.

"We loaded and ready, boys?"

"You trust this fucker to stick to the white flag?"

"Something tells me yes, but we have the surprise just in case, right?" I ask Beast, and I'm talking about the grenades each of us are carrying. I'm not sure we'd manage to get out of the mess, but they sure as hell wouldn't. *Life's a risk.* "Go big or go home" seems to be my motto lately, even if I am getting damn tired of it.

"I'm loaded," Torch says. Beast grunts, which I take to be an affirmative.

"Let's get this the fuck over, then. If nothing else, maybe the fucker will help us find Colin."

We walk together towards the bar. There's a big guy about the size of Beast standing at the door.

"Weapons," he says, and the guy is smoking crack if he

thinks I'm about to give up my firepower.

"Forget it, *ese*. I'll be keeping them or this meeting isn't happening," I tell him.

Apparently he's hooked up and monitored because I see him hold an earphone in his ear for a second, then he backs away and holds the door open. I see Torch flip the man off out of the corner of my eye. When we clear the door and I give him a look of reprimand, the bastard winks.

The room has been cleared. All the tables are pushed out of the way save one in the center of the room. There's five men at the bar and they're all older. None of them are the Saints crew I've dealt with before, but their cuts proclaim them to be part of the club. At the table are two men, one of them being Tucker.

"Beast," I call.

"Got it," he says, and then he stands in front of the men at the bar. He's not blocking their view of the table; he's just guarding our backs. I'm not going out like a punk with a bullet to the back and I don't put it past the Saints not to try and pull that kind of shit.

"Skull," the biggest one of the two says. He's a big man, and when I say big, I'm not talking about height or muscle. The guy obviously likes his beer because he has a gut on him. Still, he's broad in a way where you know he could put a hurting on a man if he wanted. He's got long hair, which at one time used to be brown in color, but now is silver-white. He reaches out his hand, which is just as meaty as the rest of him. He's got two fingers on his right hand cut off at the knuckle. His index finger is intact and carries an insignia ring with a T on it.

Tucker.

I take his hand, shaking it firm and dry. You can tell a lot by a man's handshake. For instance, Tucker's whelp Viper always had a damp hand; sweat would roll of the bastard.

I take a seat and Torch remains standing behind me.

"What's this about?"

He looks me over. I face him head-on, wondering just what the fuck his game is.

"I wanted to tell you a story," he says as I lean back in my chair.

"Never was much on books or libraries, and my school days are well in the fucking past."

"I get there's bad blood between you and Viper. It's nearly destroyed both our clubs. I hoped Viper would prove to be a good leader."

"I'd say your hopes were motherfucking dashed," I answer.

"He's weak. A product of his mother, a club whore. A man should be more careful with the woman he chooses to give his dick to."

"Is this the story you wanted to tell me? Because I have to tell you, *hermano*, I have zero interest in where your *polla* has been."

The man gives me a smile and eases further back in his chair, looking at me as if I just passed a test of some sort.

"You had a good woman for a mother. I can tell."

There's a faint ache in my chest as I remember my mama. "She was," I agree.

"And your father was smart," he adds.

"My father was a bastard."

"Most of us are," he points out, and I can't argue.

He turns his head. "Are you the one that my men tell me is called Torch?"

I feel Torch shift around on his feet behind me. "I am," he replies.

"Word is, you're marrying one of the girls Colin has a price on."

"I am," he repeats, and I feel the tension coming off him.

"I hear he's asking two million for each girl now."

"No one's touching her."

"If the purpose of this meeting was to try and gain the women, you've wasted our time," I tell him, getting ready to leave.

"You're protecting both of them?" he asks, surprised.

"They're property of the Devil's Blaze," I tell him.

The man curls his nose in distaste. "Property can be sold and bartered."

"Not in this case," I growl.

"You're very much like your uncle. Did he ever tell you how the real feud between the Saints and the Blaze began, Skull?"

"No, and I never gave a fuck once I took over. Viper struck out against my men and I retaliated."

"Just like that," he states, as if he's thinking about something else.

"A man ain't a man if he can't protect what is his," I respond, thinking if I leave now I can get back to Beth in time to take her back out to the lake.

Tucker nods his head in approval, as if I finally said something he can agree to. Maybe the son of a bitch is senile and that's why Viper took over the club.

"Which is why I stepped down from the Saints so many years ago," he begins.

"Listen, Tucker…"

"A few more minutes, son. I think you will be interested in this story."

"I'm not your son," I object, the nickname irritating me. Actually, this whole meeting so far has.

"True. If you were, then life would be much better at this moment."

Que está loco.

"A man makes mistakes, Skull. I claimed Viper's mom. Married the bitch so my son would have my name and so I could control what happened to him. It was a disaster. Hooked on blow. I had to lock her away to keep her clean while she was pregnant. That was my first clue to the weakness in her. What woman ignores the child inside of her for her next high? Still, I suffered through and did what I had to do to get my child. I thought that the club and the life I led was all there was… until I met Lilly."

"Listen, Tucker, you're wasting my time here, and I have shit to do. I'm sure your life's story is interesting shit, but…"

"Lilly was the most beautiful woman I had ever laid eyes on."

"Tucker…"

"Blonde hair, the color of summer gold, and eyes the deepest color of gray I had ever seen…"

My hand wraps up into a fist and I lean over the table to be closer to him, to study his face.

"I see I have your attention. Would you like to hear how I learned twenty years after it was done that I had not one daughter but two, Skull?"

Hijo de puta.

Chapter 47
Skull

"What the fuck kind of game are you playing?" Torch growls. I'm with him except, looking into the son of a bitch's eyes, I don't think he's playing. He's deadly serious. *Christo!*

"It is no game, son. It's a story of a mother and child working together to destroy an old man with stars in his eyes. Lilly was younger. Much closer to Viper's age than mine. I shouldn't have touched her, but I couldn't resist. Her father was in debt to the club for gambling. His choice to pay the money was offering Lilly. Sweet beautiful Lilly, who was innocent… fresh, pure, white snow. I was instantly captured by her and couldn't bear the thought of not having her near me. I forced her into my bed, kept her there, even though she hated the idea of being with a man who was with another woman. A dreamer, my Lilly, despite her circumstances. She would beg me for freedom, even as she craved the love I gave her. At times, I think she hated herself and me, but she never turned me away."

The old man is telling his story, looking out across the room. I think he's swamped by ghosts of the past and not even aware what all he is revealing. Or maybe he is, because each word is laced with regret.

"The club had some trouble in Florida. I was sending my second because I couldn't imagine being away from Lilly for a week. I was a stupid fool. We had a fight, which again ended in her begging me to set her free. I told her I'd claim her before the club. Fuck, they all knew she was mine. But she didn't like the life. She didn't like that she was sold to the club. So much she didn't like... She begged me to leave and start over with her... My Lilly was a dreamer and I was fucking tired of going in circles. I thought being gone a week would give her a chance to see what I knew. She was mine... When I came back, Lilly was gone, and so was Fox, a member of the club. She left a note telling me she never loved me and that she was using me just to get her freedom, and since I wouldn't give that to her, she found someone who would."

He sighs. When his eyes return to me, I can see the agony this caused him. *Mierda!* Is this what I am doomed to? To grieve a woman even twenty years later?

"I thought to hunt them down," he begins again with a sad half-smile that speaks of pain and even more regret. "But then she left me, and it was done. I gave her the freedom she wanted—or at least I thought I did."

"If this is true, then how the fuck did Katie and Beth end up in the fucking hands of the Donahues, and why are they in such a fucking spin to get them back?" Torch asks, taking a seat beside me. I just sit and listen, instinctively knowing whatever the fuck this Tucker tells me is going to solve a lot of my questions.

"My son and my bitch of a wife, may she be rotting in hell, sold Lilly to Redmond while I was gone. Then they set about covering their tracks and killing one of my men, just to add to their fucking bed of lies," the old man says bitterly.

"How do you know the girls are yours and not Redmond's?"

"My son is an imbecile. He records everything in a fucking journal like a moron. Imagine my surprise when one of the club girls brought it to me. When I confronted him, the bastard showed the first real sign of balls by not denying it to me. He even enjoyed telling me how Redmond thought the girls were his and forced his wife to claim the children publically so he would have heirs to the throne in the family."

"So that's why you have that cut on?" Torch asks, looking at the president tag.

"It is."

"Why the fuck is he still breathing?" I ask, because there's no way the son of a bitch would have been taking clean air if it had been me.

Tucker rubs his hand along his jaw, while he considers his answer. "I've asked myself that. It's not quite so easy, brother, when it's your own blood staring back at you."

His answer stinks of weakness. If Beth's safety was in question, I wouldn't hesitate to kill. But with Beth gone... maybe he's right. I focus on Gabby. The thought would be chilling. Could I do it?

"Is that the point of this meeting? Do you want us to finish what you couldn't? 'Cause I got to tell you, *esé*, I've got zero interest in cleaning up your messes. Got enough fucking pots on the fire as it is."

"I want to meet my daughters."

"Not happening."

"It can be where you say. I will follow your lead. I need to see my daughters."

"You're not getting me. It's. *Not.* Fucking. Happening."

"They will want to see me."

"Maybe, maybe not. What they won't do is see anyone involved in this fucked up mess until I've determined that any threat has been annihilated," I tell him, deadly serious. Torch grunts his agreement.

"Then I will work with you to make sure those threats are gone. Then, if my daughters agree, I want to see them... to get to know them."

"Why the fuck would I trust you?"

"You don't have to... *yet*. I will prove myself to be an ally. I'll do anything I need to do to be in my daughters' lives."

"I can take care of the threats without you. Why would I even think about agreeing to this shit?"

"Because I know where Colin is hiding," he says, and there it is in a nutshell, the only reason I might work with the man in front of me. I start to tell him no. The word is on the tip of my tongue. Then I realize that the sooner I get Colin, the sooner I can kill him. Getting closer to Tucker means I can tear Viper apart and find the mole. All of this fucking shit together means I'm that much closer to throwing the club Torch's way and taking my family and getting the fuck away from it all.

There's only one answer I can give.

"What's your plan?" I ask, giving my agreement without having to say the words which I would ultimately choke on.

Chapter 48
Beth

"Well, lookie who decided to drag her ass out of bed and join the land of the living girls!" Candy says, and I feel myself blush. It is late. After the work out Skull gave me this morning, I was worn out. I fell back asleep and I'm just now starting my day. It's only noon. That's not bad. Heck, after the way Skull went at me, I should be thankful I'm still walking.

"You're positively glowing," Sacks observes.

"Enough already. How are you girls?"

"Well my ass is glowing like your face, but I'm good," Sacks answers.

"Roger that one," chimes in Katie. "Torch and Briar must have both decided to punish the same way."

"Apparently. Did yours tell you he had a special lotion to take away the sting after?"

Katie snorts. "He was too busy trying to get me to swallow *his* lotion."

"You guys make it hard on a single woman to be around you," Louise grumbles.

I laugh with the rest of them as I sit down at the table. Mattah immediately puts a bowl of soup in front of me with a glass of milk. She's taken to mothering me from the minute I got here, but I don't mind. I stir the potato soup and look over at her.

"Annie have Gabby?"

"Yeah, that girl is doing some serious grieving, but our

Gabby is working her magic."

"Any word on where Latch was stationed?" Katie asks.

"Afghanistan," Sacks says, and we all stay quiet for a bit except for Mattah's mumbles calling Latch a horse's ass.

"What are we doing today?"

"Not much, I'd say."

"Why's that?" I ask, Candy.

"I'm guessing that the prospects posted at the door are for us."

"Well, hell," Katie grumbles.

"Men," Sack's agrees.

"This is why I dig chicks," Louise adds. When we're all silent for a bit, she growls. "Well hell, does this mean we aren't going after the other guy?"

"Skull says they are handling it."

"You're okay with that?" Katie asks me, because she understands as the other girls wouldn't.

"Well, I'm not saying it makes me completely happy, but he promised not to shut me out and, well…"

"And?" Candy prompts.

I give a heavy sigh. "I'm not about to get you girls hurt. Last time was much too close."

"Screw that. We're big girls, we can make our own decisions," Candy says, and everyone is nodding in agreement.

"Bethie's right. This is our fight, not yours. We need to be the ones to handle this."

"The fuck you are," Torch growls from the doorway.

I look up to find him and Skull standing there and neither one of them look happy. *Shit.*

"Skull…" I start, but he cuts me off.

"What did I tell you, *querida?*"

"If you'd just let me explain…"

"Explain what? That you're ignoring my orders again?"

"Orders?" I squeak.

"Oh, shit," Candy mumbles.

"Again, this is why I only deal with women," Louise mutters, but I can't pay attention to them right now because I'm busy staring at Skull. He seriously did not just say that.

"Orders," he confirms.

"I'm not a damn dog, Skull. You don't give me orders, thinking that's the end of it."

"I do about this. We had this out. I'll deal with it and handle it and you will keep yourself safe. There will be no more secret girl power blitz attacks. *Mierda!* You girls have watched too many fucking movies. This is not the movies, and it sure ain't fucking blanks they'll be shooting at you! What the hell do you think you're doing? It's not been two days since you promised me you'd let me handle this. Where is your damn brain?"

My head goes back like he slapped me. Which really he did, just verbally. Where's my brain? Right now, I have to ask the same question, but only because I'm wondering why in the hell I ever thought he and I could work things out.

I push away from the table, standing up without taking my eyes off of him. "If you had come in a little earlier, you would have heard me tell them that you were handling it, you horse's ass!"

"*Mi cielo,*" he starts, but I stop him.

"Don't you '*mi cielo*' me! If we're in a relationship, you aren't going to give me orders and expect I'm so simpleminded that I'll do it just for the chance to ride your cock!"

"Oh, shit," Katie mumbles.

"Damn, I wish she hit for my side," Louise says, and right now, I wish I did too; it has to be less complicated.

"You will not put yourself in danger, *mujer!*" he demands,

his eyes dark and alive with energy. I shouldn't be turned-on, but shit, *I am*.

"I wasn't! But *if* I wanted to, I would! This fight belongs to me. The shit done to me and Katie was just that: done to us. *Not you!*"

"The fuck it wasn't!" he growls.

"It wasn't!" I insist.

"My life was just as fucked up, *querida*, and if I want to make sure that you don't fucking disappear on me again, then you will follow my damned orders and stay in one fucking place! *Christo!* You would think you'd want to keep yourself safe for Gabby, if nothing else. Or did you forget our daughter?"

"Of course I didn't!"

"Then why wouldn't you do everything you could to make sure you're safe so you can be there for her? *For me?*"

"Damn it, Skull." My frustration is starting to ebb. I'm not even sure why I jumped on him so quick, except that with Skull, I seem to react first and think later. I realize he's just worried about me. It's just that I can't take being another man's prisoner, even if he's doing it to protect me.

"If that's not enough, *querida*, why can't you take care of yourself for the child inside of you? *Mierda!* It shouldn't be so hard to get you to think. I'm not…"

"I'm not pregnant!" I interrupt him, his words making something twist inside of me. My hand goes to my stomach.

"You fucking could be! Or don't you remember begging me to fill your pussy up the other day?"

"Oh, shit," Katie whispers.

I find the chair behind me and sit back down. We had sex without protection. *We had sex without protection a lot*. My hand goes to my stomach. I couldn't be… *could I?*

"We didn't use a condom," I admit, holding my head down.

"Exactly," Skull says, but he's not yelling now. I can't look at him; I'm busy staring at the floor.

"You haven't been using a condom at all," I whisper, trembling.

"I haven't," he states matter-of-factly.

That makes me drag my eyes back to him. He's standing there giving nothing away, and I have to know. I keep my hand on my stomach, not looking away from him.

"You did it on purpose," I whisper.

"Absolutely," he states boldly.

"Oh, fuck." This comes from Torch, but I don't take my eyes off Skull.

"Why?"

"Because you're mine. Your smile is mine. Your laughter is mine. Your motherfucking tears are mine, Beth. Your mouth is mine and your lips are mine. Your pussy is mine and the babies you give birth to are mine. They will always be mine and if I have to keep you knocked up from now until you're eighty fucking years old so that you're tied to me in every fucking way I can manage ... then by God, *mi cielo*, I will. You're not leaving me. You're never leaving me."

I'm trembling with everything inside of me now. There's a lot to what he said. *A lot.*

"So you're going to keep me knocked up so I never leave you?" I ask, my voice full of shock, but I doubt he can hear it because it's barely above a murmur. I don't have the energy to make it louder right now. There are too many emotions pushing through me.

"If I have to, then yes."

I swallow, rubbing my lips back and forth against each other while I digest all of this. What do I say? How did I not realize the wounds my leaving him before had caused?

"You do realize I could leave, even if I was pregnant? I could leave if I had three kids or even thirteen," I tell him, ignoring everyone around us but him.

"You will not leave me again, *querida*. Where you go, I will always follow."

"Skull, you need to…"

"You will not leave me again, *querida*," he says, and his voice is brutal, but there's a hint of insecurity in it. His eyes are shining like liquid. My strong biker has tears in his eyes.

"I love you, Skull," I tell him, trying to reassure him. I stand up to go to him, my legs trembling because of how enormous this whole situation has become. It feels monumental, but I need to fight through it. I need to make him see it.

"You will not leave me. You will not jeopardize yourself again, Beth," he repeats, and I make it to him. We're so close, we nearly touch, but not quite. I take him in. *All of him.* I reach out and bring my hand to the side of his face. I cup it, running the pad of my thumb over the groove by his lips.

"I'm not leaving you again, Skull."

"Beth…"

"I'm not leaving you again," I repeat. "I'm staying, and it's not because of Gabby or because we have more children, Skull. It won't matter. I'm staying because you belong to me. You're mine. You've always been mine and this time, Skull, I'm free. Completely free."

"Beth, you can't…"

"I'm free and I choose you, *mi mundo*," I tell him, because he is. He's exactly that… *my world.*

"Beth," he whispers, pulling me into him.

"*Te amo. Eres mi mundo.*"

His strong body trembles against me. His forehead pushes down against mine. His hands grasp along each side of my neck, his thumbs stroking up along my chin.

"*Te amo. Eres mi mundo,*" he repeats. I feel the vibration of those words into the soles of my feet. They're a promise. His hands push into my ass and pulls me up his body. I wrap my legs around his waist and hold onto him, locking my hands at the back of his neck, my eyes never leaving him. I hear the others talking as he takes me back to our room, but I have no idea what they're saying.

I don't even care.

Chapter 49
Skull

"How does it keep getting better each time?" Beth asks, her voice soft, her breath still ragged.

She's got her head on my chest, and her fingers trail over my side. If I live to be a hundred and fifty, right here is where I would want to be. At her words, I smile. Fuck, I've been doing that nonstop since her declaration.

I love you. You're my world.

Mierda! How could a man not smile when his woman tells him that? I take a breath because I need to talk to Beth. I know Torch will have already told Katie about Tucker and I don't want Beth to think I'm keeping things from her.

"We need to talk, *mi cielo*."

"No," she says, shaking her head while keeping her face buried in my neck.

"Beth?"

"No, Skull. Things are too perfect right now, and whenever anyone says 'we need to talk' it's never good. And right now, what we have is too amazing. I want to keep it longer. So, no."

"What do you know of your mother?" I ask her.

She goes still in my arms and slowly pulls away to sit up in bed. She's staring at my stomach.

"Why are you asking about my mother?"

"Are there things I don't know, *querida?*"

She sighs. "Yes, but not because I was keeping it from you.

It's not that. It's just… I didn't find out until Redmond took me and Katie back to France."

"Okay."

"And honestly, Skull, since I've been back… we've been at each other's throats, or…"

"Fucking our brains out?"

"I was going to say going at it like rabbits, but yeah," she says, laughing weakly and finally looking at my face.

"It's okay, *mi cielo*," I tell her, knowing she's worried that I might think she's keeping more things from me.

"My whole life, you have to understand, we thought that Isabel and Redmond were our parents. We may not have liked the fact, but that's what we believed. That's all we knew."

"But they weren't?"

"Well, no… not really. When we got to France, grandfather would take great pleasure in telling us what a blight we were on the family. He kept saying we were weak, that we were too much like our mother, and how blood always tells…"

"He didn't like your mother?"

"Well, that's what we couldn't figure out. Grandfather always seemed to adore Isabel, even after her and Redmond divorced and she married his brother, which personally upped the creepy factor for me. I mean, I know love is blind and all that, but that would be like me getting with Torch if something happened to Katie."

"That will never fucking happen. You stay away from Torch."

She rolls her eyes at me like I'm crazy—which admittedly I am. The thought of her being around any other man nearly destroys me.

"Please, Skull. He's getting married to my *sister*. That's just icky," she says, scrunching up her face so fucking cutely, I can't resist kissing her. I press my lips firmly against hers one more time.

"I get a little crazy thinking about anyone else near you, *mi cielo.*"

"I'm gathering that, but relax. You've ruined me for other men. If I didn't go anywhere in the time we were apart, I sure as hell won't now that I finally have you back."

My hand is at the base of her neck and I squeeze once, smiling at the joy those words send through me before letting go so she can finish.

"We soon found out that while Redmond was married to Isabel, he had an affair with a girl that the family bought… God. The Donahues are involved in human trafficking," she whispers. "They all deserve to die…"

I reach over and pull her up into my lap, hating that she looks so lost and alone in that moment. I used to feel guilt that I pursued Beth when she was so young. I'm not anymore. I was meant to find her on the street that day. I was meant to rescue her from this fucked up family and be here for her. I was meant to do all of the things Tucker failed to do when it came to her mother. Beth is my purpose. *Mierda, she's my reason for living…*

She snuggles into me, turning so her arms and legs wrap around me. I move my hands over her back, trying to comfort her. "Keep going, *mi cielo*," I whisper into her hair, hoping the heat of my body warms and reassures her.

"He got her pregnant and, normally, he would just have her and the child killed, but my grandfather's brother made moves, and they wanted heirs to ensure they would maintain control of the family long after they were gone. I don't understand, but that whole family's so fucked up, Skull. It sounds like a bad movie. He made a deal with Isabel that if she raised us as her own, he would make sure she always kept the things she wanted…"

"Meaning?"

"The Donahue name, the jewelry, the furs... Isabel was nothing if not mercenary. Katie and I accepted that, even when we thought she was our mother."

"What happened to your mother?" I ask her, pretty sure I already know.

"Redmond killed her, for daring to get pregnant," she whispers. "Our mother died because of us, Skull."

I've got my hand at her neck again, using my thumb to push the tears that fall from her eyes. There's not many, just a couple that escape, but somehow that's more heartbreaking for me to see. I squeeze my hand, forcing her head so she'll look in my eyes when I speak.

"Your mother died because the Donahues are fucked in the head. They are evil men who have to die... and they will die, *querida. Voy a matarlos.*"

I will kill them, I tell her, and I will. Colin, Viper, whoever his spy is... all of them will die.

"Katie and I decided that, too. Matthew... he and Colin, really, they worked together to kill Redmond. They wanted control of the family, but they didn't want to risk alienating my grandfather. So they made it appear like an accident. But Matthew let it slip one day when he was—"

"When he was what, *querida?*"

"With Redmond gone, Matthew and Colin convinced grandfather they could control the family and make sure everything ran smoothly. Soon, they began taking Redmond's place."

"Place in what?" I ask, but in my gut, I already know.

"Torturing us. With Redmond, it was because we proved to be weak like our mother. With Colin and Matthew, they knew the truth about us."

"Truth?"

"We weren't Donahues. Redmond wasn't our father. All this mess, Skull, and *I'm not even a Donahue.*"

"How did they know?"

"I'm not sure, or if they told us, I didn't really listen. I was just relieved. But then… grandfather found out that Colin and Matthew had worked together to have Redmond killed."

This whole story is giving me a headache. What had it done to Beth and Katie? How had they survived having their world continuously altered and out of their hands? Colin should die for that alone. I think about telling her I'm the one who did Redmond in. I will eventually, but for now, she just needs to get this story out, so I hold her and wait for her to continue. When she seems lost in her thoughts, I try and bring her back around.

"What happened?"

"He went crazy. He was so upset. He said he'd kill them for killing his son. He was shooting and waving a gun around. I thought Katie and I were going to die that day. I would have almost been glad for it, except I was carrying Gabby. I wanted to survive so she could live."

Christo!

"Colin told grandfather he couldn't kill them because his brother Dom would take over the family, as he had no heirs left," she explains. "Grandfather said he would use Katie and me and the whelp I was carrying to ensure he had heirs…"

"Let me guess: that's when your grandfather found out you weren't really Donahues."

"Yeah. Matthew delivered that news…"

"I wish we could kill him again." She smiles weakly at my words and kisses my chest, as if to bring *me* comfort. "What happened next, *querida*? Let's get it all out and we'll never visit it again. It'll be as dead as the ones who caused you this pain."

"Grandfather gave up after that. He seemed broken. But the next day, he came in and he had been drinking… heavily. You could smell it on his breath. He centered his rage on Katie, I think, because she's the one who told him who was responsible for Redmond's death. He was choking her. He was going to kill her, Skull. I had to save her."

"What did you do?"

"Matthew had left my chains off that morning. I don't know if it was by accident or if he thought he left me too weak to be able to do anything. Grandfather had left his gun lying on the table when he decided to choke Katie. I crawled to it and emptied the chamber into him…"

I want to concentrate on what she's telling me, but all thought stops when she says that one word that leaves my blood cold.

"*Chains?*" I roar.

Beth pales. I know I should rein it in and get a handle on it. I'm just not able.

"*What the fuck did they do to you Beth?*"

Chapter 50
Beth

Why didn't I think while I was talking? I start to pull away from him. I need distance from him. I need to… Oh, God. His face is a mixture of fury and misery and I know I'm the cause of it. I try again to pull off of his lap. His hands dig into my hips, refusing to let me get away.

"Tell me, *querida*."

"Skull, it's not important now," I tell him, trying to calm him. Apparently that was the wrong thing to say because his face is almost red with fury.

"It is! You're important! I need to know what they did to you!"

"Why?" I cry, wanting this entire conversation to just disappear. "Katie and I got away, we survived, and that's all that is important! I'm here with you now. We have our daughter and a second chance!"

"Because I have to know, Beth. It's something I need to be able to share with you. I need you to give it to me to carry so you can be free of it," he tells me, and I know he's making an effort to be calm.

"I am free. It's over."

"You're hiding your body from me," he states, and he is much calmer now, but that's bad news for me because he is methodical.

"Skull…"

"Torch mentioned torture, but fuck me, I glossed over it in my head. Even knowing what kind of monsters I had been dealing with, I thought since they viewed you as family, you'd be mostly safe, especially after Torch promised me they didn't rape you…"

"They didn't rape me," I whisper, seeing the question on his face.

"Then tell me why you hide your body from me Beth. Trust me this time, *mi cielo*."

His words threaten to undo me almost as much as the pleading look on his face. I take a breath because I know this is going to take every ounce of courage that I have. This may destroy me.

"Let me up," I whisper, hating that I have tears in my eyes, yet unable to stop them.

He lets me go and I slide from his lap and slowly pull myself up. I stand in front of the bed, facing him. My legs are shaking and it's all I can do to remain standing. I bite the inside of my cheek and use that to concentrate on the pain, anything but what I'm about to do.

"Skull…"

"*Créeme*," he tells me. *Trust me…*

With shaking hands I gather the ends of the long-sleeved shirt he left on me. I fist them in my hands, hating this, hating everything about this…

"*Créeme*," Skull urges again.

I close my eyes and pull the shirt over my head in one quick movement, and even when I hear Skull's curse, even when the cold air hits me, I keep my eyes closed. I squeeze them closed so tight they may never open again.

Chapter 51
Skull

Bile rises in my throat as I see the horrible marks that scar her delicate skin. They move up her stomach and over her chest and from her elbows down. They're crude and some are much worse than others. The worse ones are on her stomach. I figure the majority of that is because she was pregnant at the time. I tap down my anger, wishing I had someone in my grasp to take out my anger on, to make them feel the pain that my woman obviously endured. I push that away for now, though. Now's not the time for anger. I will do that when Beth isn't around to see it. Now, I just need to concentrate on Beth and making her feel good—reassuring her.

I drop to my knees quietly in front of her. Her eyes are still tightly squeezed shut. I want to scream at the injustice of everything she's gone through—of everything we've gone through. Instead, I put my hands on her hips, squeezing her reassuringly.

She jumps in surprise, her hands coming to cover mine.

"*Mi pobre tesoro*," I whisper… *my poor treasure*. A better man would have protected her better. She slowly opens her eyes and I see the dread there. Does she expect to see revulsion? There can be none. This is my woman.

I don't give a fuck about the scars.

"Skull…" she whispers pleadingly. "I can have surgery. The worse of them could be gone… I…"

I pull her down to the floor with me, and before she can say anything else, I stop her with a kiss. It's a pressing of lips, firm and hard, a reassuring touch. A vow to her. It's salty from her tears and the memory of it bores into my soul. Honestly, they're not all her tears. They freely roll down my own face as I imagine the hell that she has lived through. Her little hand comes out and tries to dry them from my face, shaking as she does so.

"Is this why you were afraid to come home to me, *mi cielo*?" I ask her, my voice hoarse with emotion.

"Skull…"

"Tell me, Beth. Let it out and we'll put it behind us. It will be gone."

"Skull, even if I do surgery, they will never be gone, not completely."

"*Mi cielo*, you need to listen to me. I want you to watch my face so you believe what I am saying. I don't give a fuck about the scars except that you were hurt and I failed to keep you safe."

"Skull, it wasn't you. I made choices. I…"

"Saved your sister," I finally acknowledge, and here on my knees my face in tears, I finally understand the choices she made. I release the anger I've been holding inside. Beth closes her eyes once again and she whispers words that are deeply soaked with pain and guilt. It's so thick I can hear it with every syllable.

"And nearly destroyed the man I love."

"You give me life, *mi cielo*. Your heart is so big, so full of love… that it makes mine beat. You gave me life, you gave our daughter life…"

"Skull…"

"You kept her safe and you found your way back to me. You made it in time to save me again, *mi cielo*. That's what those scars mean to me."

"I let fear make me run," she whispers.

"I won't lie to you, *mi cielo*, not now. That's the hardest part for me, but now I can mostly understand it."

"How? I let my fear of you seeing me, of…"

"You are young, *mi cielo*, and you were scared."

"I'm…"

I interrupt her, not wanting her to say anything else. "You saw those damn pictures Pistol fabricated and what confidence you had in us fled."

"But…"

"Bottom line, *mi cielo*, it just doesn't matter anymore."

"Skull…"

"Do you want to hold the choices I made while you were gone and the threats and anger I had when I first saw you against me?"

"Of course not, but…"

"It is the same for me, *mi cielo*. I finally have you back and I'm not going to let our past come in and destroy the life we are meant to have. From now on, we think only of the future."

"I love you, Skull," she tells me. Her body is trembling and there are so many tears falling from her face it hurts me, but she's never been more beautiful.

I pull her to the floor, gently kissing the largest of scars on her stomach. "Tell me about this one, *mi cielo*."

"Skull… I don't want to…"

"Tell me and let the pain out. Let me kiss them away," I tell her.

"This was the first one…"

"And…" I prompt her when she seems lost in thought.

"Katie's leg…" she starts brokenly. "The skin grafts from the explosion were still raw. I did the best I could to keep them clean, but they weren't healing properly. Redmond wasn't letting me have the proper bandages, and she needed medical care.

Matthew came in one day and demanded I brand the wound closed. He even brought the branding iron and started a fire in the fireplace. When I refused, he threatened to do it himself… When I begged him not to…"

"What happened then, *mi cielo?*" I ask her, doing my best to keep my voice from showing the anger and disgust I feel inside.

"He asked me what I would do, to keep him from doing it…"

"*Mierda*," I whisper softly, hoping she doesn't hear it, but when she flinches, I know she does. I kiss the scar again. "Tell me."

"I told him I'd take her pain. He handed me a knife… and told me to prove it." Her body shakes from the force of her tears and I hold her as close as I can. "I was so scared, Skull. I was afraid I would hurt the baby. It hurt so bad, and there was so much blood. I can still hear Katie pleading with me to stop, but she was so feverish and sick. Matthew was laughing…"

"Shh… I have you, Beth. The bastard is dead. He'll never touch you or Gabby again," I tell her, and the tears in my own eyes blind me. "*Te amo, mi cielo*," I whisper to her stomach.

I make my way to every scar, both small and large, kissing each one, praising her with each kiss for her bravery, for her courage, for just being her.

Finally when I am finished, I hold her until the tears begin to slow. Then I do the only thing I can. I slowly love her body, there on the floor, with the light on, showing her in ways no words could that she is beautiful and the only woman I will ever need or love.

Mi mundo…. My world … My pearl of great price…

Chapter 52
Beth

"Explain to me again while we're only twenty minutes away from the club, but having a picnic again?" I ask Skull. "I mean, really, there are picnic tables out behind the club."

"I told you, as long as we're on lockdown, I'm not going to let you and Gabby be far from home."

"But you're..."

"Even if I'm with you, Beth. I'm not going to risk you and Gabby for anything. But even so," he says with a grin, taking a strawberry, dipping it in chocolate, then plopping it in my mouth. I open immediately because, well, they taste good, but more than that, I love when he gets that happy look on his face. "Even so," he continues, "I want some alone time with my two favorite girls."

"Daddy!" Gabby yells, as if on cue. She's holding the bucket and shovel I brought.

Skull grins at her. "*Mi hija* is demanding me, *mi amor*."

He winks. I shake my head as he goes and plays with our daughter. It's been a week since I've shown him my scars, and each day, he proves even more that they don't matter to him. It's been a week, and I feel like finally everything is going to be okay. A week of nothing but... happiness.

I go over to sit beside Gabby and help them play in the sandbox that Skull brought. It's in the shape of a turtle, and it was all he could do to fit it in the back of the truck. Then, when we arrived here, he added the bags of sand he kept in the back.

"Can I ask what you're planning to do when she wants the sandbox at home?"

Skull turns the bucket upside-down to show the beginnings of the castle he and Gabby are building. "Make sure it's at home for her, *mi cielo*. What else?"

What else? I shake my head at his simple answer. I have a feeling that if Gabby asked for the moon, he'd find a way to give it to her. Now that Skull and I have finally worked through our issues from the past, he's much softer around Gabby. Gentler, even. She's sensed the change and the difference in how they interact is night and day.

We play for an hour until Gabby's laughter slowly changes to yawns, then we lay back on the quilt we brought and stare up at the sky, making shapes out of the clouds. Soon Gabby is sound asleep, snuggled between us. My hand goes to my stomach in sadness. I had hoped I was pregnant when Skull mentioned how he hadn't been using a condom, but I started my period a couple of days ago. No baby.

"It will happen, *querida*," Skull's deep timbre whispers against my skin, and I look up at him. He's smiling at me, even as his hand clasps mine and rests on my stomach.

"I want a sister for Gabby so she has someone who is always there for her, like I have with Katie."

"God help me," he says with a smile.

"I'd be offended … but I think you like my sister."

"I plead the fifth."

"Mmm…hmm..."

"*Querida*, I hope you don't take this wrong, but I'm hoping our next child is a son. It's going to be a fulltime job to keep men away from Gabby as it is."

"Good luck with that," I say, then laugh. I sit up to adjust a small blanket over Gabby. That's when I notice she's wearing the hair bow with the mini nanny cam in it. I just assumed that Katie had taken it out, but I can see it clearly. Actually, I'm sure she told me she did, which means she put it back in for today. She's spying on me and Skull. "That bitch!"

"*Querida?*"

"I'm going to kill my sister. She's spying on us!"

"Beth?" Skull asks, still confused.

I gently disengage the hair bow from Gabby's dark hair to show Skull.

"When we wanted to know what you guys had found out about Colin and Matthew, Katie put this little pinpoint camera in Gabby's hair bow. It's a little better than a voice recorder, so when you took her into the meeting, we would know what you were discussing."

"You *what?*" he growls.

"We had to know what you were talking about and you wouldn't tell me otherwise. You left us with no choice."

"Except to not listen into private conversations and wait for me to tell you what's going on."

"If I had done that, would you have told me where Matthew was so I could help kill him?"

"Probably not, but he still would have wound up dead."

"Then I rest my case." I shrug his complaint off. "Anyways, back to the camera."

"I should spank your ass," he grumbles.

"Feel free, later," I tell him. "I remember she clearly told me she took the camera out after you gave it back to me. Which means she put it back in on purpose, just for today."

Skull sighs, taking the hair bow and putting it in his pocket. "Soon, *mi cielo*, we will discuss your tendencies to think you are a detective, but not today. Today, I think I'm the reason she's spying on us."

"You are?" I ask, confused.

Skull stands up and reaches his hand out to me. "Walk with me, Beth."

"Gabby…" I remind him, but I stand and take his hand, wondering what's going on.

"We'll just walk a few steps. She'll never be out of our sight," he answers.

We go about ten feet. He smiles at me, and it's the type of smile that makes my heart flutter in my chest.

"Skull…"

"Just a little over three years ago, my world was rocked to its core. I saw this girl with sparkling spun-gold hair blowing in the wind, in this pure white dress looking like an angel. *Mi ángel.* She was a picture of something in my mind that I dreamed of when I was a child, and then her eyes… As a child, I wanted a woman with sky blue eyes that reminded me of a happy memory. But this woman's was a combination, a gray that look like the sky just before the rains open up. Much more interesting… more captivating."

"Skull, sweetheart…"

"*Te amo, mi cielo.*"

"That's why you call me your sky?"

"I love you, my sky," he repeats in English. "You are it for me," he says, his voice thick with emotion, and I can feel each vibration inside of me.

He reaches into his other pocket. I watch him and, almost as if everything is in slow motion, he goes down on one knee. I can't stop the tears that fill my eyes. I don't even try. When he looks up at me and shows me the most beautiful princess-cut diamond I've ever seen, I think my heart stops beating.

"Will you marry me, Beth?" he asks. "Will you have more

children with me? Will you give yourself to me forever? I swear that if you do, I promise I will bust my ass to make sure you never regret it."

All my dreams coming true in one moment... everything I've ever wanted, here within my grasp. When he holds my hand and slips the ring on my finger, I'm shaking my head up and down over and over.

"Yes! Yes! Oh, God, *yes!* Of course I'll marry you!" I drop down to my knees and fall willingly into his arms.

CHAPTER 53
SKULL

"I can't believe you got on your knees for me," Beth says as we're loading stuff back into the truck.

She's got this silly grin on her face and her eyes are full of happiness. *Mission one accomplished.* From this moment on, I will bust my ass to make sure all Beth ever has are smiles. That's my goal and my promise not only to her, but to myself. She has no idea the lengths I will go to just to make sure that all she feels is happiness from here on out, but she will.

"You can return the favor later," I tell her, and I'm rewarded with a deep blush on her face.

"I'll see what I can do."

Is this what normal feels like? Me, the woman I love, and my daughter. This right here is all I need. Fuck the rest of it. I'm buckling a sleeping Gabby in the car when I hear the squealing tires of another vehicle getting close. I secure Gabby quickly and look up just in time to see an old black truck come barreling up the road from the small picnic area we're in. This is a private road and the only cars on it would be the ones the guards would allow in the club. When the driver spots us, they throw on their brakes. The car heaves at the abrupt change, the tail-end sliding a little in the gravel.

In the next second, I see Teena get out. She's wearing a white dress that's been ripped along the side, revealing her bra. Her face is bruised and there's blood dried around her nose.

Someone has worked her over pretty good.

"Skull!" she hollers, running towards me.

"Fuck," I hear Beth mutter. To be honest, I'm thinking the same thing.

"Skull!" Teena cries again, running until she plows into me. My arms go around her in reflex.

"Teena, what is going on?" I ask, very conscious of the way Beth is watching us. I don't see jealousy in her eyes, but there's a definite dislike of Teena evident in them, which admittedly I can understand, though I thought we'd put that behind us.

"He attacked… attacked me!" she cries, taking a deep breath between the broken words. A shudder goes through her body and I pull back to look at her. She's been beaten. Not horribly, but someone's definitely left signs on her.

"Who did this to you?"

"I don't know! He was wearing a vest like yours, except it had… it had Chrome Saints on it. He was big and had blonde hair…"

Viper. *Motherfucker!* Does he know of the attack his father and I are planning against Colin next week? Had my men slipped up on doing recon? Or was it the mole I have in the group? Who the fuck is it? Briar? He, Torch, and Beast are the only ones who knew…

"Skull, he said to tell you that next, he's coming after your daughter. He was crazy. He said you turned his father against him."

"Viper? Did he say his name was Viper?"

"I don't know! I was so scared!"

"It's okay, *querida*. It's okay. Where were you when he attacked? Do you know where he is now?"

"It was at the parking garage at the hospital. I was so scared, *amante!* He left me alone after I promised to come straight to you with his message, but..."

"But?" I prompt her, my mind going over the options in my mind. I can't go back to my club first. Chances are, whoever the mole is will warn Viper we're coming. He'll never suspect me coming immediately on my own, and Torch and Beast will have the men follow me. That way, even with a mole, I'll have more on my side. It's my best chance.

"I followed them after they left. They're at that strip joint on Old Mill road, the one that shut down last month."

"How did you follow without them seeing you? Especially since you're so distraught?" Beth asks.

I get that she's jealous, and I wish I had time to work this out, but I don't. The quicker I can hit Viper, the better. I don't want to give them more time to prepare because I'm sure Viper will know I'm coming after him. The moment he brought my daughter into it, his fate was sealed.

I turn to her. "Beth?"

"Here, lover," she says sweetly—way too sweetly. *Shit*.

"You get our daughter and Teena back to the club, make sure you are safe. I'm heading after Viper. This fucking shit will end today."

"Skull!" she protests. "You can't just go! You're probably walking into a trap!"

"She's right, *amante!* You must be safe. I couldn't take anything happening to you," Teena adds in.

How did I not notice her voice was so annoying before?

"I'll be fine, Beth," I tell her, ignoring Teena's plea. "You head straight back to the club. Tell Torch and Beast only what's going on. That way, they will only be ten minutes behind me at the most. Can you do that?"

"Damn it, Skull! This is crazy. Aren't you the same man who preached to me about charging head first and..."

I walk to her, holding her shoulders tight.

"Beth. I've got this. Plans were already in place to take Viper out. This just speeds it up so we can concentrate on our wedding. Trust in me, *mi cielo*. I. Got. This. You just get you and our daughter safe and send Torch and the boys, *si?*"

"If you get hurt, I'll never forgive you," she whispers, tears in her eyes.

"I'll be careful."

"I love you," she whispers again, kissing the side of my face gently. I grab her face and hold it.

"That's not how you kiss your man, *mi cielo*," I tell her before claiming her mouth in a hard, quick kiss that can't leave any question in her mind that I need her. When we break apart, I go to my truck and get my gun that I keep in the dashboard. Beth doesn't say anything else. She just stands there and watches as I leave.

"Be safe!" she calls just as I jump into Teena's truck, slamming the door.

I plan on it. I also plan on ending this shit once and for all. With any luck, the bastard will have Colin right there for me to kill, too. I want this shit done and over. I have a life to live and a woman to finally fucking marry.

Chapter 54
Beth

I watch Skull leave in a cloud of dust. The first thing I'm going to do when this is over is tell him about his free use of the word *querida*. I know it's a throwaway endearment, but hearing him use it with her makes me want to knee him in the crotch and scratch her eyes out. I watch until the truck disappears and then I turn to look at the bitch. Riding in the car with her even in the ten minutes it's going to take to get back to the club is going to kill me. I'm already jogging to the vehicle. We need to hurry and get Skull help.

"Let's go!" I call, then gasp when she grabs me from behind, her long nails biting into my shoulder. Seriously how does a doctor keep such long nails? "What are you doing?" I growl, jerking around.

I don't have time to duck before her fist plows into my face.

Son of a bitch! Katie will scream at me for a fucking month for being so stupid. I shake my head, trying to escape the effects. Whatever else this bitch is, she can throw a punch.

She's on me quickly, grabbing me by the hair. She pulls me hard, but before she can punch me again, I throw an elbow into her. I try to angle up, hoping to hit her throat, but have no such luck; my elbow catches her boobs instead. *Jesus!* How did Skull keep from getting smothered in those damn things?

Then I think of how she slept with my man, and I remember exactly how much I hate her.

"You bitch! You should have stayed gone! You ruined everything!"

I break away from her, knowing that it cost me a hell of a lot of hair.

"What are you talking about??" I shout back. "You fucking loon! You were the one sleeping with *my* man!"

I dodge a punch. I could strike her, but I'm letting her wear herself out a little bit. She's got a heavy punch, but she hasn't had training, as is evidenced by the fact that she's swinging wildly. I remember what my instructor always told me about channeling rage: the best thing to do is use your opponent's weakness to your advantage. Besides, making her madder will only be more fun for me.

"I had him right where I wanted him, until you had to show back up," she growls, then swings at my stomach. I can't dodge that, but I kind of block it, then quickly grab her arm and twist it hard. She jerks away, but I can tell by the way she moves it that I did a little damage.

"Skull would have never been yours. You were just an easy lay to pass the time. If you think by attacking me that you'll ever get him back, that peroxide you use on your hair is destroying your brain cells."

"I don't want him, you idiot! I *have* a man!"

Whoa… What?

"If you have a man, then what the fuck are you doing?"

"Delaying you!" she brags, throwing another punch.

This one is aimed directly at my face. I'm so stunned by her answer, I almost let her hit me. I swing the opposite direction at the last second and connect my own fist into her stomach.

"You set Skull up?? Why? I thought you cared about him!" I huff, deciding I've played this game too long. If Skull is going into a trap, I can't waste time.

"I can't stand him. My man needed a way to keep tabs on him so his club could beat Skull's out of business. Skull made it so fucking easy. All I had to do was dye my hair like yours, wear those pathetic dresses you used to wear all the time, and act like a stupid kid and he couldn't chase me fast enough."

"Your boyfriend sent you to sleep with Skull to keep tabs on him? God, you're even more sickening than I thought!"

I charge into her, pushing her back against the car. I hear Gabby crying for me and my heart breaks. She has to be scared. God, I have to hurry here. Teena grabs my hair again, because apparently that's the only real move she knows. I do the same, even though it disgusts me. I can just hear my trainer now telling me how pathetic I am to be fighting like a little girl.

Still, he had another motto: whatever works.

And when she screams like someone is killing her, it seems to be working. "Let me guess. Viper is your boyfriend?" I ask her, breathing hard. Apparently, I'm in horrible shape since I quit working out.

"Listen to you. 'Boyfriend'. You really *are* stupid. He's my old man!" Teena huffs, swinging wildly once again, but unable to hit me because I have such a tight hold on her hair that she's bent sideways.

Gabby's crying grows harder, so I do the only thing I can: I ram Teena's face into the fender of the truck. Teena falls back hard. I let her hair go and she slams into the ground. I stomp on the side of her face. Not classy of me at all, but it makes me feel good.

I look up as tires screech. Katie's pulled up in her jeep. She's out before I can even wipe the blood off my face. *Damn.* I guess Teena's last hit was pretty good. I kick her face again. She's out. It's not like she'll know, and again, it makes me feel better.

"What are you doing here?" I ask Katie, rushing to check on Gabby. "Mommy's here, baby," I tell her, handing her Bingo Bear, her favorite toy.

"Mommy fight!"

"Just for a little bit, but it's okay now."

"Mommy boo-boo? Need band-baid!"

"Aunt Katie will give me one. I'll be right back."

"I saw on the camera that Skull left, but when you didn't show up, I got worried. I never did trust that cunt waffle," Katie growls, then kicks Teena in the face herself. Since she's wearing boots and kicked a lot harder, even I wince when her foot hits. "Where's your gun and keys?"

"Where do you think you're going?"

"Skull's walking into a trap. I'm going to go try to stop him while you get Torch and the boys and deal with her."

"Come back to the club with me and we can get Torch and the boys to handle it all. You can't risk yourself, and if you get caught, Skull won't be able to keep his head about him."

"Give me your gun and keys, Katie. You know damn well if it was Torch, you would be the same way."

"Bethie…"

"You're wasting time, time we don't have."

"Torch is going to kill me, and if he doesn't, then Skull will finish the job," she grumbles, begrudgingly handing me her keys. "The gun's in the glove box. Extra bullets are there, too."

"You got your phone to call for help?"

"I do. You just be safe," she says, already dialing the phone.

I run to the jeep, praying I know what I'm doing. I vaguely know where the place is that Teena sent Skull; I just hope I'm not too late. I head out on the road with one last glance in my rearview mirror of Katie kicking Teena while she's on the phone.

If I wasn't worried to death, I would smile.

Chapter 55
Skull

All the time I'm driving on Old Mill, I replay things in my mind. Maybe I'm letting Beth's mistrust of Teena get to me, but something just isn't ringing true. Her face seemed too controlled, even when she was supposed to be in a panic.

With that in mind, I stop about three miles down the road from the strip joint. If I am walking into a trap, I sure as hell don't need to make it too easy for them. I know Beth, and she'll get Torch and them out here fast. She won't take a chance of being too late; I can depend on her.

I fought against her pull at first, knowing she was way too young for me. Some things you just can't fight, though you want to. She's grown up over the last three years. I've seen it in her, and she survived shit I can't even imagine a young girl having to face. That's how I know she'll do whatever she has to now to keep her family together. I get out of the truck, carefully closing the door. I'll walk and come up on the place from the east and hopefully have enough time to scope them out before making a move. Even better, by then Torch and Beast will be here.

It doesn't take long to jog to the edge of the property that surrounds the strip joint. There are three cars in the parking lot and two bikes. I'd like to think that means there are only five people inside, but I somehow think that would be the wrong assumption.

I'm just about to make my move when I hear the voices.

They're coming from my left side and they're whispering, but I can hear them pretty plainly, which tells me they are close. I look around for a place I might find cover. There's not much to choose from: a rock or a tree, neither of which are extremely wide. I finally vote for the old oak tree, stepping behind it, my hand going to my gun. I click off the safety and wait.

"You really think this guy is dumb enough to come here and face us on his own?"

"Who knows? Viper says he will. I'm not about to chance it, though, which is why I'm carrying this instead of that damn thing you have," the other guy says, holding up a semiautomatic rifle. The other guy is carrying a pistol. I'd like to be able to take them both out at once, but I don't see how that's going to be possible. If I let them pass me and attack from behind, I have to worry about the assholes shooting right away and giving my location up. I can't afford a swarm of them all at once.

I wait until they pass me, then carefully make my way to stand a few feet behind them.

"You got two choices," I announce to their backs. "Drop your weapons and put your hands up where I can see them, or take a bullet in the back of your brain."

"Fuck!" one of them groans, but they don't make a move to do what I say.

"You're wasting time and I've got an itchy trigger finger," I warn them.

"Hey man, we don't want to die. We were paid for this shit," one of them says, still not putting his gun down. "We just needed money to feed our families."

I see the other one in my peripheral vision tightening his finger on the trigger. This isn't going easily, and I knew it wouldn't.

I just hoped.

I fire a round in the back of one of the motherfucker's heads, and he falls dead. The guy beside him jumps when blood splatters from the shot, his friend dropping to the ground. He drops his gun and puts his hands up quickly.

Idiots. They don't think I see the fucking jackets they're wearing? *"Check for their families." Christo!* I drop him too, because I know if the motherfucker gets free, he's just going to come after me. I can't take a chance on any of these twisted fuckers who have aligned with Colin. Their fates were sealed when they joined forces with that motherfucker.

I can't risk anything now that I have Gabby and Beth.

My life has never been for the weak, but I'm getting motherfucking tired of all this shit. It was different when I felt I had my brothers at my back. Now, I have no idea if they're there to help or there holding a fucking knife.

I drag the bodies off behind the trees for the crows and vultures. There's no sense in broadcasting my arrival too soon. I worried enough that they've heard the shot. Once I have that taken care of, I approach the building.

I can hear the music blaring immediately. It's no fucking wonder they couldn't hear the shots. *Pendejos!*

I walk around the club, doing my best to stay close to the sides and ducking away from the windows. I spot a window cracked in a bathroom. *Mierda!* It's like they're making it too easy. Maybe they are.

I thought Torch and the boys would have been here by now. I look in the windows a little more. Besides Viper, I see that fucker Colin inside. I hate that he's still breathing air. I have pictured myself squeezing the life out of him, breath by fucking breath. Now that he's this close, my fingers are itching to try it.

I wait a few more minutes. When there's no sign of the cavalry, such as they are, I decide to just charge ahead and let the chips fall where they may. I'll never get a better chance to take out Colin than I will right now, and I can't afford to let that fall through my fingers.

I need to do this to avenge Beth. If I die, at least I'll take Colin with me. With that thought, I hoist my body up and slip through the window.

Chapter 56
Beth

"I got this. Trust me," he had said. If we survive this, I may kill him.

Now I know how he felt when he found me at Matthew's cabin. Right now, I'm dealing with two main fears. The main one being: I'm too late to keep Skull from going into a trap.

The second is: I can't remember where this damn place is.

My nerves are on a thin string and I feel like I'm going to crack at any minute. It would help if the old country roads here had clear road signs. Half of them are missing, or heck, maybe were never there to begin with. Some have sadly been the target for bullets and the writing can no longer be read. Because I'm not sure of where I'm going, I'm having to drive a lot slower than Skull, too.

I pass the small road before I realize it. Luckily, I see the old barn with a mallard painted on it. I remember that from when Skull and I drove out here. I make a U-turn and find the small road I just passed, and sure enough, there's a small pale green sign that says "Old Mill Rd." right there with vines growing on it. I drive even slower on this road, looking along the side of the road for any sign of Skull—or anyone, for that matter, because I'm not sure what to expect.

I see a flash of blue and slam on my breaks. *Teena's old truck.* When I get my man back, I'm going to set that bitch on fire just to watch it burn. The only thing that would make it more fun would be having Teena inside of it. I pull Skull's truck alongside of the bitch's, then take off on foot, gripping my gun tightly. I keep moving north, just like the road goes, figuring that will take me to the strip joint. After about twenty minutes, I've decided that I am way too out of shape for this shit. I'm so focused on looking around me that I almost fall when my feet run into… a body.

I scream before I can stop myself. I clap my free hand over my mouth, especially when I see the second body. I can only assume that this is my man's handiwork. Why couldn't I have fallen in love with a nice, boring accountant?

I break through the timber and see the building which has a big sign of a woman with large boobs that are covered up with peaches. Above her in neon colors, it proclaims the place to be: *The Juggling Peaches*. I shake my head, then wonder why it's lit-up if the place is out of business. I don't guess that matters. I wonder why a place with such a great name didn't have a booming business, sarcastic bitch that I am.

When I make my way carefully to the back of the building, I see an open window and want to cry. *Not again! Jesus!* I'm not going to fall for that shit a second time. I go on towards the side. There's a side door where I guess deliveries used to be made. It's locked, but luckily I know how take care of that. I pull the pins out of my hair and get to work. Thank God I made Katie show me how she managed to pick all of those locks at grandfather's.

It takes me three tries, but I get it. I open the door carefully, half expecting someone to jump out and attack me. It's almost a disappointment when no one is there. I can hear voices. Yelling. I know one is Skull. The other makes my blood run cold.

It looks like I've found Colin. I hate the fear that courses through me… He's the last devil I have to face.

I can do this. I have to.

Chapter 57
Skull

I think I'm home free until I hear the gun click as someone cocks their revolver behind me. I freeze instantly, thinking what a stupid fuck I just was.

"Well, well. Look what we have here."

I know that voice. I've dreamed of ending that voice.

"Colin."

"It's good you know the voice of the man who's going to kill you. No, don't turn around. I'd prefer you not to know when the bullet's going to end you. I find anticipation makes the game so much better."

"Don't worry. I have no plan on you being the last fucking face I see. That's more punishment than any one man deserves," I tell him, trying to play the game while my brain is busy figuring out how to get out of this mess. I can't give up, not now. I have too much to lose. Where in the fuck is Torch and the others? Had Beth delivered the message to whoever the fucking mole is?

"You're being awfully brave, talking to me like that while I have a gun pointed at the back of your head. My thumb is already getting sweaty. If it slipped off the hammer of the gun…"

"You won't end me that easily. You and Viper went to too much trouble for it to end that quickly."

"Usually, yes, but just in case Viper's connection failed to make sure your men won't follow… I'm afraid time is of the essence, in this case. Don't worry, I'll take my time with Beth.

I'll make sure she agonizes for months before I send her to Hell to join you."

My hands shake at his words as true fear grips me. I try to blot out the pictures his words bring to my mind. I can't let that happen. I've let Beth down too damn much now. I can't let her endure anymore.

Colin hasn't taken my weapon yet. Maybe he thinks I'm stupid enough not to have one. Maybe he thinks he can shoot me before I reach for it. He probably could. I need a diversion...

"Bring him in here, Colin, before you end him."

The voice is Viper's, coming from the main room.

"You heard the man," Colin says.

As I make it into the main room, I see Viper sitting at a booth with some naked chick on his lap. Viper's got both his hands palming the chick's tits.

"Glad you could join us, Skull. I was beginning to wonder if Teena was going to do her job."

"Teena?" I ask, things starting to clear up in my head.

Beth had been right about her. And those feelings I had about her being too calm click into place, too.

"How do you like fucking bitches my dick has already stretched open? Never would have figured you for the type to take my sloppy seconds, but you sure got all hot and bothered over Teena quickly, didn't you? Fucking blind as a bat, too. She fed me info about your club for months before you started mooning over that Donahue bitch again."

"She's your mole?" I ask, knowing I should be relieved, but feeling like a stupid fool just the same.

"You made it too easy. All she had to do was pretend you wore her out. Then while she was 'sleeping', you talked so freely on the phone. Thanks for that, by the way. I was able to get the Ganler gun run easily from you and you never knew why. I've made a cool five hundred grand, thanks to Teena and your loose lips."

"Fuck you."

"No thanks, but then, if you got a hard-on for my dick so much, I might give it to you. That way, you can see just how much of disappointment you were for Teena."

"You went to all this trouble just to take money from my club? You're as fucked up as I always thought."

"I didn't do it just for that. Teena already caught your eye. It would've been an easy score. But then, imagine my surprise one night when she calls me and tells me that my sister is back from the dead and ready to give birth to your demon spawn. That kind of good luck just doesn't happen without a divine purpose. I arranged for Pistol and Teena to break Beth's spirit. That was an added bonus, by the way."

"You fucking pig."

"Sticks and stones," he says with a cocky grin. "Only problem is Katie. I think she might have a little more of my father's blood. She's not weak. She snuck Gabby and Beth out of the hospital early before I could get my hands on them. Took me forever to chase them down, and when I did, you still managed to get your filthy hands on them. It doesn't matter, though. Soon you'll be dead and I'll get back to work, making sure my father's bastard daughters hurt for all the pain they caused my mother. Then I'll deliver their skins back to my father as a present."

"I'll kill you!" I yell, forgetting about Colin at my back and intent only on getting to Viper and ending him. By this time though, three men have come around me and are twisting my hands behind my back. I fight against it, especially after this fucker tells me his plans for Beth. I break free, but only for a second before the hard butt-end of a gun cracks me hard at the base of my skull. My knees threaten to buckle. I fight it so I can remain standing and fight, but they pull me back and, as much as I try to kick and move, I can't stop them.

I'm about to give up hope when I hear Viper scream out in pain. I jerk up just in time to see the man fall back, his eyes wide. Blood darker than even the worn leather of his jacket stains his chest. I look behind me, my eyes blurry from the force of the hit on my head, and try to find out who shot him. I expect to see Torch there, any of them.

But what I see instead makes my dick hard. It makes me prouder than hell, but I still want to spank her ass. Beth stands there looking calm, cool, collected… and fucking beautiful.

"I have a present for you, brother," she says, then shoots Viper again.

Damn.

Chapter 58
Beth

"What the fuck are you doing here? Beth, you get your ass out of here right now!" Skull yells, but I've got my gun aimed at Colin now that the other guy—apparently my brother—is dead.

"Sorry, lover. I'm a little busy right now."

"No, you're not. You get your ass out of here," he orders, swaying on his feet as he tries to walk towards me.

"That would be more convincing if you could say it without looking like you're drunk. Oh my God! You still have your gun?"

"I told you, I had this under control."

"You really are an idiot," I tell Colin.

He's looking at me like he's ready to kill me. I'm sure if I make a mistake here, he will.

"It doesn't matter," Colin responds. "I was going to kill him; you just interrupted. There's no way you're getting out of here. If you drop your gun now, I promise to make you feel good before I kill you. We both know how much you like the things I do to you."

My hands shake, but I don't back down because I can't afford to. One wrong move and Skull and I will die here. There's not a man here, except for the one I killed, who doesn't have a gun drawn. I feel sick to my stomach. There's five men left, including Colin. There's no way to take out all five before one of them gets us. *Shit!* Why didn't I think this through better?

"Skull, why didn't you tell me I had a brother?"

"I was trying, *querida*…"

"Do not call me that again. Not after hearing you call that bitch that."

"Beth…"

Colin cuts in. "Do you think we can stop the love chat, as interesting as it is? I'm going to give you two minutes to put your gun down, Beth. If you do that, I'll let your boyfriend live."

"He's lying through his fucking teeth, *quer*—"

"I'm warning you, Skull!"

"*Dolor en el culo?* Better?"

"Pain in your ass? Really? If we survive this, I'm going to need a divorce."

"Since that means you'll have to marry me first, we'll discuss it," he says, and then he drops his voice an octave to add, "I say we shoot and run behind the bar for cover."

He said that last part in Spanish, which catches me off guard, as it takes a minute for me to understand. I hope they don't know what he's saying.

Then, it's too late. One of the men shoots. I wait to feel pain, even as I'm pulling the trigger. I take off running, but I don't get two steps before Skull is covering me with his back, picking me up and throwing me over the bar, all while shooting behind him. A second later, he dives for cover with me. I sit up and shoot again. It doesn't take long before I've emptied my clip.

I have to be more careful. I just have Katie's backup clip and then I'm out.

"How are you on ammo?" I ask Skull, not turning around to look at him.

"Are Torch and the boys on their way?"

"Should be fifteen, maybe twenty minutes behind me."

"Use this gun and protect yourself, *mi cielo*," he says. His voice is gruff, and when I turn around to look, I find him pale. I don't see any blood, so I start to breathe easier.

"You use that gun. I've got Katie's," I tell him, taking another shot at Colin's men. "We just need to hold on a little longer. I've been here ten minutes, so help will be here shortly, sweetheart." I shoot again. "He must have hit you really hard. I should have made myself known sooner. I'm so sorry."

All the time I'm talking, I'm shooting. I could almost squeal in victory when I take out one of the shooters. I look briefly back at Skull to see why he's not shooting.

"*Te amo,*" he whispers, then falls against me.

My heart feels like it's in a vise grip because only when he falls do I notice the river of red on his back. *He's been shot!* It must've happened when he played all hero and tried to cover me.

I lay him down on his side, as best I can with one hand. I shoot with the other. I don't know if I hit anywhere within the vicinity of the others. Once I have Skull turned to his side, I pull my shirt off and push it against his wound. I stay like that, applying pressure while shooting blindly every few minutes over the top of the bar.

I've just fired the last bullet in Katie's gun when I hear Torch yell.

"Skull! Beth!"

I scream, "Behind the bar! Hurry!" and then drop my gun, holding onto the blood-soaked shirt on Skull's back with all my might. "They're here, sweetheart. Your men are here. We'll be okay now. You just need to hold on. Hold on for us, Skull. Hold on," I repeat over and over, my body shaking and tears running so hard down my face that they blind me.

God, please let him hold on.

Chapter 59
Skull

"Beth!" I yell, jerking up.

Everything in me screams in protest. It takes me a minute to figure out where I am. Finally, I realize that I'm in a bed—a hospital bed, to be exact. I look around at the same time I feel a hand touch my forehead. I glance up to find Beth's gray eyes full of worry and concern.

"I'm here, sweetheart. I'm here."

"You have circles," I tell her, and it's then that I notice my voice is hoarse and my throat feels raw.

"That I do," she whispers, kissing me gently on the lips. My mouth is dry and the feeling of her lips is different than what I remember and lasts too short because I can't manage to deepen the kiss. It seems like forever since I've tasted her. Before I can protest, she looks to the end of the room. "Go to the nurse's station and tell them he's awake," she says, and it's then that I notice her voice is hoarse too, but not quite as much as mine.

When she looks back around, she has tears shimmering in her eyes.

"You're crying, *mi cielo*," I tell her, trying to tighten my hold on her arm to pull her back to me. I can't seem to even grip her though. I'm as weak as a kitten. "Stop crying. I do not want you to cry," I tell her, frustrated because sitting up seems beyond what my body is willing to do. "Why am I here?" I ask, trying to remember what happened to put me in the hospital.

"You were shot by one of Viper's men," comes a voice I recognize, though I can't understand what he'd be doing here. His words send alarm bells running through me.

"Get out of here. Beth had nothing to do with any of this…"

"Rest easy, son. I know what happened. I couldn't be more proud of my daughter," Tucker says.

I look from him to Beth, stunned. "You've met?"

"Yes," she confirms. "I'm getting to know my father quite well, actually. It's all okay, sweetheart. Don't worry. It's not good for you."

"How long have I been out?" I ask, feeling very out of my depth.

"A month," she whispers.

My hand flexes inside of hers. "*Mierda…*" I whisper, not being able to believe it. "Gabby? You?"

"We're all okay, Skull. We're great now that you've come back to us."

"What happened to me, Beth?" I ask, needing to understand everything, but before she can tell me, a nurse comes into the room and asks everyone to leave while the doctor examines me. They don't. Beast, Katie, Torch, Briar, Candy, and Sabre stand there with Beth and Tucker. "Gabby?" I ask, clinging to Beth's hand and refusing to let her go.

"She's fine, sweetheart. She's with Mattah. I'll be right outside."

"No."

"Mr. Cruz, we need the room cleared while we examine you."

"Beth stays," I tell the nurse, managing to get my hand to cooperate so I can hold on to her harder.

"Skull, I'll…"

"You're staying. I don't want you out of my sight again." She must know I need this because she doesn't argue any further.

I listen as the doctor explains how I coded on the way to the hospital and how I'm short a kidney now. I even listen as he drones on about all of the complications I went through. Bottom line, I fought to come back to Beth and Gabby. Nothing else matters, except maybe one thing. When the doctor clears out and before the others come in, I say one word to Beth.

"Colin?"

"Gone forever. They all are, except for that bitch Teena. But Torch said he had something special planned for her."

"Special?" I ask.

"Apparently Viper liked to supply women to a man in Northern Russia. Turns out, he got most of his ladies from Jane Does and women who lived on the street that check into the hospital who were unlucky enough to have Dr. Torres treat them. Torch thought it would be great to have Dr. Torres join the last bunch of ladies that Viper's crew sent."

"The last bunch?"

"Seems now that Tucker has taken control, the Chrome Saints are no longer involved in the human trafficking business."

"Fuck no, we ain't," Tucker says. I look up to see all my men gathered around. Katie and Sacks are standing off to the side, and there isn't a single one of the assholes who look happy.

Why does it feel like I might not like where this conversation goes?

Chapter 60
Beth

I feel the tension in the air. And I know the men are upset; they haven't made a secret of that in the last month. I even kind of understand why, but Skull's decisions are his own. I almost lost him and I don't want them causing him to relapse. Gabby needs her daddy to be healthy. There's so much that Skull and I haven't been able to enjoy as a family and it just seems like one thing after another keeps popping up to take that away from us.

"Not right now," I warn them, and all eyes turn to me. "We're not doing this right now."

"It's our right…"

"It's my right to have my man back. My right for Gabby to have her daddy back, and you guys will not come at him right now, especially since I haven't even had him back for more than thirty minutes. So drag your asses out of here and you can have your pissing contests later."

"Pissing contests?" Torch repeats, sounding like he thinks I'm crazy.

"She's been hanging around Mattah too much," Katie says.

"Will you two quit discussing me like I'm not even here? It's annoying. You haven't even been married for two weeks. Go have sex or something."

"I really don't need to hear that," Tucker says, and that almost makes me smile. It was a surprise to meet my real father, but it's one of the few things in my life that has been a good surprise. He's a good guy, if not completely rough around the edges. In some ways, he reminds me of Skull, so I'm thinking I'll only grow to care about him more. Gabby adores him, and he dotes on her, so that's one thing already in his favor. It's also more than I would have ever hoped for. I can definitely see Katie's crazy side in our father, which makes sense, since Tucker says I remind him more of my mother.

"Married? I missed the wedding?" Skull asks.

"We eloped. Figured if we waited around for you to wake up from your power nap, Torch would be old and gray and not able to get it up. I'd like to make sure Gabby has a cousin who will help get her into trouble and make your life miserable," Katie says with a way too-sweet smile, walking over to squeeze Skull's shoulder.

"*Dulce Jesús*," Skull mutters.

"Ten years older than you. Ten. That's just barely old enough to teach you all the tricks you need to know to keep me entertained."

"You'll be too old and gray to do those tricks," Katie tells him.

"I'll never be too old for that," Torch says, walking up behind Katie and wrapping his arms around her. He kisses the side of her neck and then settles in to look at Skull.

"You cut the club out of all of your decisions," he says in all seriousness, looking at Skull. So much for listening to me. Katie elbows him.

"I said this wasn't happening right now," I growl, not caring if I do sound like a mama bear.

"The club had a traitor. I didn't know who I could trust," Skull answers, ignoring me. I sigh and sit back down in the chair by the bed realizing he's not going to listen to anything I say. None of them are right now.

"How did you even know the club had a traitor?"

"It was the last thing Pistol told me," Skull answers Torch, looking even more tired.

"And you trusted that fucker over any of us?" Briar asks.

"He wanted protection for his sister. He knew I was ending him. I was his last chance to save his sister."

"So he gave you the info he had? Why didn't he just tell you the traitor's name?" Sabre asks.

"He died before he could."

"Funny how the traitor turned out to be the one person *you* brought in instead of your brothers—*who busted their asses to save you*. Especially since you decided to go off half-cocked and face the assholes alone," Briar says. I hold my head down and hope this blows over soon.

"Pistol was a member. I had no reason to think that there wasn't another one of my brothers out there with a knife ready to do me in."

"Pistol was a fucking problem you should have taken care of long ago," Sabre says.

"Yeah, and some of you motherfuckers were fucking close to him. I had reasons for not going to you for everything and if I had it to do over again, I still would."

"You mean me," Briar growls.

"I figured you were the most likely, but I couldn't be sure it wasn't Shaft, Latch, or any of you guys."

"Jesus Christ eating cheese biscuits, you've been fucked up about this *that* long?"

Skull doesn't bother replying to Torch.

"You're the club's president. Kind of hard to be our leader if you think we want to kill you," Sabre growls.

Skull closes his eyes and when he opens them, I see so much in his eyes that it physically hurts me. Anger, frustration, sadness... it's all there. My man has been carrying a load heavier than I even knew.

"I don't want to be."

"Be what?" Torch asks, and I know he sees the pain in Skull's eyes. He would, above all of them, because they are the closest.

"The fucking president," answers Skull. "I don't want the job. I'm tired. It's cost me too fucking much."

"Skull," I gasp before I can stop myself.

"I'm serious, *mi cielo*. If I was just someone who walked up to you that day, none of this would have happened."

"What a crock of shit! That's the biggest load of bull I've ever heard in my life," Torch says.

"He's right. This has more to do with my family than it ever had to do with you," I tell him.

"Possibly, but me being the president of Devil's Blaze sure didn't fucking help matters."

"I get it. It's hard carrying the weight of a president. Each decision is life or death for our brothers. It's exhausting." The words come from Tucker.

"You're being stupid. This club is..."

"Draining," says Beast, cutting in. "It's hard to keep yourself breathing, let alone other men, because sometimes there's nothing you can do to save anyone... least of all yourself."

The room goes quiet, all eyes moving to the tall mountain who is so somber and quiet now that it's hard to reconcile him with the laughing man I once knew. His beard and hair have grown until I'm not sure what is beneath them anymore.

"Brother," Torch starts.

"I know exactly how he feels because every day I fight to keep from leaving the club and not looking back."

"You want free?" asks Skull.

"I want to be alone. Maybe not forever, but then again, maybe so. I can't sleep without remembering. I'm tired."

"It's my fault…"

"It's not. I should have gotten rid of Jan ages ago. I could have taken my baby and kicked her out. It's on my shoulders, not yours, boss."

The room is thick with emotion. I war with myself, but in the end I push forward.

"I like being the president's old lady."

"You what?" Skull asks, shocked.

"I like being the old lady to a president," I repeat. "My father was a president, so it's in my blood."

"What are you saying?"

"I don't want you to step down. I like our life. I like our club. I want Gabby to grow up being surrounded by a bunch of men ready to lay their lives down for her. I like having my sister close and a brother-in-law in the club. I like it all. Everything about it… and I don't want to give that up."

"*Mi cielo…*"

"I'm a Devil's Blaze badass biker chick. My old man is the president, and I like it. It's in my blood. It's who I am."

"*Mierda*," Skull says, but I see relief in his eyes.

"Well, at least your woman has balls," Briar says, still upset at being thought a traitor, I'm sure.

"She gets them from her dad," Tucker says with a laugh, but when I look up at him, all I see is pride. I've never had that before. It feels really good.

Chapter 61
Skull

"Skull! Put me down! You've only been out of the hospital for a week!"

"I'm fine, *mi cielo*. More than fine, and I *need* my woman."

"Skull! It's too soon! You almost died!"

"*Las tonterías*! It's been too long, Beth," I tell her as we make it to the door of our room. Once we get through it, I kick it shut with my foot.

"But your stitches…."

"Will be fine. I'm going to be using my dick, not my back," I tell her, letting her gently down to the floor.

"Got it all planned out, do you?" she asks, but she's smiling at me.

"All except one thing, *mi amor*."

"I'm almost afraid to ask," she admits.

"I can't figure out why you have so many clothes on," I tell her, grinning. I'm already taking my cut off, lying it on a chair.

"What if I've decided not to have sex again until we're married?" she asks not-so-innocently. I would have a fucking heart attack, but I see her sliding her sundress off her shoulders.

Since that night we uncovered her scars together, she's taking to wearing her sundresses again—at least around the club. Eventually, I'll make sure she's comfortable enough with who she is to wear them anywhere; I've made that my mission.

"*Mi cielo*, I'll give you the world, but do not ask me to wait to fuck you, because that is *not* happening."

"I want a big wedding," she says. I do my best to hide my smile, although I'm pretty sure I fail.

"If you must, *mi amor*."

"You and the men have to wear white coat and tails," she adds mischievously.

"Black," I bargain, but in truth, if she demanded white, I'd bust my ass to make sure it happens. She doesn't know it, but I'm going to bust my ass to make her feel like a princess.

"I can work with that." She smiles.

"I can't speak for Torch, though. You know how that son of a bitch is," I tell her as I pull my shirt over my head.

Her dress slides down her body, pooling at her feet. Standing there with her hair down in nothing but her pale pink bra and a tiny lace scrap of fabric shielding her pussy from me, she has never been more breathtaking. I forget about everything, especially her insecurities. I must have stared too long because I hear the fear in her voice when she says my name.

"Skull?"

"You're so fucking beautiful, *mi cielo*. I'm a lucky bastard." On cue, tears spring from her eyes.

"I'm the lucky one, my love," she whispers.

My Beth, so tender she cries at the drop of a hat, but her spine is as strong as the finest steel.

"I don't know about that, but you're about to get lucky," I joke with her, trying to shake off the seriousness that has intruded on our play. Beth has had too much of that. She needs laughter… *and my cock.* I undo my pants, shove them down, then quickly step out of them, too impatient to take it slowly. I've gone too long without her and I can't wait any longer.

Beth is staring at my cock, which is rock hard and leaning towards her like the greedy fucker he is. He knows where he belongs and just where he will find heaven.

I take him in my hand, stroking him slowly. "See something you like?" I ask her.

She looks up at me, those fucking eyes that grabbed hold of me that first day and never let me go are dark with passion. Her tongue comes out and licks her lips.

"Always," she whispers, and that one word wraps around me, settles inside, and sends heat down my spine and my dick throbs. *Mierda!*

I pull her to me, taking her mouth hard and fast. She's right there with me, her tongue pushing into my mouth, tangling with mine as I swallow her groan of submission. I guide her back to the dresser, pushing the things on it out of the way. I lean her over it, letting her slap her palms down on the wood to brace herself. I step back to enjoy the view of her ass sticking out towards me. The creamy white cheeks peek out of the silky pink material. I can't resist squeezing the fleshy mounds hard, pulling them apart roughly.

"Skull," she gasps.

Pale red blooms on her white skin against my fingers, outlining where I'm holding her. It almost matches the material she's wearing. *Material that annoys me.*

I grab the ends with both hands and rip it from her body.

"I liked that pair!" she protests. "It's one of the last ones I have! Now I won't have any to put back on…"

"Now *that* sounds like a fucking plan," I growl, thrusting one finger into her pussy without warning.

"Oh, fuck!" she cries.

I love when I can make that sweet voice go dirty. Her pussy hugs my finger tight, sucking it inside her body greedily.

"Yes," she moans when I take it out and then thrust a second one back in.

"You need something, *mi amor?*"

"You… Always you," she moans, as my fingers thrust inside of her again. I pull them apart, stretching her tight little hole. My dick is dripping, demanding his turn. I slowly take my fingers out, pushing them up to slide against her swollen clit. Her whole body shudders in reaction. I rake it across again, pushing hard when I finish, her head reeling down in pleasure.

"God, *mi cielo*, you're always so ready for me. I can barely hold back long enough to prime you."

"Then don't!" she urges. "I need you inside of me!"

I shift so my hand reaches around her now so I can keep playing with her clit. I let my other hand slide under her to thrust two inside. I keep up the dual pleasure, letting her ride my fingers while I work her clit until she's riding me hard and fast.

"Skull, oh fuck… Sweetheart, I'm going to come. I'm going to…"

She can't finish the sentence as she cries out in a long, loud whine of noise as her body quakes in climax. I hold my fingers on her clit still, just applying pressure while I continue thrusting inside of her with my others. I let her ride it out, and just when I think she's about to come back down, I take away my fingers, line up my cock, and drive home hard. She cries out all over again, but this time, my groans of pleasure are louder. I pump into her hard and fast. My balls are already tight and I know this is going to be a fucking quick ride.

I manipulate her clit and angle my thrusts, letting my dick hit her G-spot, grinding into her. I can feel my cock swelling even larger, stretching her trembling walls. Just before I go over the edge, I pinch her clit, pushing her into her climax with me.

"Skull!" she cries, the sound of her voice so beautiful as I unload jets of cum deep into her, bathing her insides.

When it's over, we stay pressed together, her back to my front. I reach up and take her bra off, wrapping my arms around her so I can hold her breasts in my hands.

"*Mierda!* One day soon, I will manage to hold out fucking you until you're completely undressed."

"You don't hear me complaining..." she says, her voice hoarse and her breathing choppy.

"*Si*, but it was ill-done of me. Time to make it up to you."

"Oh, fuck...."

"Did I tell you, *mi amor*, how much I love it when you curse?" I whisper in her ear, right before I carry her to bed.

Time for round two.

Chapter 02
SKULL
ONE MONTH LATER

I was starting to think this day wouldn't happen, but finally I get to make Beth completely mine. Today, on Gabby's third birthday, we're finally going to be a family.

We're getting married at the spot that reminds me of where Beth and I made love in Georgia. I had a dock built just for the occasion. It feels like we've come full circle. In the past month, life has been calm. I sent out word to the Donahues that Colin and Matthew were taken care of and that Beth and Katie belonged to the Blaze, though Tucker had me tag on the Saints, too. It appears the old bastard and I are going to be tight allies. I'm okay with that. Tucker is a good man, and he would die in a heartbeat for my wife or my daughter. You can't ask for more than that.

The club itself has been healing slowly. My relationship with Briar is still a little stilted, but we're working through it. Torch wasted no time knocking Katie up and, though she's barely more than a month along, he's making sure she's spoiled. Hell, he barely lets her walk anywhere, insisting on carrying her all the time. I half expect him to carry her up the aisle today.

She deserves it. Beth has finally let me in on everything. Though Beth might have more scars on the outside, I'm sure Katie is carrying around some deeper ones on the inside. Redmond, the bastard, actually put Katie on the boat that was rigged to explode. That's why I thought I lost Beth that day. Katie survived, but not without some heavy burns and a damaged hip on a leg that was already hard for her to walk on because it was a little over an inch shorter than the other. Some of the stories Beth tells me of their time under lock and key with the Donahues still give me nightmares. One thing good about it: I'm obviously marrying a fucking strong woman. Sometimes, I wonder what I ever did to deserve her. I'm a lucky bastard.

That thought only repeats when I hear the piano music start. I'm standing under an arch of roses on the dock. The minister is here as well as Torch, who is serving as my best man, and Tucker, who is standing up for me, too. He's not walking Beth up the aisle; that was her choice, but she still wanted him to be part of the wedding. It works for me. Besides, I like the bastard. Go figure.

"I did this right by eloping. This fucking tie is about to get me," Torch whispers. I tear my eyes away from the area the women are supposed to march in from to look at him. He's pulling out a bowtie, which is attached by a piece of elastic around his neck, like an idiot.

He's wearing tux pants, like me. His shoes are shined and he's even wearing the suit coat with long tails, but he's not wearing the standard white shirt underneath. He's wearing a black and white t-shirt which has a cat lying on its stomach, all four legs bent, with the words "Need someone to pet pussy" above it. There's a man beside it wearing a tux that says "Best man for the job". *Christo!*

I tear my eyes away from him as the music picks up tempo. A horse-drawn carriage glides up. I'm giving Beth a princess wedding that even Cinderella would be jealous of. Out first is Katie. She's wearing a soft pink dress, her brown hair brushed straight until it glows and one white rose pinned in her hair. She walks slowly, giving me a brief smile, but then shifting all of her attention to Torch.

"Fuck me. Maybe I should rethink this and do this whole wedding thing," he whispers and I grin. I dreaded it, but even *I* have to admit the thought of seeing my woman walk up the aisle to me is something I'm looking forward to. When Katie is in place, the music shifts again.

Another carriage pulls up outside. And slowly, my woman is assisted down. She's bent over and I see our daughter beside her, holding her mother's hand. My girls. My world. They start walking along the white silk path that has been created. Gabby drops little pink rose petals, and she's dressed almost exactly like Beth, except her dress is pink like Katie's.

Beth. *Dios mío.* She takes my breath away. She's wearing a white dress that hugs her curves. It's all white silk. I'm a man, so I know shit about these things. It hides every inch of her, but at the same time, lets a man know that the valleys and curves underneath make men find religion and pray to God to touch.

Her face is hidden under a veil, but my daughter's is smiling broadly. When they make it to me, I reach out my hands to both of them. My family.

"I threw flowers, daddy!" Gabby says.

I laugh. "You sure did," I tell her, picking her up for a kiss. "I love you, *calabaza.*"

"Pumpkin!" she giggles.

"That's right! You're daddy's pumpkin. Happy Birthday," I tell her, kissing her again before Katie takes her away.

Now I turn my attention to Beth. Carefully, I raise the veil showing me her beautiful face. She's smiling, and the happiness in her eyes—knowing I'm the one who put it there—means the world. There's a few tears running down her face. My thumb shakes as I wipe them away.

"I love you," she whispers shakily.

"*Mi cielo, tu eres mi mundo*," I tell her. "You are my center. My compass. Without you, I lose my way. Without you, I merely exist." As I say the words in front of all of our friends and family, in front of my club, Dragon and his men, Diesel and his new woman Violet, and even the Saints, I have no shame when my own eyes cloud with tears. My heart is too full. Finally, I have everything I've ever wanted.

"My world," Beth whispers, reaching up to kiss me sweetly, and we turn towards the minister—toward our future.

Chapter 63
Beth

"I do," I whisper.

I'm having trouble catching my breath. My heart is beating crazily. I think I'm coming down with the flu, but I wasn't about to let anything rob me of this day. The wedding, everything Skull has done, is like something I used to dream of as a child. When I hear his deep voice whisper, "I do," I tighten my hand against his. I'm finally his wife.

The priest motions for us to turn around. As I turn, the world begins to spin. I fall to the side against Skull. He smiles down at me, thinking I just stumbled, but that's not it.

The world starts spinning and I lurch forward this time.

I hear Skull yelling my name. I feel his arms go around me and then… the world goes black.

Chapter 64
Skull

"I don't give a fuck if she's being examined! That's my wife and I want in there!" I yell at some wet-behind-the-ears security guard. I'm about ready to rip his goddamn head off his shoulders.

"Sir, if you'll have a seat, they'll let you see her in just a minute, otherwise we'll have to escort you from the hospital."

"C'mon, man," growls Dragon, clapping his hand on my shoulder and motioning me toward the seats. "Sit the fuck down. Last thing Beth needs is for you to be going ape shit. It's probably nothing."

"I didn't see you calm when Nicole was in the hospital."

"Yeah, well, motherfucker, my woman was shot and dying. Yours passed out. She's probably just knocked up or something. Nicole is always doing that shit when she's got a bun in the oven."

His words would comfort me, but it wasn't just two weeks ago I was complaining I couldn't have her pussy because she was bleeding. We found other ways to pleasure each other, but not being able to fall asleep while I'm still inside of her fucks with my head. I need that every fucking night with Beth. Shit, I'll need it when I'm ninety and popping pills just to make it possible.

"That's not it, man. It's not possible. Beth hasn't been feeling good for a while. She's been sick. She's been trying to hide it from me, but she's losing weight."

"Maybe she just has the flu. It's been going around," Nicole whispers, trying to reassure me.

"What if it's the cancer? Shit, I've been so focused on getting rid of all the threats against us... What if...?"

"Don't borrow fucking trouble," Katie growls. I look up at her—a face that looks so much like my woman, but so different. "Beth is strong. She will be here to watch her nephew get into this world."

Torch leans into her. "Katydid, you're not far enough along to know it's a boy."

"Trust me," she shoots back, "only a boy would already cause me this much trouble, Hunter."

I do my best to hold onto Katie's words. They're all I have and they are true. Beth is strong. She's so much stronger than I ever gave her credit for. We wait for another fifteen minutes and I'm slowly going insane before I look up after hearing my name called.

"Mr. Cruz?"

"Yeah?"

"You can go in now. You'll need to..."

I don't listen to him, and I don't particularly give a fuck about what he's saying. I make a beeline for the room that I saw them wheel my woman into. The security guards who stopped me from following her into the room are there. They stand far away from me now—and that's smart of them. Still, I flip both of the fuckers off, shove open the door, and go to the bedside of my woman.

She looks pale in the hospital bed. Her beautiful dress has been exchanged for a blue and brown standard-issued hospital gown. She's smiling. Even sick, she's the most beautiful woman in the world.

"Are you okay, sweetheart?"

"I'm fine, Skull. The doctor just needs to run some additional tests and then I can go home and we can…"

"Beth, don't worry. Whatever this is, we can face it together. It doesn't matter. We've already beaten so many odds; this is just one more hurdle."

"Skull, sweetheart…"

"I mean it, Beth. I'm right here with you," I tell her, holding her hand. "It doesn't matter, even if it's your cancer coming back. I'm here with you, and together, we're strong enough to wipe out anything standing in our way. We've already proved that."

"Skull…"

"We'll just prove it again."

"Skull!" she yells.

I go still. "What's wrong, sweetheart?"

"I'm not sick! It's not the cancer!"

"It's okay, honey, we can… Wait, you're not? It's not…?"

"No, sweetheart. It's nothing like that."

"Well, what in the heck is it, then?"

"I'm pregnant."

"It doesn't—" I belatedly hear the words. "Wait. What… What did you say?"

"I said I'm pregnant!"

"How is that possible? You just had your monthly thing, and…"

"The doctor said some women continue to have what appear to be light periods for a few months before the pregnancy makes itself known. There's even one lady on file who had periods clear up to her seventh month."

"*Christo!*" I murmur, my mind whirling. Beth… pregnant.

"Skull, this is a good thing. Gabby needs a brother or sister she can grow up with, and this way, the child will be close to the same age as Katie's. It's perfect."

"*Christo…*" I murmur, even softer.

"Skull? Aren't you happy? I thought you said you wanted another child," Beth asks worriedly.

My hand trembles as I move it slowly to her stomach and hold it where, even now, my child is growing inside.

"I'm happy, *mi cielo*. I'm ecstatic. We're going to have a baby."

She nods her head yes, smiling and crying at the same time.

"We're going to have a baby," I whisper again.

"We are," she confirms.

"I'm going to be a daddy again."

"You are."

As everything settles into me, I close my eyes. When I open them back up, I know she can see exactly how I feel because Beth has always been inside of me—a part of me.

"I'll be there this time, *mi cielo*. I'll be with you every step of the way." I wrap her hand around mine and kiss her fingers. "*Te prometo*," I say as I kiss her forehead. *I promise you.*

"We'll be there together," Beth says, bringing her lips to mine. I deepen the kiss, sliding into her mouth with a groan. My hand goes to her neck, fingers rubbing against the pulse.

"Okay, I've waited long enough," Katie exclaims, barging through the door. "What's going on?"

I pull back just a space from Beth's lips.

"My sister has very bad timing," she whispers, her dark gray eyes close to mine.

"*Muy mal*," I agree, staring back into her eyes. I remember the vow I made as a child. Everything I ever wanted, here in my arms.

Por siempre…

I'll bust my ass to keep it forever.

EPILOGUE
KATIE & TORCH
KATIE

"Breathe, Katydid. We're almost home free."

Breathe, he says, like that's so easy. Let him try squeezing an eight-pound baby through his pee-hole and then talk to me. I close my eyes tightly. Beth made this shit look so easy with Gabby.

"Bite me," I growl, wincing as the contraction starts again.

"I will later, sweetness," Torch promises, and if he didn't look so adorable with his hair all mussed up and wearing his "Proud Dad" t-shirt, I'd probably punch him in the junk. Instead, I stick my tongue out at him.

"You doing okay, Katie?" Bethie asks.

I look over at the next bed. Beth is there with Skull feeding her ice chips. She's a month early, and I'm a month late, but these kids are bound and determined to come out together. I don't know who Skull and Torch paid off or threatened—I'm not even going to ask. But, somehow, they broke every rule and put us together in the same birthing room.

Peanut, which is what Torch has taken to calling our child, is bound and determined to come out first. I'm in so much pain, but I'm okay with it—totally good, if he would just fucking hurry.

"You didn't tell me this hurt so fucking bad."

"Some things you shouldn't know until you have to." Then Bethie gasps, and I can tell she's just started a contraction.

"You remember that time you made me stick a lighter to that turtle's ass to see if it would make it shoot out of his shell like in the cartoons?"

"*Christo!*" Skull mutters.

"Made you? That was all on you! I told you, turtles don't do that in real life," Bethie huffs.

"What was it you got the big idea for, then?" I ask her, knowing what she'll answer, but we both need a distraction from the pain.

"I made you snails, remember?"

"Fuck me sideways," Torch mutters. I attempt to give him a grin, though that takes a little more effort than I have left in me, I'm sure.

"She roasted them with a lighter. Just saying, Hunter, I'm never going to France and ordering snails."

"I'll make note."

"Fuck!" I growl as a contraction hits harder than it ever has.

"You're crowning, Katie," the doctor informs me. "I just need you to really push when this next contraction starts, and we'll have this baby out of here in no time."

"You loved those snails. You ate every single one of them!" Bethie cries.

"There was only… *Ahhhh!*" I break off to yell. "Two!" I finish while the doctor and Torch are screaming for me to push. "And I only ate them… *Motherfucker!*" I scream again. "Because you dared me!"

"I know. I could literally dare you to do anything and you would. That's how you got your first kiss from Johnny Paul. You're welcome, by the way."

"Johnny Paul?" Skull asks, and I'm trying to focus, but God, this having-a-baby thing is not the cakewalk I thought it would be.

"Take a breather, Katie. This next push will get him out. I need you to push him out this time. Get ready," the doctor says.

"You got this, sweetness. I'm so fucking proud of you."

I look up into Hunter's eyes and breathe, taking my strength from him and the sound of Bethie's voice.

"Fish-lips Johnny," I clarify. "All the girls said his lips felt cold and slimy. Bethie dared me to kiss him to find out." I huff, feeling the contraction start.

"Were they?" Hunter asks.

I can't answer because I feel the contraction slide from my back all around my stomach and I know this is the big one. I'm pushing my baby out now. I can do this.

"Turns out, he was more of an octopus tongue. Felt like he had eight of those in your mouth at once," Bethie cries.

"How the fuck do you know that?"

"Well, after Katie bragged, I had to try it too, Skull."

His response is lost as I scream until I'm sure I strip a vocal cord. I bear down as hard as I can, then feel the baby leave my body. As the doctors declare my victory, I fall back on the pillow, exhausted. I open my eyes when I hear my baby's cry.

"Is he okay?" I ask, my voice hoarse and weak.

The nurse comes over holding a naked, squirming baby boy, placing him on my chest.

"He's beautiful, Katydid. Just like his momma," Hunter says, his voice hoarse as he comes back to me, brushing his hand across my hair and kissing my forehead. A few minutes later, a nurse comes over and places the baby on my chest.

"Ten fingers and ten toes, I'd say he's perfect," she says.

I look down at our beautiful baby boy with a small patch of sandy blonde hair on his head and these perfect little lips and tiny fingers, trying to wrap around one of mine. He's so quiet, staring up at me and Hunter as if he's trying to decide if this is a good thing. I see a little smile almost come across his lips. Can newborns smile? My son can. I look up at Hunter, feeling completely at peace for the first time in my life.

"Look what we did," I gush, my happiness boiling over with tears in my eyes.

"It's what *you* did, sweetness. All you. He's perfect."

"Hunter Bartholomew Evans," I whisper.

"Bartholomew? *Mierda!* Why are you giving him that name? He'll have to beat up his whole school for picking on him with that name!" Skull says. I grin up at Hunter, my husband, my partner, my rock.

"Katie and I are going to call him Bad Bart," he says with a wink. Only he and I know that Bartholomew is Hunter's middle name. A small secret. It's okay, his secret is safe with me. Just like I know that our child and I will always be safe with this man.

"I love you," I tell him, and those three words seem like so little when you realize what they encompass. He gives me air to live.

"I love you too, Katydid. I always will."

With my life, I never thought I could believe in a man, let alone a promise he gives me. I know that no matter what, I can always trust in Hunter's, though. Peace, just one of the gifts he gives me.

"Bethie you better hurry up over there. Hunter's getting lonely."

"Working on it," she huffs, and I wink up at Hunter, right before the nurse comes over and starts giving breastfeeding instructions. I get ready for even more blessings that having Hunter in my life has given. I do believe my cup runneth over… and if the big sloppy tears of joy falling from my eyes give me away, no one comments. Least of all my husband, who has the same tears in his face as our child suckles from my breast.

EPILOGUE
BETH & SKULL
SKULL

"Beth, are you ready, *mi cielo?* We're going to be late for Thomas's birthday party," I call before walking into the bedroom of our new home.

I had our new home custom-built right by the dock where Beth and I got married. Torch and Katie are right up the road, too. Far enough away so I won't have to kill Torch, but close enough so our children can be together, because one thing has shown itself in the last two months: these kids are going to bond. They somehow instantly sense when the other is in the room.

Diego Cruz was born exactly fifteen minutes after little Bart made his appearance. He's got Beth's blonde hair, my dark eyes, and a mixture of both of us when it comes to his personality. He's perfect, and Gabby is fascinated by her little brother. She's walking beside me, her little hand in mine, and it never fails to make me feel like I'm ten feet tall.

"Mommy's sleeping, Papi," she whispers. She calls me Papi. There was no coaching, nothing; she just picked it up one day and it clicked, and I've been Papi ever since. My daughter is the smartest child on the planet, and I'm definitely the proudest.

"That she is, *calabaza.*"

"So is Dee-go."

I smile, picking Gabby up in my arms. Her little hands come around my neck and she kisses the side of my face, giggling.

She's turned into daddy's little girl, and I couldn't be happier.

We're supposed to go to Dragon's little boy's birthday party. Nicole had a little boy they named Thomas and he and Dom keep him and Nicole completely on their toes. I hate to miss it, but Diego has had trouble sleeping through the night. Looking down at my beautiful wife and my son, there's no way I'm going to disturb them. I let Gabby slide to the floor and then I pull the cover up around Beth and a sleeping Diego, who is napping, spooned by Beth. *Mi mundo.*

"How about we skip the birthday party and go fishing on the dock?" I ask Gabby.

Her face breaks out in a big smile. "Can snuffles go?"

Snuffles is her teddy bear that her grandpa Tucker bought her. Tucker, who bought the property across from me and set up house there just to be close to his family. Tucker is a pain in my ass, but the best grandfather a little girl could ask for, and we won't even begin to talk about how he's trying to spoil Diego and BB—which is what we call Torch's and Katie's son, but then again, I warned them not to name him Bartholomew.

"Absolutely. We can make him bait the hook."

"Snuffles can't do that, daddy!" She giggles as I pick her up. When I get back to the door, I look back at Beth and Diego and smile. My heart feels so full it's about to burst.

Mi familia…

Life couldn't be more perfect. The pain, the hurt, the ghosts from the past… They have been released, and all that we have around us now is love.

The End.

LEARNING TO BREATHE

Beast's Story
Fall 2016

I look at the small, rundown shack and disgust curls in my stomach. All the money that Pistol made through the years and this is how his sister lives? When Skull approached me and asked if I wanted to head to North Carolina to check on Pistol's sister, my instinct was to say no. I was done, really. I didn't want to have anything more to do with anyone. When he offered me the cabin on Whitler's mountain in the deal, I finally agreed. A cabin in the mountains away from people seemed like heaven.

I could care less about Pistol or his sister. Pistol is part of the reason my child died. Whatever happens to his sister, I figure she deserves. I don't give a fuck if she does live in a shack. It's probably more than she deserves. Especially if she's anything like her brother.

I'm going to get back on my bike, go to the top of my mountain, and that's it. I'll email Skull and tell him the chick is living in a shack... maybe.

I walk back to my bike, veering off at the last minute to take a leak. I've got my pants unzipped and my dick out when I feel something jab me in the back. I look over my shoulder to see the long end of a shotgun barrel pointed at me. I follow it until my eyes land on a woman holding the gun.

She's five foot nine, maybe ten. She's got fiery bronze hair that falls down in waves almost to her elbows. There's a beat-up-looking brown hat on her head and the clothes she has on are butt-ugly. She could be decent, but it'd take some damn work. She's curvy. There's not a skinny thing about her, least of all that ass. She's got breasts that are just as large and in your face, but perhaps the biggest thing on her right now is her obviously very pregnant belly.

My dick drained, I shake off the excess and slide him back in my pants and zip up as I turn around to face her.

"You always take a whiz on other people's private property?"

"Only when my dick demands it. You want to lower your gun?"

"Not especially, since you're trespassing. Who are you?"

"I'm living in the old hunting cabin on Whitler's Mountain."

"You look like a mountain man. I didn't know they sold that cabin."

I grunt, walking around her to go back to my bike. "You should leave the gun-handling up to your man. It's dangerous to pull a weapon on a stranger; it could get you killed. You need to think about your baby."

"I don't have a man."

"That watermelon in your stomach would seem to argue that point," I tell her, my voice straining. I don't talk that much and I hate the hoarse sound that comes out of my throat sometimes when I speak. It's a reminder, and I don't need any fucking reminders.

I look over at the woman one last time. Her gun is down and she's rubbing her hand over her stomach. When she looks back up at me, there's a sadness in her eyes that grabs hold of my attention.

"Looks can be deceiving," she says.

I shrug and start up my bike. She spares me one last glance and then takes off walking. I watch her almost against my will as she heads back to the old shack I had just been looking at.

Guess I just met Hayden Graham… Pistol's sister.

AUTHOR'S NOTE

Thank you for reading. I hope you all love Skull and Beth's happy ending as much as I do.

xoxo
J

GLOSSARY OF TERMS

Cagar	shit
Christo	Christ
Créeme	trust me
Cuidadoso	careful
Dios mío	oh my God
Dolor en el culo	pain in the ass
El cabrón	the bastard
Estúpido	stupid
Hermano	brother
Hijo de puta	son of a bitch / motherfucker
Jesús Cristo de mierda	Jesus fucking Christ
La violo	raped her
Las tonterías	foolishness
Lo prometo	I promise
Madre	mother
Maldita perra	damn bitch
Me escuchaste	did you hear me
Me voy de aquí	I'm out of here
Mi amante	my lover
Mi amor	my love
Mi cielo	my sky
Mi dulce tortura	my sweet torture
Mi esposa	my wife
Mi familia	my family
Mi hija	my daughter
Mi mujer	my woman
Mi mundo	my world

Mi pobre tesoro	my poor treasure
Mierda	shit
Muy mal	very bad
Niña	girl
Padre	father
Por siempre	forever
Que así sea	so be it
Que diablos esta pasando	what the hell is going on
Que está loco	that's crazy
Que mujer estúpida	that stupid woman
Querida	dear
Tan bueno	so good
Tan jodidamente cansado	so fucking tired
Te amo	I love you
Tu eres mi mundo	you're my world
Vivir peligrosamente	living dangerously
Voy a matarlos	I will kill

Made in the USA
Middletown, DE
01 July 2016